A RUIN, GREAT AND FREE

A NOVEL

CADWELL TURNBULL

BLACK STONE
PUBLISHING

Copyright © 2025 by Cadwell Turnbull
Published in 2025 by Blackstone Publishing
Cover and book design by Kathryn Galloway English

The characters and events in this book are fictitious.
Any similarity to real persons, living or dead, is coincidental
and not intended by the author.

Printed in the United States of America

First edition: 2025
ISBN 978-1-0941-7590-4
Fiction / Fantasy / Contemporary

Version 1

Blackstone Publishing
31 Mistletoe Rd.
Ashland, OR 97520

www.BlackstonePublishing.com

To all the ones we've found.

THE NIGHT LADY

PATRICE PAIGE
TORTOLA, BRITISH VIRGIN ISLANDS

EARTH 0016

JUNE 27, 2049

TWENTY-FIVE YEARS AFTER THE MASSACRE OF MEN

Patrice knocks twice.

"Coming," the caretaker shouts from inside. Footsteps approach—the delicate clump-clump of low-heeled shoes Patrice can hear keenly through the reefs. Then the door opens.

"Hello, Arla," Patrice says.

"Governor Paige. My, my, it been long, no? I sure he gon' be happy to see you."

Patrice is grateful for the warmth in Arla's words. If she wanted to, if she chose to, Patrice could allow herself to believe, if only for a moment, that this is a home that welcomes. And that feeling might last all the way up until she sees the old man.

Patrice leaves her shoes at the door, then walks down the short hall behind Arla, listening to the woman spurt trivialities at a mile a minute. How is St. Thomas? Tortola has been so quiet, sleepy. Arla misses the old days, when things used to happen here, though she supposes she is grateful that prosperity has granted them the luxury of boredom. Now she has to be satisfied with idle gossip. One of her friends has taken a young lover, she confides. And—can Patrice believe it?—he's twenty-three! A full forty years younger. Though Arla supposes that Michelle has been taking good care of herself; the age difference is barely noticeable. All these fancy age-defying treatments!

Patrice makes appropriate small noises at the right moments.

"You looking great yourself," Arla says.

"Thank you."

The house feels both bigger and smaller, her younger self superimposed on this older self. Her father has lived here for twenty-five years, since the Ynaa left, since he survived the Massacre of Men by fleeing here. In that time, Patrice has changed a lot. Mostly on the inside.

They're going down another hall and then through a doorway that opens up into a second living room—smaller than the first one she passed, though not by much. The large windows make the room feel spacious, and the furniture—antique, even when the Ynaa were still present—gives the room a quality of being stuck in amber, preserved for some time traveler to step into.

Her father, Jackson, is by one of the expansive windows—not in his usual rocker, but instead in a hospital-model bed that can fold itself to prop up its occupant with the press of a button. And this is how her father is displayed: half lying, half propped up, the afternoon light glinting off his balding scalp, the wisps of gray hair catching that light and transmuting that hair to gold. Patrice has never seen her father so small. It's as if he were shedding himself by inches, as if there is no lower limit to this expulsion of self.

The television is on but muted. An animal documentary of the New Amazon: lush foliage, a jaguar slinking through the understory. Her doing—with the help of the reefs, of course. She allows herself a little pride. She *has* done some good. It hasn't all been acts that have darkened her soul.

He fixes a polite smile on his face. "So, you're here," he says, his voice lacking any friendliness.

"I am," Patrice says.

"I'll leave you both to it." Only then does Arla's warm mask slip, an expression of worry appearing and disappearing in a blink before she hurries from the room, leaving Patrice alone with her father.

Quietly, Patrice grabs the office chair from his worktable, which looks as if it hasn't been used in years. Three copies of *The Night the Men Died* are stacked at the right back corner of the desk, next to a printer, both under a layer of dust. It is the only book her father ever finished writing, but its impact alone overshadowed his subsequent failures. Other people wrote about the Massacre of Men, but her father's account stands above them all. He was there. He escaped. And he knew the people to talk to, the stories worth telling. He was a good writer too, made even better by the reefs, when he allowed himself to have them, to use them. His inability to follow up his great book is partly due to his stubbornness and pride.

Now there is just this man, falling to pieces.

Patrice rolls the chair stiffly over to the bed. When she sits down, the old coils in the seat protest her weight.

"What is it this time?" her father asks, all politeness spent.

"Can't I just come to see you?"

"I made myself clear the last time."

"You did," she says lightly.

His eyes are milky with cataracts. He isn't actually seeing her, just looking in the direction of her voice. "Have you stopped killing people?" he asks.

Somehow Patrice isn't prepared for the direct question. Not knowing what to say, she changes the subject. "How are you feeling lately? Any new pain?"

His frown seems plastered on, the skin molded completely to that one expression, all the age lines severe, monstrous.

"I hope the medications have been helping. I want you to be comfortable," she says.

"So I can die nice and quiet. Save you any grief."

"You know that's not true."

"Do I?" A smile of amusement forces away some of the frown lines. "I asked you a question."

Patrice bunches her hands into fists. "Daddy, will you stop antagonizing me for a moment so that we can talk like family?"

"We aren't—" He stops himself from saying it. Bless him for that much. "I will not be complicit."

"Talking to me is not complicity, Daddy."

"All this 'Daddy' stuff. Trying to butter me up for something. Or . . ." His milky eyes fix on her. If there is something behind that stare, it remains properly hidden beneath the plaster of her father's face.

"I haven't had to hurt anyone in years," she lies, softly so that Arla doesn't hear, even though she knows—through the reefs— that Arla is two rooms down, watching a soap opera on her phone.

"Listen to yourself," he says. But just as quickly, he is done with that route of antagonism for the time being. "How's my grandson?"

"He's good." She doesn't dare insult her father with any promises of Derrick visiting or lies about Derrick missing him. Derrick misses no one.

"Good," he says.

"Daddy." She is stalling, but she wants to try one last time to defend herself. It is important, especially now. "Dad, they killed almost all the men on the island. We were so powerless. It was a fluke that the Ynaa didn't exterminate us all. We may not be so lucky the next time."

"The next time it may not be the Ynaa. The next time could be better."

Patrice laughs before she can pull it back. That optimism sounds so wishful. It reminds her of her onetime best friend, now dead.

"The Ynaa could be the exception," her father continues. "Other aliens could be kind—"

"If that's true, we're even unluckier than we think."

"*And* it might serve us better to be slow to conflict. You—" He coughs violently.

Patrice waits until he is finished.

Clearing his throat, he says, "You learned the wrong lessons from the Ynaa."

"Daddy, it is better to be ready in case we're not blessed with these benevolent aliens of your imagination."

"Watch it," he says, before being racked by another bout of violent coughs. He is slow to speak after, his eyes closed tight, the creases at their corners multiplying. He breathes slowly, wincing through some inner pain. "Look, we've had every different version of this conversation. You've made up your mind. Nothing I can say will change it. I've made up my mind too. Even if the next invaders are worse than the Ynaa, it don't excuse what you done in humanity's name. You took away everybody's choice."

Patrice notes that quick slip into St. Thomian, unusual for the former English teacher with prescriptivist tendencies. He must be angry. Or in terrible pain. Or both. She says, "Dad, what I've done will save us." She thinks, *It could save you.*

"And if it doesn't? Then all you've done is visit evil on your own kind."

Patrice pushes down her frustration. That's it, then. The same impasse.

To his credit, he looks a little remorseful. "You're my daughter," he says. "But I can never support you in this."

"If you loved me, you'd support me."

Silence stretches between them.

She knows she isn't being fair. All relationships have conditions. Every person has a line they won't cross. This is her father's. She has yet to encounter hers. So what is left to say? Nothing. Eventually, Arla will have to come back to give her father his medication. There is no time to fix what is between them. And now, looking at him, she knows it can't be fixed.

That leaves . . .

When Patrice removed the reefs from her father's body, he aged terribly fast. He should be only in his mideighties. He looks older. Having lost the reefs so suddenly, his body went into a state of slow shock it never recovered from. Patrice can remember every sign of age as it appeared on his body, in his body. And each time, she had to fight the urge to help, to ease the harsher edges wrought by time. A simple nudge here or there, and he would be sitting before her, graceful in his old age, still on the way to death, but gently. She held back, though. Because she feared he would know and hate her more for it. Because she feared that his own helplessness to stop her would lead to a resentment so great that he would burn what was left of their relationship.

Still, she's here now. To finally end this pointless suffering.

Her father knows it too. His face is so stern, so dignified. He will not let her have any show of weakness. Even if his body is weak, his mind is in there, hating her.

Tears. She lets them fall. He will see it as a manipulation. It doesn't matter.

She drops any remaining pretense. "Are you ready?" she asks.

No answer. His milky, unblinking stare.

"I love you, Daddy."

Just the slightest tremble of his lips, a stifled moan, barely audible, picked up by Patrice's enhanced hearing.

She waits a little longer to see if he will say it back, say those words he has withheld for so long. But he can't say them, *won't* say them. Patrice understands. This is the one power he has, not to let her off easy. She can survive this much. She can bear it because she loves him.

"Will you ever stop?" he asks her.

Patrice answers honestly. "As soon as I'm sure humanity won't destroy itself—or won't be destroyed in spite of itself."

Her father nods, closes his eyes in that pained way. Even if he understands, he'll never agree. "If there is a heaven," he says, "I hope I can meet your mother there, so we can share in our disappointment of you."

One final admonishment. For the rest of her life, which might be forever, she'll be hearing these final words from her father. But it can't be undone, only endured.

"Well, go on, then," her father says.

Patrice lets the tears fall as she stops every organ in his body all at once. Softly. No violence. A gentle release into death.

Her father's head slumps back onto the bed as if sleep had suddenly taken him. It isn't sleep. Patrice decides to wait a moment before yelling for Arla, so she can think through what she'll tell the woman when she comes back in. She'll say that her father refused to speak to her, which Arla will understand because she's witnessed Patrice's father doing this enough times, freezing Patrice out, ignoring her. Arla may not know what caused the falling-out, but when Patrice tells her that he turned his head away and went to sleep, she'll believe it. She'll believe that Patrice respected his personal space, that she did not approach his bed until she was readying to leave. She'll believe that only then did Patrice notice something was wrong.

People die suddenly all the time. People don't use alien technology to kill their own fathers. She won't suspect what Patrice has done. She can't.

"Arla!" she yells, putting real emotion into her voice.

Patrice allows herself to cry. The tears will help.

In 2019 they arrived. Patrice was on the porch that day with her
father. She saw the spaceship descend, stopping to hover over
Water Island. She remembered that it looked like a seashell—
blue-white, oscillating streaks spiraling down toward the central
point of the ship. She remembered thinking it was beautiful,
even though she was terrified.

The Ynaa came speaking human languages, and with an ambassador who had been secretly living on the planet for hundreds
of years. Because of her experience with humanity, Ambassador
Mera became the intermediary between Ynaa interests and human
beings. In accordance with her role, she was the one who told humanity what the Ynaa had to offer: cures to several diseases, for
example, and clean renewable energy. In exchange, they wanted
to study Earth for a discrete time, no more than twenty years.

They left in five, having killed tens of thousands of people
(mostly men) and having found the secret to immortality—
what they called *Yn Altaa*. Mera revealed this secret to Patrice

in fucked-up atonement for the loss of life, specifically that of Mera's human lover, Patrice's best friend.

The gift itself was also left to her: a dozen medicine capsules, each containing millions of reefs, all encoded with Yn Altaa. The reefs were superintelligent cybernetic cells the Ynaa used to manage and maintain their bodies and, on the night of the massacre, to kill twenty-five thousand men and boys.

Patrice briefly considered that the gift might be a ploy, but if the Ynaa could kill thousands of people at once, leaving no visible trace, it was certain that every living human body already had reefs lying dormant inside it. But more than the certainty that all humanity was infested with Ynaa technology was the certainty that Mera's grief was genuine. Patrice hated Mera. She also believed her. Nothing to be gained by leaving a note behind. The gift was real, no question, and Patrice decided she would use that gift, even if she could never forgive Mera.

Patrice gave one of the tablets to her son, who at the time couldn't consent to it. She regrets that choice now, but back then trauma had made her commit to the decision. Two others accepted the gift: her father and Derrick's sister. Two turned it down: her best friend's grandmother, who was sick at the time but unwilling to take alien gifts even before the Ynaa killed her grandson; and Patrice's own mother, who had no interest in living forever.

Nine years ago, her mother died in a boating accident. Patrice felt her drowning through the reefs. She could not stop it; she could only kill her faster. So she did. In her grief, she confided in her father what she had done, what she had to do, and he comforted her. But that was when he started to suspect her. That was when he started paying attention.

A year later, he came over to the house with his gathered evidence. "Take it back," he said. "I will not be complicit."

Hours of fighting. Eventually, she did what he asked: She took away her father's gift of living forever. And then today she took away her father's life. Because nothing mattered more to her than preventing another Massacre of Men—not even her relationship with her father, not even his life.

On the drive home—the actual driving done by the reefs—Patrice diverts her mind from what has just happened, by thinking of the road ahead. Her big project is to become president. This won't be the most difficult thing once the US Virgin Islands get statehood. But she'll need to make sure she can use the office to its highest possible advantage. She will have to quietly take control of the House and the Senate—a process that has been gradual so far but will have to intensify within the next decade. She'll have to seed more influence internationally as well, which will require more aggressive action on her part. Blackmail, certainly. At this point, there's no secret spoken that she doesn't know. Plenty of levers to pull. And if those fail, a heart attack should do, an ischemic stroke, a brain hemorrhage. Ease power quietly into more pliable hands. She will also have to increase her wealth substantially, granting herself more resources, access to the world's elites, better opportunities for investment. More than doable with the help of her reefs.

Up until this point, she has been careful, amassing only millions instead of billions, secrets instead of obvious power. And busying herself with local politics instead of on the national and international stage. She wanted her ascendancy to seem plausible.

But to prevent humanity from destroying itself, she will

have to seize control of all its methods of self-destruction, then reform or dismantle them. And to do that requires a greater sense of urgency.

Ultimately, she has the Ynaa to thank for both her urgency and her power.

At home, Patrice slumps near the door, sliding down the wall and onto the floor. She is looking up at the high ceiling, feeling the profound weariness that she experiences a lot lately. She is sleeping well, and the reefs alleviate all her fatigue, so it isn't physical exhaustion. It is something else. She is mind-tired, heart-tired, tired of thinking or feeling or being. She takes a slow breath in and out.

Can we help? the reefs ask.

A decade ago, Patrice might kill a warlord to feel better. Nothing like a small correction with a significant impact to lift her spirits. But warlords are a vanishing race. Her doing.

Patrice shakes off her fatigue as she walks through her house. She climbs two flights of stairs to her son's room. The door is ajar. The bright lights of the room assault Patrice's eyes. On every wall, filling the space, are the usual monitors, all turned on, every one of them displaying a different image: the news, television dramas, films (one so old it's in black and white), televised government sessions, two audiobooks (one a pulp crime novel, the other a book on plate tectonics), prices on the global stock exchanges, and at least a half dozen online videos. None have sound, but Patrice knows he is listening through his comically large headphones. She has no idea how he can listen to all of them at once. It must be with the help of the reefs, but how much? He's been using reefs since before he could speak. How has this affected the development of his brain?

"Good evening," Patrice says.

"He's dead, isn't he?" Derrick says without turning or taking off his headphones.

Patrice nods, though she isn't sure he can see it. "It was peaceful."

"Of course." Derrick spins around to look at her. "You're handling it better than I thought you would."

She wants to say something, defend herself, but there is no judgment in her son's eyes, only understanding. Her son, though distant as ever, isn't without empathy. For those he has chosen to care about, he can display immense social intelligence. Before, when he was younger, she would call him "Little Derrick" to differentiate her son from his namesake. But now he looks very different from his namesake. And he *is* different, in about every way except for that empathy. She didn't expect him to look like Derrick—they have no relation, except in her heart—but somehow she had hoped there was something in the name, some transferable quality so that she didn't have to miss the other Derrick so damn much.

"I *am* sad," Patrice says. "But it was going to happen anyway. At least he didn't have to hurt."

Derrick nods. "At least." His voice is deep—what Patrice imagines he would sound like at his true age, although he presents as a teenager.

"Anyway. I didn't want to interrupt."

"You're not."

"Still. I'll let you get back to what you're doing."

His eyes are on hers, trying to read them. "It can wait."

So much empathy right now, but if she were to leave for a month, Derrick would not miss her. He would simply accept it and carry on existing, accumulating knowledge, continue being an ever-growing island unto himself.

"No, it's okay," she insists. "I'm tired."

Derrick picks up on some microexpression on her face and comes to his own decision. "There's dinner in the fridge if you get hungry," he says, and returns to his work or whatever it is he's doing.

Patrice slinks away to her room, feeling, if anything, like the child of a distant parent.

When she reaches her room, she falls onto her bed. A flash of her father's frowning face leaps to her mind. "If there is a heaven," he had said to her, "I hope I can meet your mother there, so we can share in our disappointment of you."

Well, for there to be a heaven, there would have to be a god. Patrice remains unconvinced of that prospect.

The Ynaa believe that the universe is a black prison. She has learned much about Ynaa philosophical beliefs by talking to the reefs. Dutifully, they supply answers to her like gifted students, eager to please. They tell her that the Ynaa meant nothing by the harm they inflicted. Their true enemy is the universe itself—this thing that pits life against life, that enjoys death so much, it visits this plague on all living things.

Well, not all living things, not anymore. Inherent in the Ynaa discovery of Yn Altaa is a contradiction. If immortality can be found here within the enemy that is the universe, then how can it be said that the universe values death and destruction above all else? The immortality of the Ynaa gives the lie to their foundational belief. What kind of adversary would grant life everlasting when it could continue granting *death* everlasting?

Patrice laughs to herself. Foolish to personify the universe in this way. Things within the universe are alive. The universe itself isn't.

The reefs stir like the diligent pupils they are. They say, *To be alive, or to be possessed by aliveness: What's the difference?*

She sends her thoughts to them: *It is very different. My cells are alive, and I am alive. The stuff of me, and me. But life inside dead matter doesn't make that matter live.*

They say, *The universe is alive. We promise.*

Explain it.

We can't. It is . . . above us.

Patrice can hear the struggle in their collective voice. Whatever they are talking about, it is truly beyond them.

She wants to believe them, but Patrice has abandoned the idea of god. Could they be talking about something else? But what? A thought crosses her mind, but Patrice shakes it away. Nonsense. All of it.

Put me to sleep, she tells the reefs, and they gently push her down into quiet, dreamless darkness.

In the early hours of the morning, the reefs pull Patrice back from sleep.

What is it? she asks.

She's outside.

Grogginess passes quickly, thanks not just to the reefs but also to this information. She is outside. Again.

Patrice finds the front door open. When she steps out onto the porch, she sees Derrick, leaning over the railing, staring out at the sky. She goes over to him before she follows his gaze.

And the reefs are right. She is there, hovering in the sky, just as the Ynaa once hovered over Water Island. Silent.

"The Night Lady," Derrick says. His expression is unmarked by surprise or fear, but there is a little bit of wonder, and it looks alien on his face. At most, her son is amused by things, responding to everything—major or minor marvels alive—with a soft, knowing smile. Never wonder. Never except for these visitations.

"What do you want?" Patrice asks the being hovering there. An angel of absence, a being of void.

Again, as always, she does not answer.

"She wants to take you someplace far away," Derrick says as if he has heard something that she hasn't.

Patrice doesn't know what to say to this. Should she laugh? Should she believe him and politely decline the offer? *Is* it an offer? Or an order? Patrice is prepared for a great many things in this world, but not this, whatever this is. And if something happens to her, if she is taken, who will protect her son? It is a silly thought, really, one born of old instincts instead of observable facts. Her son may once have needed protecting, but not anymore.

"I'll be fine on my own, Mother," he says.

And not for the first time, Patrice wonders if he has hacked the reefs inside her own mind and bent them to his will. Or maybe he just knows her too well.

"I know you're fine."

"But you're not," he says. There is a moment's pause before he elaborates. "A terrible burden, guiding the world to actualization. But what about *you*?"

"What about me?"

Whatever assessment he has made, he keeps most of it to himself. Instead, he says, "You should go with her. Actualize *yourself* further."

Patrice knows that her son is only affecting youthfulness. But still, these words, coming from his lips, are . . . *strange*. And the effect: Patrice feeling utterly exposed.

Mera offers nothing. She continues to hover there. Actualized.

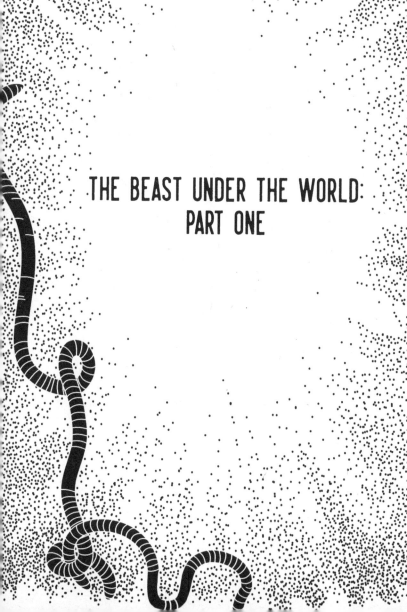

THE BEAST UNDER THE WORLD:
PART ONE

THE BEAST UNDER THE WORLD:
PART ONE

3

DRAGON
SOMEWHERE IN THE MIDWEST

EARTH 0539

JUNE 12, 2028

NINETEEN MONTHS AFTER THE BOSTON RIOTS

It is sunrise over Moon, and Dragon climbs onto his roof. At this time of morning, Dragon has Moon completely to himself. It is quiet, except for birdsong and a gentle wind blowing through the trees. But if one stretches the ears to hear, hushed conversations are stirring within the rows of houses of the hidden town. It is the start of summer. Dewy grass and coolness will soon turn to persistent heat as the sun claims the sky. In the diffuse morning light, the vestiges of the ghost town are stark against the new wood of freshly constructed houses, their paint still unchipped. The newly paved streets are arranged in a grid. Some of the old roads and signs remain, interrupted, pushed aside, fragmented by the new town made on top of the old one.

Perched with feet inclined to the roof's edge, Dragon stoops to a crouch, readying himself. He is naked, of course, his other form too large to tolerate the restriction of clothing. And with a thought—no, something faster than that: like deciding to lift an arm or leg purely by instinct, like deciding to walk and simply, instantly doing so—Dragon unfurls his wings. Beneath his human feet, etched into the roof tiling, are the familiar claw marks of his talons. And that's the other cue. Dragon submits his legs and feet to the change, the appendages becoming something else, something more. His whole body borrows from this other self: subtly scaled flesh, each muscle in him rippling from the oncoming expulsion of energy. His eyes change too: the spots of red at their center, the pitch black that has claimed the whites. Now he is prepared. Now it is time. He tucks his wings tight against himself like two knife blades aimed skyward, and Dragon leaps into the air.

He ascends, shooting up and up from Moon, wings beating furiously, until he can feel the cold between the slight indentations of scales on his skin, and still up, ever heavenward, until tightness closes around his chest when he tries to breathe. He isn't in his full form—he knows better, his other self having gotten so big—but he wonders how far up he can go if he submits completely, becomes the dragon fully. If a plane passes—and this has happened—he'll have to tuck his wings back into himself and surrender to free fall, dropping below the plane's belly, away from view. But on this morning, there is nothing for miles, and now he has left the birds far below. He ascends through the low clouds and then beyond the final cloud layer, the sky opening to vastness above, the low atmosphere a navy-domed roof over the world. He looks to the east as the sun pierces the cloud layer beneath. The rays speckle his sight. He could do it. He could change fully right now. No one would see him. Dragon tries a triumphant yell, but the sky receives it and draws it thin as a whisper. He keeps flapping his broad wings, catching air beneath him to keep himself aloft, deciding, trying to decide. But the air is so thin here he has to exert extra energy even to think. The cold is numbing. Dragon tries to hold fire in his chest, to keep his core warm, but even this, what with the lack of oxygen . . . It's too late; he has to fall, or he will die.

Dragon tucks his wings to himself and falls like an arrow to earth. He waits until he is below the clouds to expand his wings again, the action jerking him steeply back up before he rights himself into a gliding descent, right to left, like a leaf wafting down from a branch.

Moon is visible beneath him. When he gets close enough to the ground, he flares his wings and steps out of the sky. As planned, Dragon lands in front of Ossi's house, on the south edge of Moon, right up against the forest. He walks up the path to the door and knocks.

Inside, the floorboards creak. "It's open."

Dragon tries the door, enters. Staring at him from the darkest corner of the living room is Ossi, in her cat form. The sunlight through the open door glints off her black coat, flashes in the bright yellow of her eyes.

"Good morning," Dragon says.

Ossi stands on her hind legs, and in the dark, it looks like a very large house cat reaching up to bat at the air. But then she lengthens, undergoing her change, the sheen of fur turning to the duller gleam of bare brown skin.

She steps out of the shadowed corner, naked and unselfconscious, and says, "Pass me my robe, would you?"

Dragon looks politely away, reaching for her robe hanging from a hook near the door while he grasps his own bag of clothes hanging right next to it. He tosses the robe to her and then gropes through his bag.

One full outfit remains. As he dresses, he notes that he'll have to bring clothes by later tonight.

Now robed, Ossi asks, "How was your flight?"

There is no humor in her tone, and Dragon wouldn't have gotten it anyway. He has never flown in a plane. "I went higher this time," he says.

Ossi falls back onto her couch, sighing. "You'll kill yourself," she says, her usual halfhearted warning. Each time she says this, there's less concern in her words. The room is dark still, but sunlight is beginning to lift some of that darkness.

Dragon doesn't bother defending himself. He takes the wooden chair by the door, moved from the dining table for his benefit.

"Any news from the outside?" Ossi asks.

Dragon shakes his head. There is news, but it's the usual kind. More unrest, more dead monsters, or dead people suspected of being monsters. And otherwise, more of the same petty events and conflicts that have always plagued humankind. Dragon has given up caring about that stuff. *Humankind* has nothing to do with him.

"Okay . . . anything *at all* you'd like to talk about?"

Sitting there in the faint light, Dragon can see a little of Ossi's brother in her face. In the eyes, for sure. Except that Dragon remembers Tez smiling constantly. Ossi rarely smiles, but when she does, as she is doing now (with a sort of amused curiosity), even that is the same, which always makes Dragon a little sad. Thoughts of Tez inevitably give way to thoughts of Sondra, who has locked herself away in a cabin on the north side of Moon, accepting no visitors. In a way, she has also been lost to him. And the Wallaces too, his would-be adopted family. Murdered. And Smoke. He really doesn't want to think about Smoke.

Ossi continues observing Dragon. Weirdly, this is something he likes about her. He can see her trying to read him, because she doesn't pretend otherwise. Ossi isn't polite. She isn't nice. But she is kind—the sort of kind that is hard to see if you're only paying attention to the surface. Ossi's kindness is in the subtleties.

"Not in the talking mood, I see," she says.

Now, for example, even though he knows that she can tell something is wrong (more wrong than usual), she will leave it alone, quietly take in the information for later, when she drops by his place on her way to take a "stroll through the woods." And if he decides to go with her, she might ask a question that will be an invitation he can receive if he chooses. Even her showing herself noticing is an invitation.

Truth be told, Dragon isn't sure what is wrong. He has been feeling for some time now that this place isn't right for him. It has been good in a lot of ways; the quiet of Moon has allowed him to pick up on the subtler aspects of being a person. And he knows himself better now, knows what he likes, what he doesn't—an ever-lengthening list. But what he is really coming to terms with is this resistance in him toward the path he has been on, this path that has been at the whim of others. He wants to make his own way in the world, find his own path. He can feel in himself an expansion, or at least a desire to expand.

He has the strength now to be on his own, and he desperately wants to be on his own.

But he can't leave yet. There is something he has left to do here. He has a sense that there's something on the horizon, and people here worth protecting. Mostly out of obligation, but also, in a few instances, out of love. He knows that Ossi would understand this, but Dragon isn't ready to talk about it.

Ossi reaches for the familiar drawstring pouch on the coffee table between them and spills its contents. The checkers fall in a pleasant clatter, some onto the checkerboard that always sits open on the table.

Dragon grins and pulls his chair closer to the board, and it is as if years of trauma melt away, the child who never got a chance to truly exist springing from a secret place inside the teenage boy.

"Better," Ossi says. "You can go first."

Before Moon, Ossi lived with an Inuit tribe for decades, as a sort of guardian. They accepted her despite her physical differences from them. The acceptance wasn't based on superstition—they didn't mistake her for a spirit, or any such nonsense. The tribe had a slippery view of reality, a more agnostic sense of what it entailed, having its own long history of monstrosity, of strangeness. Ossi was surly but not dangerous. Over time, she became fond of her tribe, and they of her, and she committed to watching out for them. But with modernization came climate change, and life outside the tribe called the young people away. The tribe dwindled. Ossi, used to moving on, moved on.

The first game ends quickly, with Dragon as the winner.

"You let me win," he says.

Ossi smirks just a little. "I got distracted."

"By what?" He is careful when he asks this but trusts himself to know when he can press Ossi for information.

And it seems to be a good time. Ossi says, "The night sky in the north. It is beautiful here, but up there it is so clear you feel like you can drink from it, like it can just pour into you. I know that's a strange thing to say."

Dragon shakes his head. "No, I think I get it. That's why I go so high."

"I wanted to ask if you could take me sometime. Up there."

"Yes. But I think I'll have to shift to do it. *Fully* shift."

Ossi nods, her amber eyes shimmering. Even in her human form, there's still a bit of the cat in those eyes. "On a cold night, when everyone's inside, so it's safer."

They play several more games of checkers. Dragon wins a couple of times, but by the end, as always, Ossi has claimed the majority. He shouldn't like this, losing so often, but he has learned vastly more from playing with Ossi than he would from someone who took pity on him. Ossi doesn't throw games out of pity, and Dragon hates being treated like a baby.

On his way out, Ossi asks Dragon if he will come back later this evening. For a walk. Dragon chuckles to himself. "Sure."

The air outside is still cool, but the sun is fully out. And Dragon can see people in the distance moving about the little town, some heading off to the community center or for a morning walk, or just gardening in plots outside their houses. In a couple of hours, Moon will be bustling with life, the calm faces of adults idling in front of each other's houses, children running and screeching.

This tiny bubble of tranquility in a roiling world, its soft film so easy to pop, given the right pressure. Just one glimpse from an outsider with evil intent, and this sanctuary could collapse. Dragon tries not to think about that, but in his experience, peace is not a steady state. It can't be maintained forever.

His thoughts are disrupted by the sight of Georgie, a few houses ahead of him, chopping wood with an axe that reflects the morning sun. She buries the axe in a stump and waves him over.

Dragon obeys the beckon, frowning. He can guess what this is about and begins to dread the course of the conversation prematurely.

"Will you help us this afternoon?" Georgie asks.

Yes, it is exactly what he thought she would ask.

"With jam making," she adds, likely mistaking Dragon's affronted look for confusion.

"Maybe," Dragon says. What if he simply walks away right this moment? On a scale of one to ten, how inappropriate would that be?

Georgie smiles at him, all warmth, her big eyes shining. "Connor and I would love if you dropped by."

Does knowing this change anything for Dragon? A little.

"You know," Georgie says, watching him, trying to figure him out while trying to hide it, the way everyone is always trying to figure him out while trying to hide it, "you could join us full-time, as a worker-owner."

"Aren't I too young?"

"In the outside world, sure." She grins. "But we're not in the outside world, are we? We can do whatever you like. We should have been paying you anyway."

Dragon has done work at the jammery a handful of times. He never expected money. It is something to do when he's trying to find things to do. Today he simply wants to exist.

"You can think about it, anyway," she says. "Come by today or tomorrow, whatever. How about books? You like reading, right? I've seen you reading."

"I do," Dragon says. "But I don't want to work at the bookstore either." Dragon doesn't know if that's what she was getting at, suggesting that he join Ridley at the bookstore, but he realizes that the "either" implies that he also doesn't want to work at the jammery.

Georgie's smile falters a little bit. "It's just," she says, "we've seen you spending more time with Ossi, and, well . . ." Dragon can see her choosing her words very carefully. "She's withdrawn, and you've been starting to withdraw too."

"I'm not withdrawing. I'm just growing up."

"Right, yes, we've noticed. That's why we want you to feel like you're a part of the community." She studies Dragon's face. "I'm being pushy, aren't I? I'm always doing that. I don't mean to. I'm sorry."

"It's all right."

"We like you here. And we want you to feel like you're among family. That you're, you know, taken care of. No, cared *for*. You know?"

Georgie has always been overly invested in everyone's well-being. Something she has in common with Connor, in fact—that syrup-sweet caring.

But something about this moment, the purposeful way she's looking at Dragon, feels as though this is a more serious kind of concern. "You're worried about me," Dragon says. "Worried I might harm myself?"

"I saw you this morning," Georgie says, and the words just spill out of her as if she's been holding them in for the entire conversation. "I've seen you several times, actually. You go up"—she points to the sky—"straight up, and you disappear. And then today I saw you falling back down, opening your wings only when you were close to the ground. You're young, I told myself. Well, okay, this is what people do when they're young. I was no stranger to risky behavior myself. But. But . . ."

Dragon says nothing.

"I just want to make sure you're not doing it for another reason."

Like trying to kill himself. Or deciding to kill himself and changing his mind at the last instant. He actually has to consider that, weigh it in his mind. Is that what he's been doing? Playing with the thought of ending his life? He can certainly see how it might look that way from the outside. He remembers Ossi saying, "You'll get yourself killed doing that," and wonders if she's worried about this too: his emotional stability.

But when he really considers it, he truly believes that what he is doing in those moments—flying up to the limits of Earth and free-falling back down—is the *opposite* of wanting to die. What he wants, is desiring with all his heart, is to feel alive. He is reaching *for* life.

"I didn't mean to make you worry," he tells Georgie.

"Like I said, I wasn't worried at first. But you've been so withdrawn. And today . . ."

"Honestly, I've just been figuring myself out. That's why I've been withdrawn, I mean. I've been figuring out what I want."

"What do you want?"

To not be here, Dragon thinks. To travel the world. To have the choice to do that. To be a person not confined, not moving from one form of confinement to another. He wants to be . . .

And it is such a silly thing. No one is. No one is *free*. But some people are freer than he is, have always been freer. Dragon has always been in a cage.

"I don't know," he finally says. Because, in a way, this is true too. Because what he wants is the freedom to not know, the freedom to find out.

"The offer is open. Come make jam with us anytime."

And those bright eyes tip him over the line of indifference, into true caring. Those eyes make him want to try not withdrawing completely. "Okay."

She reaches out, puts one hand on his shoulder. He is taller than she, has grown so much in the past year, so she has to reach up. But somehow the gesture is loving. Motherly. On the wind, though he knows it isn't there, could not be there, Dragon catches the faint scent of blood. Bees swarm in his ears. A man's grinning face. The scent of blood overcome by the whiff of burnt flesh, a whole circle of people on fire. A door tries to open in his mind, and as he has done so many times before, as he did then, he slams it shut.

"I should go," Dragon says.

She can see that she has somehow misstepped. "Seriously, no pressure. If not today, come by tomorrow. Really, it's an open invitation."

When he returns to his house, he calls out. No response. Alex must be resting—no surprise there—but he wishes he could talk to her, hear one of her lengthy stories about her missions abroad, places he has never seen, people living in ways he could never imagine on his own. Dragon sits on the couch, not bothering to call out again even though he wants to. Sometimes he'll spend a day or two without interacting with Alex. Her room is in the heart of the house—blacked-out windows, door closed to keep out the light. Alex will sometimes go on walks at night with Ossi and Dragon. He wonders if she might this evening. Ossi and Alex get along, which is a relief to Dragon. They're so different, all of them, but on the walks, they seem to align on so many things. Mainly, they agree that eventually they'll need to be proactive about the threat to monsters. They just don't know how yet.

He could go to the community center later, see if anyone is there, if June or Nat are playing a video game he can jump in on. They're teenagers like him, human children of a witch, but he finds conversations with them to be vapid, useless. Video games he likes, though, and they let him play with them. But is he in the mood? He might have to go to the jammery in the afternoon after all, or stop by Ridley's to grab another book. A whole day lies ahead, and Dragon has nothing to do. Sitting alone too long will only invite thoughts he does not want.

He thinks of all the days stretching out before him, days in which he'll have to continue choosing between activities to pass the time, and he has to fight back frustration. He has to do something. Something needs to happen. If he doesn't figure out how to quiet this feeling inside him, he's going to explode.

LAINA CALVARY

It is 8:00 a.m., and Laina is sitting in a rocker by her bed-room window, staring out at the rows of houses, the dense trees beyond, with a steaming mug of milk tea cupped in her palms. Rebecca is still asleep, her soft, intermittent snoring a backdrop to the muted noises outside the window.

People are up. Laina watches two neighbors idling on the front porch across the street, talking. One of them is human, the other a dryad witch with a green tint to her skin in a certain light. The latter neighbor, Jesmeen, is one of Laina's casual acquaintances. Even that might be a stretch. They exchange gardening techniques, though Jesmeen has more to offer than Laina ever could, considering what Jesmeen is: a dryad . . . and a witch.

She loves the early a.m. quiet. Most mornings, she is at this window, watching the orange sunrise cool to morning blue. She got up a little late today, but the sight is still beautiful. For a time, she felt claustrophobic in Moon, but she has now settled into the solitude of this life among mere dozens, with no anonymous faces. No *true* strangers.

Even when new people arrive, they feel familiar. Those same reluctant expressions, mixed with anxiety.

Moon isn't very big. The town houses forty-eight residents, four of whom are new to Moon—two just this week—and there will likely be more before the end of the month. With each arrival comes news from the rest of the world—news not easily found on social media. Only the darkest corners of the internet tell the truth about what is happening to monsters and their sympathizers outside sanctuary intentional communities like Moon.

New residents bring their own stories, having left communities that became increasingly hostile to monsters and their sympathizers. First are the messages, out in the open for anyone to see: on utility poles, on community bulletin boards, graffitied on the sides of buildings. Usually a simple question: *Do you suspect that someone you know is a monster?* The wording isn't always the same, but these messages always come with a website to visit or a forum to join or a number to call. The threat of what will happen to the people who have been reported is left hanging in the air.

The new Moonites tell of rallies in public spaces, anti-monster sentiment spreading like gossip in their workplaces, the signs of danger becoming louder and louder, the feeling that threats are wrapping around them, circling tighter and tighter. Was that person really watching them? Did they imagine the hostile look on that neighbor's face? Then come the unambiguous signs: people standing outside their apartments in the dead of night; acts of vandalism to their businesses, their homes, their possessions; someone following just out of sight or loitering in the darkness beyond the streetlight, watching.

And just as they feel this final pressure—eerily so—they receive a message. Sometimes from a friend, or an envelope inside their mailbox, or a card slipped right under their door. Not a threat but a lifeline. Per the instructions, all they have to do is text the word *ESCAPE*—just like that, all caps—to a number. A response will not come from the phone number itself. There will be no invitations to meet in a dark, secluded place. These terrified people would hardly agree with a request like that anyway. Simply text the message, and something will happen. And this part is very important: Do not tell anyone who does not wish to escape.

What reaches out is not a person. It is an arthropod—an ant or spider or bee or beetle—with an offer of sanctuary. All they have to do is say yes. A leap of faith. Some take the leap right away. Surely, whoever has sent a talking insect to them isn't a human, could not possibly be involved in the anti-monster movement. Others decline at first, due to the strangeness of the invitation itself. Terrifying, really, to be visited by an insect. And why does it look like that, as if its carapace were made of metal? But almost always the offer becomes less terrifying than the clear and present threats they face in their own lives, and when the insect or spider returns every day with the same offer, they eventually accept. Then something even stranger happens: A ring of ants appears on a nearby wall, their hindquarters glowing, and a portal opens in front of them—just like that, a hole in the world, leading to another place entirely. They simply have to walk through. By this point, most people do, lured by the magic of the moment and the promise of safety.

Of course, the residents of Moon have no idea what happens to the ones who don't choose to step through the portal.

Not every resident of Moon is a monster. Kirsten, the woman outside Laina's window talking to Jesmeen, is merely a vocal sympathizer. Before the vise tightened around Kirsten, she was a YouTube personality who investigated potential hate crimes and also monster disappearances, some of which were people who had escaped to Moon. She had a popular series on Karuna Flood because, well, who doesn't start there? No interest in the woman herself, however, who actually lives in Moon, because "she gives me the creeps."

Humans like Kirsten make up one-fifth of the residents. Kirsten has become an especially valuable member of the community, hosting movie nights for the eleven kids in Moon. Laina and Kirsten aren't as close, but Rebecca likes her. They've even discussed Kirsten joining their pack of shifters.

When Kirsten first came to Moon several months ago, she was startled by her own shadow. But, as with most other residents, her fear has softened as she has slipped into the sleepy day-to-day priorities of the town. Everyone's terror dulls eventually. Now Kirsten has redoubled her efforts into monster investigation, publishing audio-only podcasts on her website through a virtual private network. Laina does not like this, hence the lack of closeness. She wishes Kirsten and those like her would get over their interest in things happening outside Moon or, if they are dead set on torturing themselves, to do so quietly. Rebecca, unfortunately, is among the people concerned about what's happening outside, but at least she's smart enough to lurk on forums instead of drawing attention to herself.

Laina's only real concerns are Rebecca and Ridley, and the ongoing safety of the town. She likes her peaceful mornings that stretch into languid days of idleness, or routine work at the small bookstore downstairs. She likes that their lives have become uneventful. She has yet to miss the threatening anonymity of the city, the way dread lingered on in those years after the Boston Massacre. It started with Lincoln's death, the persistent fog of low-buzzing panic. The panic, the worry, only grew with the mass shooting a year later, and the riots a couple of years after that. She began to see threats everywhere. Anyone who looked at her too long became a secret enemy; any sudden noise became a potential assault. The ever-increasing fear that anti-monster sentiment would spill over into something that could harm her or the people she loves. So much noise she had to filter out—or pay attention to in case paying attention might save her life.

Until Moon. Here, she can tune out everything and not worry. Here, she can pretend everything is okay.

A box drops downstairs, startling Rebecca awake—Rebecca's wolf turning the sound into gunfire, Laina supposes. Or something worse.

"Damn it," Rebecca says as she settles into wakefulness. "I've told him to stop tossing those boxes around." She stretches her back, and Laina hears the pop of vertebrae.

What Laina understands is that Ridley can't stop throwing those boxes around. She sees him try not to, but when he's angry enough, with nothing and no one to direct his anger toward, boxes of books receive the punishment. It is one of the only outlets Ridley allows himself under the cover of expediency. Why set a box gently down when you can quickly drop it on a stack of other boxes? Saves time, right? It is why Laina hasn't brought it up herself. When another box smacks loudly into its neighbor, she knows that Ridley is having a particularly bad day.

"Jesus," Rebecca says under her breath, and then: "Hey, you made some tea for me too, right?"

Laina nods. "There's some left over in the pot on the stove. You'll have to get it from the kitchen, madam."

"What happened to bed service?"

"You'll get that when I get mine," Laina says as she turns from the window, her smile all mischief.

"You're such a tease."

"Who says I'm teasing?"

Rebecca grins and leaps out of the bed to sit on Laina's lap. They share a kiss with all the passion of their first. The press of Rebecca's body in her nightdress. The softness of her lips. They separate, breathing hard, Laina a little dizzy from forgetting to breathe.

"We should go out for the day," Rebecca says, taking a sip of Laina's tea while ignoring Laina's glare. "Leti and some others have been sneaking away to a nearby town, you know. We should go with them."

No, she didn't know that Leti and her stupid friends—because she can guess who these "others" are—had left Moon. And the suggestion of going with them quickly turns her mood.

"What?" Rebecca says, noticing the change.

"That little girl's crazy, is what."

"She's twenty-two. Hardly a *little* girl."

"You remember what you were like at twenty-two?"

Rebecca opens her mouth to argue, then takes a second to consider the question. "Fair point."

"And I bet Tash went with her. She should know better."

Rebecca keeps her mouth shut, which tells Laina she's right.

"Who else?" Laina asks.

"Now that you're on a warpath, I'm not saying."

"It's reckless."

"So you're not interested in ever leaving Moon again?" Rebecca asks.

On impulse, Laina almost answers honestly. No, she has zero interest in leaving the safety of Moon ever again. And why should she? All the people she cares about—a vanishingly small number even before their escape—are right here. She's been wondering for a while if she would change somehow, has waited patiently to feel the change within herself, to feel the restlessness begin. But it hasn't happened yet. This hidden place, with all its smallness and petty dramas and predictable daily routine, feels large to her. Inside it, she has everything she's ever wanted, but most of all, she has peace.

"No, it's not that," Laina finally says. "I just think, if we leave the town, we should go somewhere far away. And it should be spread out, as if at random, not routine visits to nearby towns. How many times have they gone out?"

Rebecca sighs. "Leti said a few times, which makes me think it's actually been several."

Laina stifles a curse.

"Yeah," Rebecca says. "I'm beginning to see the problem."

And how could the problem not be seen? It's obvious. Yes, the residents of Moon never talk about what to do on excursions outside. But that's because no one leaves, since everyone here is hiding from the outside world. Okay, that's not entirely true. People *do* have to visit friends and family during emergencies, attend funerals, get health checkups if they're uncomfortable being ministered to by mechanical ants. But in those cases, they use the goddamn portal! Which, sure, comes with its own risks. Moonites, for example, could be spotted by neighbors while leaving the empty apartments in any of the major cities the portal is linked to. But that's far less conspicuous than regularly dropping into a small town in rural America, where everyone knows fucking everyone. And in come Leti and Tash to the local diner each week, chomping down cheeseburgers with their clearly not-from-here accents, the locals asking each other, "Are they living in town? Did you see where they came in from?" All it takes is one local getting the bright idea to follow Leti and Tash back to the monster town hidden in the woods.

"You are *so* pissed off," Rebecca observes.

Laina gulps down her tea so she won't have to respond.

"We can't tell people they're forbidden from leaving. Which is why we don't."

Laina puts her mug back on the windowsill.

"We're not prisoners."

Laina stares out the window.

"The town is hidden by magic."

But what does it look like to see people drive into a magically hidden town? Or leave it? Laina decides not to say this part out loud. She turns back to Rebecca, changing the subject: "How about we go to the lake later?"

Rebecca pouts.

"What? You like the lake."

"Fine. But let's wait until the morning chill has lifted."

There's another noise from downstairs.

"Now Ridley really *does* need to get out of here," Rebecca says.

"You think he's unhappy?"

"I know he is. You do too. You're just too content to disrupt his 'I'm okay' performance."

If someone else had said this, Laina would have felt a little hurt by the implication. If she's willing to ignore her partner's suffering for her own contentment, what does that make her? But she hears no judgment in Rebecca's tone, only loving observation. Maybe even a little good-natured conspiracy.

"You're right," Laina admits. "He's been restless. I haven't seen him pick up his wood-carving tools in months. He's been pouring all his attention into the store."

"We should help him more with that."

"I've tried taking on more shifts," she says. "But he still spends all day and night downstairs doing busywork. And where would he go? Except for the project with Karuna, he's been quite antisocial here. It's really unlike him." Laina has an idea, and it is out of her mouth before she musters the good sense to stop it. "If we do go out, we should make it a road trip. Take a week or two and put some miles between us and this place."

"I'd love that. And with Riddle, I know we'll be supercareful."

Laina is sure of this too. With Ridley present, this version of Ridley especially—having had the experience of being cornered by the Black Hand, guns pointed at all of them, ready to fire, his bookstore burning behind him, before a literal hole opened up in the world, thus saving their lives at the very last moment—Laina is certain that he will do everything in his power to keep them safe.

But then again, no form of caution, however vigilant, could ever compare to staying here, inside Moon.

She holds this thought back as well. She has already made the road-trip suggestion. Instead, Laina smiles and kisses Rebecca softly on the cheek, getting a whiff of her morning scent.

If Laina says nothing, if she lets the conversation end here without more plans, this might remain a *someday* thing. Someday plans can easily be forgotten.

5

HAROLD SHINER

There's an itch inside Harry's ear. He reaches to scratch it and realizes that he has tried to use his phantom hand again, just as the scarred end of the stump touches his earlobe. He has to tamp down the frustration, which leaves only the embarrassment. He looks over at Karuna, and as always, she looks completely comfortable at her desk, writing with her nondominant hand in her yellow notepad. The light from the window has set her short-cropped hair aglow. She looks like an angel—if that angel might just decide to kill you on a whim.

Karuna and Harry are writing a book together. Under the pseudonym S. A. Nine—*S* for *Six*, *A* for *Alfred*—and about . . . what *is* it about? So far Harry's contribution has been a first-hand account of his time underground, the events leading up to and after his imprisonment, his impressions of the Cult of the Zsouvox, the secret conspirators behind the Boston Massacre. Karuna is writing about the history of secret societies, fitting within it the history of two dueling orders of monsters. Harry's part is really about his trauma. And so is Karuna's, if looked at from a certain light. But their approaches are different. Harry's contribution, although its voice is at a remove, is still very personal: leaps of conjecture, occasional anger, the clear intention to exonerate the mass shooters as pawns in some greater game. Karuna's contribution is more distant, as seemingly cold as the woman herself, but engaging, dynamic. Sober and brilliant in equal parts, providing ample context for her conclusions about the monster secret societies and their history within the larger secret society ecosystem. What the book will look like when it comes together remains to be seen.

The book is not the only complicated aspect of their life. Over their time together, Harry has come to admit to himself, and to Karuna (though more indirectly), that he is desperately in love with her. And Karuna, who seems very much aware of his affection, has made it clear, without saying it outright, that their relationship will remain a friendship, will not be burdened by even a casual romance. Harry—suffering from a deep and chronic lack of self-confidence due to his disability and, according to himself, to his "ungraceful aging"—has accepted this dynamic stoically. Though he loves her, he recognizes that they have become life partners in a platonic sense, with a mutual tolerance of each other, and even, perhaps, mutual respect.

The house they share is a standard Moon two-bedroom—a single story, a reasonably sized front room with a connected kitchen and dining area, a short hall with a large bedroom on one side and a slightly smaller bedroom and bath on the other. Broad windows to let in light. Modest. Comfortable. Certainly better than the cabin Harry and Karuna hid away in for three years before coming here.

If they had a family or small business, they'd get a two-story house with three or even four bedrooms. The occasional five-bedroom for the really big families, but even those houses, though bigger, could also be described as modest. When Harry broached the subject of sharing a house, Karuna nodded curtly. "We have a good living relationship," she said. "I don't mind a roommate." Harry interpreted that as strong interest.

While living in the cabin before the ants transported them to Moon, they had gotten used to helping each other out since they each were missing a hand. And, as was previously established, Harry loves Karuna and didn't want to be in another house. He has gotten used to getting up in the morning and seeing her at her desk, already working on the manuscript, a cup of tea slowly cooling next to her notepad. Karuna always writes longhand now, since the "amputation." A computer or a typewriter, although quicker in one respect, feels unnatural, she says. Harry still uses a computer, sometimes dictation software, and very occasionally a notepad when he wants to work in the same room as Karuna, who is prickly about noise: the clatter of keys, his voice, even loud breathing.

Karuna is at her usual spot, one leg folded under her so that a knee juts out at an awkward angle. Harry's foot would fall asleep if he sat in that position. She is writing furiously, brow creased in deep concentration. He passes as quietly as he can manage, goes to the kitchen to have a cup of the coffee Karuna has made. He sets the steaming mug down on his desk in the living room and pulls his notepad from one of the drawers. All these things he does one at a time so that he need only use his one remaining hand. He doesn't like using the stump, even now after many years of watching Karuna navigate the world using hers as stoically and unceremoniously as Karuna does everything.

When Harry isn't in love with Karuna, he hates her.

An hour like this, in complete silence, Harry trying to focus, sneaking glances at Karuna. When Harry looks up, yawning and stretching both his writing hand and the missing one, Karuna is looking at him.

"Can I ask you something?" This in the inflectionless way that lets Harry know that she will ask anyway, no matter what he says or whether he chooses to say anything at all. And so: "The Ritual of Knowing—do you think that was a literal thing or not?"

Harry waits for Karuna to explain further. He doesn't know what she's getting at, but he is already sure he won't like it.

"Did the Cult of the Zsouvox actually believe that having Dragon eat our hands would help them understand the Beast-under-the-World?"

"And bend it to our will," Harry says through shudders. These were the exact words the leader of the Cult of the Zsou-vox used before they each lost a hand.

"That," Karuna says, "I think, is also a part of the extended metaphor—'beast' meaning true reality, and 'bend to our will' meaning manipulate reality to their own ends. Or something. But how does the ritual help them *understand* reality?" Her eyebrows crease, but before Harry can respond, she shakes her head. "No. I don't think there was anything to the taking of our hands. Only ritualized cruelty."

Harry has turned fully to her—his whole body instead of just his head. At this moment, he can pine openly. And use his pining over her to ignore the thrum of phantom pain coming from where his hand used to be. He focuses on her face. Karuna keeps her hair short on the sides, less short on top. She has let it turn gray, but her face remains quite smooth, youthful—at least compared to Harry, who has recently turned fifty. Her appearance isn't of great concern to her. Still, unadorned though she may be, Harry finds her beautiful.

But it doesn't matter, because he is hearing her words and is considering them, and a thought is slowly coming to the surface. It is a big thought, at least to Harry—a breaching whale. "Collective unconscious."

Karuna looks at him.

"The Beast-under-the-World. What if 'beast' isn't 'true reality' but is instead 'the collective unconscious'? Maybe too fine a distinction, but . . ." He takes a beat to find the right words. "In that case, the Beast-under-the-World would be the collective unconscious invisibly guiding humanity. The Cult of the Zsouvox's mission: Come to understand the collective unconscious. Come to bend it to their will."

Frowning, Karuna says, "And the ritual would do that . . . how?"

It isn't a real question she is expecting Harry to answer. Her gaze has gone inward, thinking over the puzzle.

He answers anyway. "Heat."

"You obviously have to say more than that."

"Are you familiar with how bees ventilate their nests?"

Karuna nods. "Tell me anyway."

Harry sighs, forcing himself to continue the analogy. He hates analogies. "Bees don't consciously cool their nests. When a bee is hot, it hovers, beating its wings. This creates local warming. Heat where the bees are fanning. More bees draw to that heat, flapping their wings, eventually cooling the nest. It is emergent. If you step far enough back, look at society from a far enough remove, we are built—human society is built—on the same emergent properties."

Her eyes on him, sharp. "You're saying—"

"What would happen if they created heat? If we, the perpetrators of the Boston Massacre, were the heat."

She nods.

"And our missing hands. Think about how that one detail magnified everything, encouraging endless conspiracy theories. If the attack was heat, all the unanswered questions were fire."

Karuna says each word slowly: "The Cult of the Zsouvox wanted to engineer a human-supremacist movement." Then her eyes widen. The expression on her face is both epiphany and frustration. Harry knows her well enough to know why the frustration is there. This answer seems obvious now that it has been said out loud. Internally, she is kicking herself.

Harry doesn't think it was obvious, but already he is on to the implied next question: *Why would a monster organization want to engineer a human-supremacist movement?*

They are looking at each other, considering the unspoken question between them.

"I think the Cult of the Zsouvox wanted unrest to hide their true objectives," Harry says.

"They were creating background noise," Karuna says. "But why? For a monster war? It doesn't make sense. There hasn't been one, not really." She pauses. "Not yet." Karuna rests her chin unselfconsciously on the stump of her arm, deep in thought. She says, "Okay, they had two objectives. A psychological operation on the human population. An attempt to draw out the

Order of Asha. Stretch their resources out; wear them down. But why attack so indirectly? Why take all this time?"

"Well, hasn't it been effective so far? We look cornered, hiding away in Moon. The Order of Asha looks cornered hiding us here. Especially as unrest builds outside Moon."

Now Karuna is thinking, like *really* thinking, her stump under her chin and the other hand across her forehead—a deep, pensive expression, completely disappearing into herself. Long minutes elapse this way, Karuna inside her own mind and Harry looking on, waiting. He is secretly proud of himself for being the cause of this particular moment of contemplation, because he often worries that he isn't smart enough to be in the same room as Karuna, let alone in the same conversation.

Suddenly, she is looking at him again, another epiphany on her face. "Another reason they'd do this: Their power isn't limitless. They need noise to keep institutions busy: law enforcement, governments, intelligence operations—at least the parts they don't control—while parts of the conflict spill out into the world. Noise to hide other noise. And. And . . . If they can control a part of the noise, then they can worry less about the parts they can't control."

"Then they're damn lucky we weren't captured by the authorities," Harry says.

"I have a feeling we wouldn't have been able to reveal anything. We'd been with the Bone Witch so often down in that basement. No telling what magics they put on us, *in* us, over all those months to make sure we kept our mouths shut."

To Harry, the answer is still unsatisfactory. And for Karuna too, apparently, because she has disappeared into herself again.

Harry is thinking, to his surprise, about Dragon. He is thinking that he's never talked to Dragon about his part in all this, never asked him what he knows about Trapp's dungeons, his life there, or his interactions with the Order of Asha. Harry has talked to Ridley and has gotten very little out of him. He got much the same from a couple of other people in Moon, who knew next to nothing. But he's never talked about any of it with Dragon, the one person in Moon who would know a lot, even if he doesn't know what it means.

Karuna, by contrast, has talked to Dragon often, has taken copious notes, but has also assured Harry that Dragon doesn't know much. And Harry believed her, still believes her, but he wants to ask Dragon a specific question: What is his earliest memory? He is wondering this because first memories tend to be important—the moment that you become aware and start seeing yourself as a self, moving through the world, experiencing, only you're there experiencing yourself experiencing the first metamoment of your life. Harry's was on a car ride with an uncle, when the uncle turned to him, put his hand on Harry's head, and told him, "Aren't you a smart boy. You're going to be someone someday."

Harry was too young to understand all the layers of meaning in the statement, but he knew by his uncle's tone that it was important, something to remember—something his uncle wouldn't say often or to just anyone. It might have been what made Harry think he could be an apiologist and an academic despite being the first in his family to go that route. The memory, to put it mildly, was formative. He wonders if Dragon had a formative moment like that, a memory that could be an important piece in this sprawling puzzle.

Harry looks to Karuna and asks her if she's ever talked to Dragon about his early memories.

"You should ask him yourself," she says. And in her expression—in that sharp-eyed way that she looks at him when she is saying something under the words and is looking through him at the same time (getting to his core)—he knows that what she's really telling him is that it is time to settle things with Dragon. Harry doesn't have it in him to tell her that he has tried to talk to Dragon. It didn't go well.

Instead, he says, "Maybe we can get Ridley to reach out to Melku about some of this."

"I've asked. The Order of Asha have refused an audience with anyone. Even Melku has ceased communication. Ridley has been a little uneasy about it, actually."

"So much we don't know, may never know."

"How is that different from anything else in life, in *everyone's* life? I've never met my real parents. My whole line stretching back to humankind's Eve is a mystery to me. We use what we can get to enrich ourselves, but we will die incomplete, with vast chasms of ignorance in our decomposing brains."

"Jesus." Harry sometimes forgets how strange this woman is, and then she says something that shocks him out of all familiarity, and he realizes it again. He is certain he will never fully understand Karuna. She will always and forever remain a mystery.

"What do we do?"

Karuna shrugs. She turns back to her desk and begins writing furiously.

A fitting response from this woman, his platonic partner. He returns to his own work.

Five minutes later, she says, "You should talk to Dragon. Again. I think it will help the both of you."

Of course she knows. He nods agreement. Yes, he'll try again. Maybe it'll be different the next time, he thinks. He doesn't find the thought especially motivating.

6

RIDLEY GIBSON

Midmorning and Ridley is still busy downstairs, unpacking boxes of books that were brought in through the portal last night. On the front of the house, which doubles as a small bookstore on the first floor, is a sign. On it, a name: *Anarres Books*. This two-story house lies along the central vein of the town, the main road where Moon's stores reside. For a time, Ridley considered calling it Anarres Redux instead. But no—Anarres Books hadn't quite risen from the ashes like a phoenix. The new bookstore was a ship rebuilt in miniature, a ship in a bottle. Now that they live in a secret intentional community called Moon, *Anarres Books* seems even more appropriate, almost prophetic. Perhaps the first store was always meant to burn down and be built again here, in this secret place. Perhaps, when he decided to start the cooperative, he had taken the biggest step toward becoming what he is now. But sometimes Ridley has to tell himself that nothing was lost in that transfer from Boston to this place, that he himself remains undiminished by that transplantation, that though he is hiding, he is still every bit the person he was. Sometimes the telling himself is enough.

Ridley stabs the tape securing the box a little too hard with the X-Acto knife. He swears, hopes he hasn't damaged anything as he tears the flaps free of the torn tape. Inside, one of the covers of *Lost Heaven* is nicked, but everything looks fine. Still, that's a book he'll have to discard or put on the free table.

Again Ridley has the thought that it wouldn't matter anyway. In this bubble reality he's hiding in, free of expenses such as rent and groceries, what does he need money for?

He starts taking out books from the box, dropping them heavily on his work desk. He will spend the rest of the morning unpacking boxes sent here through the portal and packing other boxes to send back through.

There is a small warehouse on the other side of the portal, which everyone in the outside world believes is all that remains of Anarres Books. The warehouse ships to another, larger warehouse, the regional hub for Book Indie, a platform cooperative for independent booksellers. As far as the outside world is concerned, the actual brick-and-mortar Anarres Books burned down, and now the owners take only online orders. It is a fiction that must be encouraged.

The current Anarres Books is much smaller than its predecessor. Now its in-person clientele is under fifty people, the residents of Moon. Happily, most of Moon actually patronizes the store, even if they buy only a handful of books with their disposable income from their other businesses. (They all do this—support each other with the money they make from outside the community.)

At the moment, Ridley is packing a single big box for a

patron in Oregon. He has suspected for a while that this patron buys exclusively from Anarres Books and must be a supporter, not just of the store but of monsters too. Many of Anarres Books' online orders are from sympathizers, or people who know what happened to the store, or previous clients who want to stay loyal to their local indie—another useless political gesture. Anarres Books isn't local to anywhere.

He cuts open another box, emptying the contents onto his desk and the floor before organizing them into more outgoing orders and books to go on shelves. And then it's 10:00 a.m. Time to open.

Ridley goes to the front, which isn't far. He is remembering the two floors of Anarres Books—the first one, the one that got burned down by Black Hand. All that space, enough to have more than one shelf in each genre. Enough to have a small bar-café and places to sit and idle. Enough room to host events from visiting authors. God, *visiting* authors—when would that happen again? He tamps down his own sense of claustrophobia as he unlocks the door and turns the sign over so that *Open* faces the street. Not a street, really. A road between two rows of houses, some of which double as storefronts. Ridley will be closing by 2:00 p.m.

You're lucky, he tries to remind himself. *You're alive*. But his life has gotten so small. He goes back behind the desk to fill another box. So *small*, this life.

The bell over the door chimes at 10:25 a.m., and a voice calls out as the store door closes: "Ridley?"

But then their eyes meet, because the bookstore is so small, and Ridley is standing behind the desk, adding a sticker to a small package. One book, *The Fracture Effect: Redux*.

"Here," Ridley says anyway, recognizing Leti, a short white woman with tan skin and green eyes.

"Just wanted to pick a new book," she says. "I'm finished with the last one you recommended."

"Oh, great," he says. "What did you think?"

"I loved it."

"Another recommendation?"

"Yes, please."

It was a new novel with characters that are monsters. A slice-of-life contemporary realist novel—because here, in this particular universe, it could be realist—where monsters are not openly persecuted (so not altogether realist). A novel about young people in a Midwestern city, dealing with breakups and crises of faith and new jobs and finding one's place in the world. They just also happen to be monsters. The book, titled *Monster Town*, was written by Kilah Allen, a young writer doing her first novel after a realist collection. A quiet story dense with the inner lives of its characters.

Ridley likes the book because it imagines a world where monsters have normal problems, and indeed this is the reason Allen wrote the book. It is a subtle political statement (maybe not so subtle)—a sort of wish fulfillment for a world where monstrosity doesn't have to be a dividing line. Ridley tries to keep up with news about Kilah. So far, she has avoided any great misfortune. She has been threatened, of course, and "looked into" by the Black Hand and other, lesser human-supremacist organizations. But there have been no direct threats to her life.

"Nice day outside," Leti says.

True. But Leti looks . . . "What is it? What's wrong?"

At first, she tries to pretend she's fine. Then she says, "Something has happened."

Ridley waits, because he understands that in a moment like this, no prodding is the best prodding. *Something* has happened—the inexactness a balm over a fresh wound.

Finally, she says, "We went to a nearby town," before losing courage again.

Ridley tries to fill in what's missing, but all the thoughts his mind leaps to are more horrible than whatever she's fighting with herself to say out loud. At least, he hopes so.

She takes a slow breath. "Okay . . . So, yeah, we went to a nearby town. Only, everywhere we went, people were looking at us. A week had passed since our last trip to town, but something had changed. Eyes on us in the grocery, on the street, in the park where we'd settled down for a picnic lunch. We were so unnerved we left midafternoon. And I know what you're thinking. We checked several times, winding back and forth on our path. We'd biked there, so we took every manner of detour until it was starting to get dark and we had to cut straight home."

"Who was with you?"

She confesses a handful of names: Espeth, Tash, Anton, herself. Ridley suspects that is not everyone but doesn't press. Leti explains that early on they argued against any excursions like this, but it soon became clear, at least among her friends in Moon, that occasional outings were good for their mental health. People didn't want to feel trapped, even if they were. Leti and her group had decided on daytime trips with circuitous routes back to the settlement. They agreed to use cars from the community garage. Leti herself had advocated for cars over bikes because it gave the impression that they were just driving through. Bikes might imply they were coming from nearby. But after several outings with no incidents, everyone had loosened up. Yesterday they discussed going on a long bike ride, and once they got going, it didn't seem unreasonable just to drop into town.

This, Ridley is thinking but not saying—not just yet anyway—was a mistake. He leans against the table in front of him and says, "I wouldn't worry. If you weren't followed—"

"We weren't," she says, a little too confidently, a little too quickly.

Ridley smiles. "Even if you were, we have a glamour over this place, and technology to obscure your reentry." He isn't saying anything she doesn't already know. But his goal is to be reassuring. What he doesn't want to say is that there are limits to the magic, that if someone had looked at just the right moment, they would have seen Leti and her little contingent enter the woods and glitch right out of existence. They would know that something wasn't right. But could outsiders enter without the residents knowing? Ridley asked the ants once, and their answer was no, but they also said they had opted against any violent response—no sirens or hidden weapons or booby traps—just in case it was a friendly entry, a monster seeking sanctuary or a resident returning from a private excursion. But would the ants be able to warn them in time?

Leti blinks at Ridley.

"Sorry," he says. Was she saying something? He must have been silent too long.

"It's just . . ." She hesitates. "You look worried. Like, really worried."

"I'm not," he says. "I promise."

This is the wrong thing to say. He's gone too far to appease her, slipping out the other end. Her expression tells him that he has done the opposite. What to do now?

"Ah, *there* it is," he says. "Book's in the back." He steps away, going through the doorway to the storage room. He pretends to search for a minute before pulling the book from the top of a pile. All the while, he's trying to figure out the best way to re-approach the situation.

Ridley steps back out and hands the book to Leti. "It's a good one," he says. "I'd love to hear your thoughts."

She nods absently.

"We'll keep a lookout," he adds. "Don't worry. Nothing will happen."

Again his reassurance does next to nothing, her smile as false as his words. "Thanks for the book."

"Of course."

After she leaves, the silence is a tangible weight, a thrumming vibration inside his skull.

Laina and Rebecca leap from the dock. The midday water is still freezing, the rush of electric cold running through them as they splash in, go under, kick back up to the surface. They swim out to the middle of the small lake, splashing wildly, taking turns pushing each other underwater. As usual, they swim in their underwear, and every once in a while, they steal a kiss. Today they are careful. Manny is on the bank reading a book. He isn't looking at them, or he appears not to be looking, his long black curls falling over his eyes. But neither of them wants to make him uncomfortable—hence the careful, glancing displays of affection.

Before the change, Laina wouldn't have been able to bear the cold, but now, with encouragement from Rebecca, she has come to enjoy the chill, the shock of wakefulness it provides. And, of course, she has the wolf and the magic to reassure her that she won't freeze to death.

Rebecca is close to Laina, her body heat carrying just a little through the water to Laina's skin.

Quietly, Rebecca says, "I think he's angry at me."

Laina continues her kicking beneath the water to stay afloat. She whispers, "Did you fight? You didn't fight again, did you?"

"No," Rebecca says, shaking her head, "but he's in one of his moods."

Laina doesn't need to be told what this means. "His moods" is code for "wishing he were anywhere else than in a community full of monsters."

Before, he could have left, had almost made up his mind to leave, but then Rebecca's mother arrived, and Manny, torn between his prejudice and his protectiveness, chose to stay. And now he resents everyone for it, especially Rebecca. Most days it's fine. But today Manny is apparently in one of his moods.

"Mom told me he was dating someone," Rebecca says. "Apparently, he had to break it off."

"That's terrible."

"Don't feel too bad for my brother. He's an idiot. None of his relationships last longer than a few months anyway."

Manny has his head down, staring into a book in his lap, intermittently reading and staring off—in thought, Laina supposes—before returning to his book. The pulpy crime novel, unimaginatively called *Bite Marks*, is about a killer who leaves bite indentations on the wrists of her victims. Laina likes to think the killer is a woman. She hasn't read the book in its entirety, but since she noticed Manny reading it, she has read the first six chapters just so she can bring it up in conversation whenever Manny chooses to talk to her. *If* he ever chooses to talk to her. The subtext of the book, of course, is that the serial killer is a monster.

Rebecca splashes Laina in the face.

Laina laughs sharply to hide her surprise. "Cut it out."

"Look at me, not him."

"I *am* looking at you. I had to take a break."

More splashing, Laina laughing and playfully trying to escape from Rebecca, but not *too* earnestly. She wants Rebecca to catch up, and so she does, wrapping her arm around Laina's shoulders. Laina is staring away from the bank where Manny sits. And so is Rebecca, hugging her from behind. Both of them stare at the line of trees on the far bank, darkened by the dense foliage. It isn't creepy, even though it might be easy for someone to watch from under the cover of that not-so-distant tree line.

"I'm going to ask him if I can read that book after he's done," Laina says.

"You don't need to be friends with my brother."

"I want him to feel comfortable here."

"He'll never feel comfortable here," Rebecca says.

"And you're okay with that?"

"I'm not okay with a lot of things. But this is the world we live in."

They know that Manny can't hear any of this; he's too far away. Still, they look. But under his shroud of hair, Manny could well be asleep.

"I love him," Rebecca says, "but there's nothing either of us can do."

Laina wants to push but doesn't. She has no family now: mother dead, brother dead, father excommunicated from her life. Ridley is also estranged from his family. Ever since moving here, Laina has fostered a pleasant relationship with Rebecca's mother. And she wants to do the same with Manny—and thinks she can, if she can just manage to break through the tough exterior. She can see cracks in the armor, and if she makes the right nudges, she can break through. But the biggest reason she hasn't been able to get close is because Manny is angry at his sister, and their distance extends to her. And, yes, some of her desire to push Rebecca into healing the relationship is born of selfishness. She can admit that this is some sort of proxy thing: her living vicariously through Rebecca's familial relationships, or, possibly, her turning her own frustration at her missing family toward something more productive.

"Maybe if I get him drunk, he'll talk to me," Laina says.

"We're so failing the Bechdel Test right now."

"I think there's an exemption for little brothers."

"I don't want to talk about Manny."

"Okay, okay." A short silence. "But *would* he get drunk with me?"

Rebecca pushes Laina underwater, and when she rises a few feet away, coughing and spitting, she yells, "Asshole!"

Rebecca pursues. Laina turns to swim away, splashing loudly, her laughter echoing.

Manny, head lowered into his book, rolls his eyes.

That afternoon, Dragon does end up helping at the jammery. The bottom floor of Georgie's house has been transformed into one large kitchen. Every time Dragon is there, several industrial stoves are going at once. This time is no different. When he enters through the open front door, Georgie and Connor are running around as if they were in an episode of *The Great British Bake Off.* This is also not unusual.

"Go help Connor stir," Georgie says.

Dragon nods enthusiastically. Stirring is good. Dragon can stir. He hopes he can skip the jarring part.

As Dragon approaches, Connor is at one of the stoves, moving between two large copper pots. He is holding a long wooden spoon in one hand and has another spoon pressed between his teeth.

At the sight of Dragon, his eyes go wide. "Hey! Garb gatwan!"

"What . . . ? Oh." Dragon grabs the spoon from Connor's mouth.

"Grab that one," Connor repeats.

Dragon starts to wipe off the spoon with his shirt but thinks better of it. He rinses the spoon in the sink, then begins to stir the other copper pot.

"Thanks, little man," Connor says.

"If Georgie catches you again with a spoon in your mouth . . ."

"That's why it's our secret, right?" He winks at Dragon.

Dragon resists smiling.

"Make sure to get the bottom, okay? Or it'll burn."

"I'm not an idiot."

"No," Connor says, "but I am. Mess that up all the time."

The pot is nearly full with dark blackberry goo. The jam is beginning to set, and the scent is rich, spicy. It's Georgie's secret recipe that she refuses to share with anyone, even Connor. In the end, the jam will be peppery-sweet and tart, with a faint nutty aftertaste.

After a minute of stirring, a white foam begins to settle on top of the jam. Dragon knows what to do. He takes the shallow spoon from the draining rack and skims the froth off the top, then quickly cleans the spoon and returns it to the rack. All without having to put the stirring spoon in his mouth.

"You're a natural," Connor says.

"It's easy."

"And yet I botch a batch almost every week. Take the compliment, little man."

Dragon wishes Connor wouldn't call him "little man" and loves hearing it at the same time. He says, "How many more today?"

"Lucky for you, this is our last round."

Dragon hides his disappointment.

After another ten minutes, Connor says, "What you think? Done?"

Dragon lifts a small glob of the jam up with the spoon. He could do the plate test, but he is confident that it's done. "Yeah, I think so."

He looks to Connor, and Connor nods. "You got it. Go and back up Georgie. I'll finish up over here."

Dragon goes over to Georgie's workstation. She has three pots going. He grabs a spoon.

As he is stirring Georgie's signature raspberry-pepper jam, Dragon finds the courage to ask a question that has been on his mind for a while. "Why do it this way when you can have the ants make the signature jams?"

This is a good question because there's a large shed in Georgie's backyard that has been retrofitted to produce jam at factory volumes, but she only uses it for standard jams, not any of the fun flavors.

Georgie smiles at the question as if she has been waiting all day to answer it. "Because," she says, stressing the pause with an even brighter smile, "it makes me feel connected to the world. And myself."

Dragon stares blankly. Surely there must be more, because he isn't getting it yet.

"You might think . . . well, I don't know if you do, but I've heard others say, 'We're trapped here.' And, yes, that's sort of true. We can't leave for any long period of time without risking our lives in some way. But I think part of the reason we feel trapped is a matter of perspective. For most of human history, people stayed in their little village or town, never venturing far from the river or lake or valley or island or mountain settlement of their birth. And yet they had full lives, full of any sort of drama you can imagine. Depth of experience isn't only about how far you can roam; it is about how deeply you can live. And for me, making jam the long way is a form of living. It isn't just a thing to do. When I make jam, I feel connected to the world beneath my feet and to the people who are eating my jam out in the world. I feel connected because I am contributing to a network of life and living and experience, and while doing that I am having an experience. This is as valuable as any big thing you can do out there. Value is in the heart and the hands. I know what I am doing and why I am doing it, and it has meaning to me.

"So," she says, touching Dragon gently on the arm, "I've untrapped myself. I am as wide as the universe."

Dragon nods. Often, he needs time to gather all the meanings of a thing someone has said. But he can feel the trueness of what Georgie has just told him. It isn't bullshit, or it isn't *just* bullshit. Something in it is worth his careful consideration.

"Show me," he says. "I want to learn."

And this has Georgie grinning even brighter, if that is even possible. "I'd be honored."

9

That night in Moon, many are gathered in the community center: kids and young people sprawled on the floor, couches pointed toward the large bedsheet hung on the barn's southeast wall where a children's movie is projected, older folks loitering in the kitchen or around tables near the northwest wall, drinking tea or coffee, beers and ciders, harder stuff. The barn is one big room, and voices and sounds travel across the space between these smaller gatherings, mixing into the static of background noise. The size of this cavernous space makes it bearable.

Ridley, Rebecca, and Laina are in the kitchen, drinks in hand, voices low.

"I've been on the socials," Rebecca says. "I know, I know. Don't start. My point is, things are getting pretty scary on even the normal channels. Anti-monster sentiment is growing even as the monsters are retreating."

"But why?" Laina asks. Lately, she responds with incredulity to all news from outside Moon.

"The riot in New Orleans got pretty bad," Ridley offers. "Video evidence of monsters harming humans."

"In self-defense," Rebecca adds.

Ridley's glower doesn't have the same bite as in years past. "Of course. But that doesn't matter to the human supremacists. Anyway, the relative quiet from monsters in recent years has made people itchy. Paranoid. It doesn't help that so many accused monsters have vanished over the last year."

Ridley has been dreaming about Abyssia lately. Visions of roiling planets, burning suns, falling through the cold void of deep space. Now, within the context of the current conversation, the dreams feel ominous.

"Isn't it obvious to the world why we're in hiding?" Laina asks. "Isn't it obvious that we are afraid?"

The question strikes both Rebecca and Ridley as naive, but Ridley understands what lies under the words, under the petulance: fatigue. They are all tired without giving name to it. The real question is, what will be enough? What else can they do to appease humanity other than to cease existing?

How much worse must it feel to the born monsters? Ridley thinks. How tired must they be? Or do they have the stamina for such things? He tries to answer Laina, saying, "I suspect that to humans"—implying, as always, that monsters are separate from humans, which is more than a little reductive—"our absence seems threatening. Like we're readying ourselves. We weren't particularly visible before. Now we're invisible again, or mostly so—gone back into the shadows, as far as they are concerned. Only they know we're here now, without a doubt. They must feel like eyes are on them, that at any moment they may be pulled into the shadows themselves."

Laina has no trouble imagining this. She knows how uneasy she is sometimes at night, staring around Moon with the worry that people are out there, that she will wake from sleep with a knife at her throat.

Rebecca, for her part, can feel only anger. It is crowding out all other emotions. She finally voices an uncomfortable thought that she knows will change the whole timbre of the conversation: "Black Hand have been telling their people to keep their eyes open for small, isolated communities." She lets that be the end of it because it's not hard to draw the logical connections from there. And she is right; this does change the timbre of the conversation. Ridley and Laina are looking at her and each other with a shared expression of disbelief. Their faces say, *Could it be something else? Please let it be something else.*

But they know this is wishful thinking.

"What are you all talking about over here?" When no one returns Georgie's smile, she says, "Just getting a drink—don't mind me," and quickly retrieves a cider from the fridge before slipping away again.

They resume the conversation once they think she's out of earshot.

"If they were followed . . ." Laina says.

"They said they weren't," Ridley says.

"I don't know if we can trust that," Rebecca says.

Ridley, frowning: "Nothing to do but be on the lookout. If the next week goes by without incident, then maybe we can relax."

"What we have here," Rebecca says, giving voice to another uncomfortable thought, "can't last forever. If we fail to keep this place secret, there's nowhere for us to go."

In the dining area, the part of the barn with long tables connected end to end, three people are putting labels on jam and peanut butter jars. Lunar's logo is a crescent moon the width of a fingernail clipping, against a dark background with one five-pointed star drawn as if it is shooting across that background. It is one of several small businesses within Moon, all of them a part of a cooperative association. They pack the last of the jars in the boxes and walk them over to the portal room. No bots are in the room at the moment, but they know that soon enough, something will come and retrieve the boxes and take them through the portal to the Lunar warehouse.

By the time Harry arrives, near the end of the movie, the dining area sits empty. He stands in the back of the large open room, looking for Dragon. He isn't here, and a frisson of relief and disappointment shivers through him. Harry grabs a beer from the community center fridge. Some other time, then.

Outside the barn, it is mostly quiet: music coming from one of the houses, two people talking on the covered porch outside the community center, backdropped by the chirring of crickets. A cottontail on the grass outside Connor's house. Two more nibbling on some grass near Georgie's place.

Farther off, on the edges of Moon, they walk: Dragon and Ossi. And Alex, who has joined the stroll at the very last moment. First, they circle the periphery, taking two laps around the outside of Moon until they reach, for the second time, their preferred path into the woods. They veer off into the trees, Alex in front, Ossi and Dragon in the back, all of them moving easily in the near darkness. A thing they all have in common: exceptional eyesight, which has helped them during their night strolls.

The night is uncomfortably still and warm, but it is cooler

under the trees and alive with noises: small animals scurrying through the brush, a hoot of an owl. The scent of soil and grass and bark. Pine cones. The musk of fungi. Overhead, bats dart in jagged paths, catching their fill of flying insects.

Georgie is right, Dragon thinks. The world is infinitely complex right where they are. And still, it is too small.

"I've been following the Democratic primaries," Alex says.

Dragon and Ossi look at each other.

"Yes," Alex says, not looking back. "You both have made it your business to ignore current politics."

"Current? I've never been interested," Ossi says.

This gets Alex to spin around to look at Ossi. "All right, fair enough." She spins back. "But we have a unique opportunity right now, don't we? There are two Democratic candidates running on monster-friendly legislation."

Dragon slows his pace. Ossi grins, slowing her pace as well.

"One of them is a centrist," Alex continues, "and her idea of 'monster-friendly' involves registration. But the other candidate is a senator from Massachusetts, Shaya Joshi, and she's progressive. And, not a big deal or anything, but I happen to know her. We, uh . . . grew up together. I could maybe arrange a conversation? Who knows, given the right kind of pressure, she could . . ."

When she turns and sees Dragon and Ossi several feet behind her, they burst out laughing.

"You both suck," Alex says.

Ossi wipes a tear from her eye. "Well, you're ruining our walk."

Scowling, Alex stops so they can catch up. "Forgive me for caring about improving our situation. Dragon, you've said yourself that you want to get out of Moon."

Dragon startles. "Have I?"

"Well, not in those exact words, but I've gotten that gist."

Dragon looks at Ossi, and he can see by her expression that somehow she's gotten that gist as well.

"Listen, we could get real protections under the law," Alex says. "And then maybe we wouldn't be trapped here."

"There'll be strings," Ossi says. "There are always strings. Sure, we might get some protections, but they'll want assurances that we're not dangerous." She smiles wickedly. "I don't know about you, but I'm definitely bad news under the right circumstances."

"They're already afraid," Dragon says. "One incident and they'll turn their backs on us."

Alex shrugs. "Can't argue there."

"Can your friend even run on monster legislation without risking her campaign?" Ossi says "your friend" with a note of something Dragon can't decipher.

Alex is quiet a moment, then says, "She's careful. Well, no, she's not careful. Her platform is bonkers, actually, which paradoxically gives the monster stuff better cover. Universal health care and housing. Free college. Banking regulation. There's some co-op stuff that I need to talk to Ridley about. Would be lost on you two."

This is mostly true. Dragon did some cooperative work in New Era, but he didn't understand it then. A little more now, but since he was in a hole most of his life, he can't really appreciate cooperativism from a revolutionary perspective.

Alex continues: "A cap on high-end wages while raising the federal minimum by a lot. Social reform based on race, gender, orientation, class. Better protections under the law for those with marginalized status. That's the one to pay attention to. It includes monsters. But she's clever enough to keep it on an even footing with everything else."

"They'll destroy her in debates," Ossi says. "Universal housing. Banking regulation. Wage restrictions? Come on."

"I thought you said you don't pay attention to politics."

"I don't," Ossi says. "But I didn't emerge from a cave a year ago. I've been around a very long time."

"Tez used to say that," Alex says. "He was also suspiciously careful about disclosing his actual age."

A longer-than-usual silence, each of them processing the emotions that the mention of Tez brings up.

Naturally, Alex is the one to break the silence. "Yes, her monster support might come up, which will frighten some people. But fear isn't always a bad thing."

"And why is that?" Ossi asks.

"Everyone has an idea about how powerful we are. What they don't know is how many of us there are. And this is why most people don't talk about us, and if they do, they're careful what they say on camera."

"What about the Black Hand?" Dragon says.

"Supremacists are idiots," Alex says. "But they understand what I'm saying too. It's why they keep calling on the military to act despite many of them being anti-government. Also why hate crimes appear to be so random, so unexpected. Even the supremacists are careful."

"Still bad for us," Dragon says. But he is considering what she's saying. Would he call the supremacists *careful*? And just as he asks himself the question, he understands. Random, surprise acts of violence are careful if you think your enemy can kill you easily—*especially* if your enemy were to see you coming. And this, above all else, causes another thought to surface in Dragon's mind. *We could kill them all if we tried. Every single one of them who might hurt us.* It is the first time in years that Dragon truly scares himself. But even as the thought scares him, he feels the call of it. Powerful stuff, this thought. Liberating in the face of so much loss and pain.

He sees Ossi looking at him, but just as he returns her gaze, she looks away again.

"What I want," Ossi says, "is the means to defend ourselves proactively. That's something we'll have to do ourselves."

The words carry more meaning, given what Dragon was just thinking.

"You know we're on the same page," Alex says, "but we're also talking about routes that might take. Useful *and* effective approaches. A diversity of tactics protects us in the short and long term."

Ossi's declaration isn't exactly what Dragon was thinking, but it's close. And better. Emphasis on the self-defense part. Dragon walks himself back from the other, more hard-line way of thinking. He can kill to protect, but he won't kill out of fear. He won't become the Black Hand.

Alex suddenly stops ahead of them.

"What is it?" Ossi says.

Alex is tensed, silent. She puts out a hand to stop them from coming forward. Dragon peers into the darkness ahead and can see something stirring there. But his eyes aren't as sharp as Alex's, and he's farther away.

He's only a little worried. It's not as if they could summon the Black Hand simply by talking about them. Noise in these woods is always a deer or possum or some other critter. Sometimes Ossi hunts these woods, but never so close to the settlement. She wants the animals to build up an association with this part of the woods. Avoidance, paradoxically, could draw interest. But Ossi has brought venison back to Moon on more than one occasion, keeping most of it for herself since the nonshifters are disturbed by the practice.

He sees when Alex's shoulders ease, the tension leaving her body. She straightens. "Deer," she says.

Ossi nods in agreement.

Dragon can't relax. Something still isn't right. "Want to start heading back?" he says.

"We're not even halfway to the lake," Alex says, but she is still looking around, still searching.

Dragon follows every subtle shift of her body. "There's nothing here," he says. "Probably just another deer." He very much wants this to be true.

Alex doesn't answer.

"Not funny. Whatever you're doing, cut it out," Dragon says.

Alex turns fully in their direction. "I feel . . . off," she says. "I swear, the hair on the back of my neck is standing straight up right now. Anyone else feel like something is about to happen?"

Dragon looks to Ossi, who is also tense.

"I don't feel anything. Can't see anything out of the ordinary. But," Ossi says, locking eyes with Dragon, "I can smell something." Ossi's eyes sparkle in the night. "Smoke."

Confusion. Fear. Dragon's mouth is suddenly dry. "What?"

"Oh, no, not him. *Actual* smoke. Fly up above the trees and tell us what you see."

Dragon takes his shirt off and unfurls his wings. He is up over the canopy in seconds.

His heart sinks. "Moon," he shouts. "Moon is on—"

A VISIT WITH
A CHILD OF ASHA

You're really not looking so hot, friend. See, right there—and there! You're flickering. Not good. Here, have a seat. Whoa, lost you again there for a moment. Mother of the universe! What happened to you?

Damn. I tried to warn you, but of course you didn't listen. I can't be mad at you, though. We're similar. We walk right up to the pit to see what's inside, can't help but fall in.

Oh, this? It's my death shroud. Relax, I'm kidding. To tell you the truth, the suit is inspired by something I made a long time ago, in another life. Actually, from where we're standing, that long time ago would be your future. I know. Confusing. But let's stick to right now. Keep you *rooted*. I also grew up on St. Thomas, you know. Something we have in common. You've learned by now how monsters are made, so I'm sure it doesn't surprise you that I was an orphan. From before I could remember, I was being prepared for what I am. And before I had a mind to think differently, I already was a monster.

Oh, there you go again—flicked right out of existence.

Fine. I'll stop if you're going to be so sensitive about it.

No, no, there was no such thing as a tech mage, not before me. They'd intended for me to be a light mage, but I was defective. That's the word they used in the beginning, when the applications for my abilities weren't clear yet. I could talk with machines, but at first, I lacked the ability to communicate exactly what I was doing. I couldn't explain that I saw each part of a made thing and could understand not just its use but how it *could* be used, what technology could become or not become except through me. Light mages are matter manipulators, you see. These mages can move matter because they can see and manipulate matter itself. What you might call telekinesis. I can't see atoms, but I do see circuits, gears, bolts. And I can move them with my mind, alter them. It was still magic, a spark of creation molded by the parts of me I'd forgotten, the parts of me hidden away.

We'll get there, promise.

Magic is slippery. Sometimes the child doesn't believe the story it is meant to believe, and the magic doesn't take. Sometimes the magic doesn't take for no reason at all. Sometimes the indoctrination text ceases to work. This happened with the fifteenth-century faerie books. Just stopped working on children. No one knows why, really. Sometimes books don't take, or start failing to take, and the blight can jump across a whole series, volume after volume turning as useless as a book of fairy tales—hence being the common example. In my case, it must have been a combination of factors. Me, for one—I was never a normal kid. Also, the Book of Light was more incomplete than the other mage books, many of its pages lost to time. That is why the Order risked an indoctrination attempt on only one of us.

No, my minders weren't cruel. Though the Order of Asha had abandoned the slower (more humane) method of making monsters for the faster European indoctrination model, they didn't abuse children. Well, mostly. They didn't steal them away either. They ran Saint Ash like a standard orphanage, nestled away on a backstreet of Charlotte Amalie. We weren't allowed to go outside. There were eleven of us: five elemental mages, three obeah practitioners (made the new way, the European way), a shadow mage, and a light mage (me). Oh, and a sight mage, like Mother Inness.

What can I say about sight mages? You know them as well as I do.

In any event, back then the elemental mage books still took. It was twelfth-century magics that came up out of the alchemical schools. Before you interrupt me, yes, our order was around then, but it wasn't us who made the books. That was one of the dead societies. Many of those were eaten by the Order of the Zsouvox, folded into that then-sprawling secret society during the Third Consolidation. There was another, smaller splintering later on, but eventually we settled into four monster societies: the High City, the Sisterhood of Sight, the Order of Asha, and the Order of the Zsouvox (now called the Cult of the Zsouvox since that faction within the society took control). You know the latter two. High City is truly a neutral party, so there's not much to report. It's made up of old monster families with their own systems of governance and protections, exclusionary by nature. They did not wish to be involved in this conflict. The Sisterhood, well . . . they're complicated. Cassandra was the sight mage the Order of Asha made, but she was not, and could never be considered, part of the Order of Asha. All sight mages belong to each other. Their goals have always been their own, no matter who makes the mage.

What happened to the other mages? They're dead. That outcome might have been avoided if the Order of Asha hadn't tried to make a shadow mage. Shadow mages always turn rancid.

The night Smoke killed the other orphans, I was developing the second generation of my portal ring. I had on headphones, so I didn't hear him moving from room to room, taking each child and setting them on the moon. Maybe some of them screamed before he grabbed them. I don't know. Cassandra reached me first. She pulled my headphones off and told me to use my portal ring. I hadn't tested this one yet, but she assured me I didn't need to. I asked her how she knew. Cassandra hardly ever emotes now, but back then she did it more than hardly ever. She watched me like I was an idiot. I used the ring; we slipped through the portal to Water Island.

Cassandra didn't tell me what happened until the morning. I cried that whole day and the next. There was a boy named Abel. My brother. I mean, he wasn't my brother, but I loved him like a brother. And Elsie, who occasionally made me feel things in my body. Not love. Curiosity that heats you from the inside. I loved the others too, but differently. I didn't really like Cassandra at first. I just didn't understand her, you know? But she loves me in her own way. And I love her in the only way I can, given that she doesn't speak to me unless I ask her a question. One thing I'm grateful for is that she told me what I would have to do. And she gave me time to accept doing it.

I won't answer that. It will happen soon anyway.

Yes, I thought you'd forgotten. We've gone all the way here.

I knew it wasn't just the Book of Light that gave me my power. Even then I was waking up to the other parts of who I was.

Yes, you've guessed: I once lived in Akasha, the world above. I lived there early in what is called, in Akashan, the Era of Final Peace, sometimes called the Era of Sacrifice. Time is different in the world above. There are no seasons, no revolutions around a sun. The sunmoon spins without beginning or end, and so we measure time in eras. Eras of peace or tumult, and then degrees of calamity when more nuance is needed. The naming of eras is comically literal. For example, the Era of First Peace lasted a long, long, long time and ended with the making of the Zsouvox. What followed was the Era of First Tumult, which ended with the Era of Second Peace. Yes, I know, not particularly imaginative. During the Era of Second Peace, after they trapped the Zsouvox for the first time, gods had to sacrifice their children to the Zsouvox. Every hundredth turn of the sunmoon, as a sort of appeasement. They were very afraid, you see, that if they didn't, the Zsouvox would simply decide not to be caged. And so they did the sacrifices for a very, very long time.

A lottery system. There were billions of us at that time, and millions of young gods that could be sacrificed. Many of the gods made children precisely for that purpose, should the need arise. And it was an ugly thing. Those children assumed a very special status among the gods. They were feed for the Devourer. I was not feed. I was Asha's only child then.

Please stop interrupting me.

Asha is a very old god, the first of seven created by Maker, and in all her existence she had created only two other gods. Every god in Akasha descended from the other six. People suspected that I was for the Zsouvox, but she impressed on them that I was not. This was foolish, they said. If her line was ever chosen . . . But she didn't want to hear it. On principle, she would not subject any child to that fate, even hypothetically. But eventually the time did come when a child from her line was chosen. Asha refused. And though everyone was grateful to her for creating Akasha—don't interrupt!—they tried to take me by force. When the mob came to our home, Asha went out to confront them. And what can I say? I was young. I was frightened. Other gods had been known to flee into their verses, but I had none, so I stuck my head into yours: Asha Verse Seven. It was only for a moment, but then I . . . fell in? Look, this is very hard to explain, but the experience was something like leaning over a bathtub and sticking your face underwater. In this case, the tub had no bottom. I lost my footing. I fell to Earth. By the time Mother found me, I had become part of this place, my molecules dispersed, at once distinct and indistinguishable from the "water" around me. She knew I couldn't come back out again—not until Yun decided to release me.

You know who I mean. Think about it.

Damsel filled me in on what happened after I left Akasha. Asha took her verses and disappeared, but not before sacrificing a part of herself to the Zsouvox. This was a mistake; Asha was too powerful, and it made the Zsouvox too powerful. Eventually, the Zsouvox decided *not* to be caged, as was feared. And then: the Era of Second Tumult; the Era of Quarantined Cities; the Era of Greatest Calamity; and the one we are now in, the Era of We're-All-Fucked-If-This-Doesn't-Work.

I truly don't know. That is the purview of the Sisterhood.

No, Cassandra isn't a god, though she is another class of being. Something above human or monster. But these classifications don't matter, as far as the fate of the universe is concerned. Despite my origins, her role is more important than mine. It is she, by what she chooses to tell, who will decide how this ends, whether for some . . . or for everything.

THE BEAST UNDER THE WORLD:
PART TWO

SONYA PAIGE

It is a room with a chair, a table, and a bed. Three lamps overhead, a small bathroom in the corner, with a shower curtain she can draw around herself, the whole thing enclosed within a transparent box, a glass cage.

It is not really glass. She has tried to escape, but her cage did not break like glass, did not sound like glass when she hit it. Outside her transparent box is a larger room, with bare gray walls cracked in places. Sonya was abducted without her skin, and, after being there so long, she is used to being without her skin, walking and standing and sitting without her skin, making her as transparent as the box she is trapped in. She doesn't feel exposed. But here, in this empty place, with nothing to do most of the time but sit in that chair, the discomfort is beginning to creep inside her. It isn't the fear, though there's a little of that too—the thought of what they will do to her after they get what they want (or after they realize they *won't* get what they want). She thinks she can feel her skin withering from thousands of miles away, nestled in that chest, hidden from anyone who might want to do it harm. She knows that it is safe—Melku made sure of that—but the magic that holds her together has . . . needs. In simple terms: affection, the need to feel needed, companionship, intimacy. The longer she goes without it, the quicker age will start to creep into her skin. She was so busy before the abduction that she had no time for intimacy, no time for carefully managed relationships that would end right when they needed to. It was easier with Melku, but Sonya loves Melku too much. It made things complicated.

The longer she stays here, the more damage to her skin, and the more she will feel the edges of her body bleed into the environment around her. Before long, she will become not just an invisible creature but a ghost. How does she know this? She doesn't. But the feeling is beginning to seep into her—an ancient knowledge resurfacing.

The door opens abruptly, and the man comes in. He takes the seat right outside her prison. The sound of the metal chair protesting against his weight comes to her as crisp and clear as if there were nothing between them.

For a moment, he stares at the spot where she should be. He has gotten unnervingly good at seeming as though he can see her. "You feel like talking today?"

Sonya says nothing.

"I'll bring in some food after we have a chance to chat."

She maintains her silence. This is another of his tricks. The promise seems to be that if she talks she will get to the food more quickly. But Sonya is used to hunger.

She knows he will eventually start taking up the silence with his own talking.

And he does: "I've been alive for a long time. I know a little of the magic that created you."

Sonya fights against the sudden eagerness that springs up within her. She knows very little about her own magic. She was too ashamed to ask even Melku, who likely knows more than she does. But she will not give this man, this enemy, the satisfaction of knowing her ignorance.

"A lot of the folk magic," he continues, "comes from stories told over generations, gaining solidity over time. On the West African coast, there were stories of women who could remove their skin. It might've started with an exiled woman and her unborn child. Perhaps it was a strange pregnancy. Troubling in some way. Paranoia too. She was sent away. And as the story gained strength, it acted on the pregnant woman—made her give birth to the monster the people thought she'd conceive. Our method—and I mean the Western school of magic, of monster creation—is more deliberate, predatory. Weaker too—an unfortunate by-product of our approach. We tell a child a story for the child to believe. We call the practice indoctrination, as you might know. Sometimes that belief simply doesn't hold. But the indigenous African magics—and this is also true of the indigenous Eurasian and American magics—first start with the people and what they believe, what they imprint on each other without knowing. Spiritual belief. Unconscious belief. And so it gains a strength that our methods lack. Even me suggesting this to you, that your magic was 'made up,' will have no effect on you, right? Or I'd be seeing you now. But if I did this to one of our monsters, it would likely unravel them."

Sonya remains silent.

"I find these more collective magics fascinating," he says. "It is a hardier way to make a monster, but less predictable. Who knows what particular combination of superstition and paranoia made you. That sort of specificity becomes lost. I can only come up with theories at best . . ."

Sonya studies the room. She tries to focus on anything but his face, but before long, she's looking at him again. He is an older man. Older because, presumably, that was when he was turned. He has that vampire look about him, his wrinkles smoothed away as if by tastefully applied plastic surgery. But the gray in his beard and hair remains.

"They're often weaker monsters, in a certain sense, these communal creations, though I've met quite a few variants that terrified me. For example, during a storm, the weredog can be quite dangerous. But because they're not intentionally designed, they have certain weaknesses or limits that can be a hindrance. Like someone putting salt on your shed skin, for example."

Sonya goes rigid.

"You have to hide it, right? Your skin. Dangerous to leave it out."

Sonya replays her favorite fantasy of late: tearing this man's head from his body.

"Don't worry. You've hidden your skin well. I don't think we'll ever find it." His eyes are staring directly into where hers should be, keener now, the wistful expression gone. "I am not your enemy, you know. Or it's more that you and I have a common enemy. The Zsouvox."

Sonya doesn't speak but almost leans forward in the chair.

She stops herself, afraid the subtle creak of her shifting weight might give something away.

The man stands. "We'll talk more tomorrow."

• • •

He returns the next day. Interestingly, he doesn't pick up where he left off.

"I used to be a revolutionary in my youth. I use 'youth' now to mean everything before I was turned. I was not only young but also ignorant of the way the world really worked. As a revolutionary, I wanted to change everything. Create my own version of utopia. Sometimes I dabble in that version of myself, revising some of my ideology for the sake of the exercise."

Sonya continues listening.

"When I was alive—this was over one hundred and fifty years ago now—I helped found a political organization called the First International. During that time, I learned a lot about the pitfalls of idealism. Most political organizations fail. Or they reform themselves until they reach a spiritual death. Eventually, those organizations fail too.

"Anyway. The First International started to dissolve within a decade. It was partly because of a rivalry I had with another radical of that time. Radical, but in a different way. We were both influential. He might have felt threatened by me. Perhaps I also felt threatened. Back then, I thought like this, that the world wasn't big enough. I've learned my lesson.

"My objective in the First International was to further my revolutionary cause. Perhaps I succeeded. Depends on how you look at it. I could explain what I mean, but then you'd surely know who I was back then. Or maybe you already do, hmm?"

Sonya doesn't know. She keeps her silence, the only card she has.

"I've been careful with that prior life. Now I'm Valter Trapp, or Thirty-Two—my designation within the Order. That other person is just a distant part of my current self, though he lives on in people's minds. When I 'died,' I decided to bury him, leave him behind, become a new person. My new goal: understand everything. And I've spent my afterlife devoted to that goal. Endless reading and study and observation. Meticulous planning so that one day I would know what to do with this world, fix it so that it would never break again. Do you understand? You might dislike my methods, if you truly knew them, but our goals are the same."

"We are nothing alike."

"*There* you are." The look of satisfaction on his face. Like a hunter's, finding a trap he's set, with a critter inside. "Okay, we're not the same. You would know. But we want similar things."

"No."

"No? So talkative today!"

Sonya stifles a reply.

"The thing that eventually undoes any organization, secret or not, is the conflicting goals of its members. That's why it is important to remember who you are apart from the organization, so that if you're lucky enough to outlast it, you'll have learned the right lessons to take forward with you, to use toward your truer goals. I'll say it plainly. The Order of the Zsouvox, or the Cult of the Zsouvox, or whatever it wants to call itself, will someday die. Hopefully, our universe won't die with it. Your order will eventually die too. Some might say it's already got a foot in the grave. You must ask yourself: Who will you become after? And who do you want to stand by your side? It may not always be the person you like. You might want someone like me on your side so I'm not opposing you. Trust me—me on your side is better than the alternative." The man stands, finally releasing the tension in the room. "I'll let you think about it."

For long moments after he has left, Sonya replays the conversation, trying to commit everything to memory, trying to find the underlying meaning. So many different threads to untangle.

He's trying to confuse me, she thinks. It won't work. He has no idea what he's talking about.

• • •

The next day: "You know something I've always thought about? The beginnings of our orders. How old are they—over four thousand years old at this point?" Valter waits for an answer that doesn't come. "Not talkative today, hmm?"

He lets the quiet settle before continuing: "Do you know the story of how your order began? We have a record—a second-hand account, really—of an ancient Egyptian slave happening across a talking cat. A black cat with a strange collection of feline features. We don't know what the cat said, but we do know that this woman escaped Egypt and gathered monsters from across the continent—a difficult task in that era—to start the Order of Asha.

"Now, here is the strange thing. You listening?" Sonya remains silent. "Good. The Order of the Zsouvox started around the same time. We know this because one of the early members of the Order of Asha helped found this organization. His real name is lost, but our early texts call him Two. There is no record of One."

He sighs. "There's also no story for our founding. Trust me—I've looked. Somehow we"—he claps his hands together; the sound echoes in the spare room—"popped into existence. Somehow we knew what the Zsouvox was. Somehow we knew that it would come and either rule the world or end it."

He stands suddenly, and Sonya startles.

"I have two theories. Either the Order of the Zsouvox is a splinter organization, which fits what I've just told you. Or—and it's really a variation on the first theory—the Order of Asha created the Order of the Zsouvox.

"There are some less compelling alternatives, not worth mentioning. And sure, I'm reasonable. I know four thousand years is a long time to keep records. I know that records get lost all the time. But you know what? I like to trust my gut. And I think, well, these missing pieces aren't accidents. They're . . ." Valter turns for the door. "We'll talk tomorrow."

• • •

The next day: "When I was young, my politics were strongly opposed to systems of power. But I did consider authority as an intermediate step, a way-stop on the road to true self-governance. Well. Power is corrosive. When people have power, they want to keep it. And the people without power begin to look like a dull mob. Isn't it better if a select few carry the burden of rule for the sake of the many? Easy to shift 'everyone should have the power' to 'let me be the good steward.' You see what I mean? Corrosive.

"I became disillusioned. I realized I couldn't figure out how to break that very human impulse, even in myself. I wavered, yes, but I was no ally to Western-style democracy or capitalism. So why, then, would the Order of the Zsouvox induct me into its ranks?"

This is the first time he stops. His eyes float down from the ceiling to the spot where Sonya is standing in her glass cage. Where she is *actually* standing. "Any great power," he says, "needs a balancing mechanism. Conflict is necessary for the tightening of control."

Sonya holds her body completely still.

"Higher power is a counterbalancing of many powers, an interplay. To rule over, you don't just gather one power to your corner. You gather and manipulate *all* powers. When they found me—defeated, jaded, old—dying—it was just the right time, exactly the moment I was at my weakest and likeliest to join my stake to theirs. And I was arrogant then; I thought I could come into this new and dangerous place and have my way. But I found myself among people with lifetimes at their disposal, with wisdom and resources amassed over centuries. I quickly realized I needed time to do the same. Time to build. Time to find the right circumstances."

"How do you know they're not listening?" Sonya asks.

"This is my house," he says. "And they know my methods of interrogation are unorthodox."

"Meaning you say whatever you need to say to manipulate the other person."

"Yes."

"And now that I know this—"

"How can you trust me? You can't. But what I am saying

could be useful, no? Could enhance your own thinking on certain matters. You've already begun to do just that—reconsider
things."

"You couldn't possibly know that."

"And yet I do." He stands to leave again.

"I think I know who you are."

His eyebrows rise. "Well?"

"I can't say it. I'll sound ridiculous if I say it out loud."

He laughs. "Then you're probably right."

After he leaves, time stops.

Sonya considers the question she is compelled to answer, and
says, "If you can hear my thoughts, then it is already too late."

ALEXANDRA TRAPP

JUNE 12, 2028

NINETEEN MONTHS AFTER THE BOSTON RIOTS

Alex watches Dragon take off in the direction of Moon. In the direction of the fire.

Alex and Ossi follow on foot. As they arrive, they find Dragon standing over the body of a man. Wordless, Alex approaches, looking down at the body from over Dragon's shoulder.

"I found him like this," Dragon says.

Which he doesn't need to say. The flesh of the man's neck has been mangled by sharp teeth. A canine's.

"Well, we know what he is," Ossi says, gesturing to the single leather glove the man is wearing. "Black Hand."

"And we know who killed him," Alex says.

They look up to the one inhabited house on this street. Sondra's house. As always, the lights are off inside. Alex's sense of smell isn't as good as Ossi's, but blood is the one thing she can follow for miles. The scent of blood leads directly to Sondra's door.

"One of us should go in and talk to her," Alex says distantly. It has been a long time since Alex took blood from a living person. And the scent is everywhere. God, her mouth is watering.

"There's no time." Ossi is peering at the tree line. "We have to track down the other trespassers and—"

"Kill them," Dragon says—cold, resolute.

The words pull Alex out of the noise in her mind. "What?"

But there is no time to discuss it further among themselves; others are arriving. The wolf pack arrives first: Rebecca, Ridley, and Laina. Georgie and Connor are close behind. As they approach, Alex can hear everyone's heartbeats.

"What happened?" Ridley asks. But then he looks at the ground.

Alex isn't here. Suddenly, she is back at the riot, her teeth sinking into the neck of one of the Black Hand, fresh blood staining her shirt, coating her throat. Thick and sweet and—

"You're suggesting you go after them?" Ridley asks. "And then what?"

"You know what," Ossi says.

"No, we can't do that."

"They know where we are now. What do you think is going to happen when they get out of these woods one person short? I'll tell you what will happen."

"Are you okay?" Dragon is asking Alex, close enough to whisper the words.

Dragon has always smelled different, less appetizing. With him so close, the urge lessens. Alex closes her mouth, swallows down her saliva, her hunger.

"I'm fine," Alex says. "I'm just . . . surprised."

Of course, Dragon knows more than she wants him to. He touches her arm—a soft caress. "But you're under control now."

Alex nods at the nonquestion.

"We don't have time to argue," Ossi says. "Their scents are fading fast."

Worry crosses Ridley's face.

"Listen," Ossi says. "We can still say we're defending ourselves."

"This is something else," Ridley says. "If we consent to you doing this . . ."

Laina says, "We'll be consenting to hunting human beings."

"And we'll be the monsters the humans think we are," Ridley says.

"We *are* monsters," Ossi says. "And if we let them go, the Black Hand isn't going to give us any points for our kindness. They'll send an army in here and burn everything to the ground."

"She's right," Rebecca says.

Alex sees the look of betrayal on Ridley's face.

And Alex is sympathetic, but: "There are still seven of them. Next time there'll be many more unless we . . . stop them now."

"How do you know there's seven?" Georgie asks.

Alex looks at the woman. Once upon a time, Georgie had thrown Alex a lifeline. She referred Alex to her aunt, a powerful witch who helped Alex retrieve her stolen memories. Since then, they've been friendly, but Alex can see by Georgie's face that she's asking a question she knows the answer to. An answer she doesn't like.

Alex knows there are seven Black Hand because she can smell them, like prey. She says, "Three set the fires—one dead, two more not so far away. Five more deeper into the woods."

"I'm going to kill them," Ossi says. "You can thank me later." She's already shifting by the time the final words are out, the last bit coming out in a growl. In a blink, she is sprinting into the woods.

"Dragon and I should go," Alex says. "Make sure nothing happens to her."

Everyone is stunned silent. Ridley just looks away.

No time for more discussion.

As Alex sprints ahead, Dragon takes off again into the air.

Ossi has gone straight, so Alex veers left, where she knows that the two Black Hand are fleeing. She's at the tree line, slipping between trees with ease—fast, graceful, all action a merging of intellect and instinct, both happening at the same time. Her senses are keener now too. She can hear all the noises in the surrounding woods and see far ahead despite the dark. She sees two men, illuminated in the moonlight. Weave and dodge and weave again, her superhuman strength propelling her through every turn.

Alex comes upon one of them as he stumbles through the underbrush. So much noise but not nearly fast enough. She reaches him. He notices at the last moment, just as she grasps his head, twisting. The snap is quick. Like a felled tree, he pitches forward. She is gone before he hits the ground. The Black Hand ahead is faster, but he's breathing hard from exertion. She jumps, pushes off a tree, and shoots forward, flying through the air and colliding with the man's back. There's a snap of shattered vertebrae. She doesn't prolong his suffering. Taking hold of his head, she finishes him with a quick, brutal twist.

She rushes forward. Dragon is above the trees, and he swoops down on a Black Hand just as Alex spots him scrambling through the brush. Alex runs ahead, moments later hearing the scream of that Black Hand as he plummets back to Earth behind her.

Trees brush past her in a blur. A shout from her right pulls her attention. She slows when she spots Ossi, releasing a Black Hand's neck from her jaws. With a chuff of acknowledgment in Alex's direction, Ossi takes off at an oblique angle, closing the distance on another Black Hand some yards ahead. Ossi is a perfect predator in her pursuit—not a single wasted movement. Ossi catches the Black Hand in the shoulder. He yells out as the impact brings him to the ground. They skid to a stop, Ossi's teeth in the muscle of his neck, just above the collarbone. She bites down, blood spraying.

The sound of a snapped branch. Ossi and Alex turn in that direction: a man, gloved hand clasped over his mouth. Ossi crouches to pounce just as Dragon swoops down between the trees and plucks the man up into the air. The screams grow distant, then crescendo as the man plunges to his death. Slack and bent, the Black Hand lies where he fell.

Dragon drops down. He doesn't speak, just surveys the ground. The dispassionate way he observes the bodies makes Alex feel a mix of emotions. Worry, yes. Guilt? This boy, barely a man, has discarded something in himself. Maybe a little pride too? Because, like her, he has accepted what must be done to survive in this world. Earlier in life than she had to, but can she fault him for learning the lesson? The world has certainly been less kind to him. She isn't completely comforted by this new Dragon, but there is some relief. She wants him to survive, and to survive he can't hold himself back from doing what needs to be done.

Then why does the human part of her want to cry?

Dragon seems to be having less inner conflict. "I couldn't find the last Hand," he says. "Can you smell him, Ossi?"

Ossi moves her head from side to side in a facsimile of the human gesture. For a moment, Alex's mind struggles to accept what she is seeing. Since she came to Moon, these moments happen a lot less frequently, but occasionally the part of her that is human, that understands the world as it should be, still must exert effort to accept the fact of magic.

"I'll fly ahead," Dragon says. Great wings unfurl again from his back, and he shoots up in a sudden gust of wind and displaced leaves. When he clears the treetops, he sets off in the direction of the road.

Alex and Ossi follow. Minutes later, they find Dragon standing on the roadside. Alex sniffs the air, searching for the human scent.

He was here, and now he is gone, their fears realized.

Ossi shifts back into her human form and rises from her stooped position.

"I could try to catch up with him," Dragon offers.

Alex shakes her head. "We don't want anyone to see you."

"I wish I could disagree, but . . ." Ossi doesn't finish the thought. "We should head back."

They take their time returning to Moon, but when they arrive, even more people are standing near the body, which is now covered by a sheet. As the residents watch, the three of them approach, defeat on their faces.

"We've called the ants," Ridley says. "To dispose of the body—bodies, I guess?"

"Yes. Plural," Ossi says. "They're in the woods. Hey, Connor, eyes up here."

"Right. Sorry." Connor glances to Georgie, but her eyes are on Dragon, then on Alex.

Alex pretends not to notice.

"Did you, uh, *find* them all?" Rebecca asks.

"We killed all but one," Ossi says. "Got away by car. Which means we're fucked."

"Why are you looking at me like that?" Ridley asks.

"Because we wasted time."

Alex notices when the ants start to arrive, seemingly from every corner of the town. They swarm the body. Are likely doing the same to the others in the woods. As they begin to break down the corpse under the sheet, Alex looks away. The ants are efficient, but the scent of blood perfumes the air.

"Anything *you* have to report?" This from Georgie, glaring at Alex.

What the hell? "Umm, no," Alex says. "Like what?"

Georgie doesn't respond.

"Won't they know where we are now?" Connor says as if the thought had just occurred to him. The loveable idiot.

"Well, they won't go to the authorities," Ridley says. "Worst-case scenario, he takes it to the forums, and we have dozens, if not a hundred, Black Hand beelining to our location."

"No," Ossi says. "Worst-case scenario is that the authorities are involved and we have hundreds of Black Hand and law enforcement coming to burn this place to the ground."

"We're being hyperbolic here, right?" Connor asks, looking from one somber face to the next. "Uh . . . right?"

The sheet covering the body now looks as if it is covering a square of flat ground. The blood smell is gone, replaced by the scent of soil after a fresh rain. Alex doesn't know whether she should be disturbed by this.

"And now they know that we will kill them, which opens us up for criminal charges," Georgie says, again looking at Alex.

Jesus, what is her problem? Alex points to the sheet. "There's no evidence."

This has a nearly imperceptible calming effect.

"Let us hope the authorities won't be involved," Laina says.

"What do we do?" Connor asks.

"We abandon Moon," Ridley says.

"You can't be serious," Ossi says.

Ridley raises an eyebrow. "Wasn't that the point of your own dramatic worst-case scenario?"

Ossi huffs. "And we'd go where, exactly?"

"One of the other settlements," Ridley says. "I'm sure if we just explain the situation to the ants—"

"I've asked the ants," Georgie says. "They won't do it. They say they *can't* do it."

Silence.

"Given that our options are limited," Rebecca says, "I have to agree with Ossi on this one." The look of betrayal on Ridley's face is once again very hard to miss. "We shouldn't run from this. What message are we sending if we run and hide?"

"That we value our lives," Ridley says. "That we value other people's lives. I mean, I'm sorry, but . . . what are you all proposing exactly?"

"We defend Moon," Ossi says.

Rebecca nods.

"Oh my god," Ridley says. "That's . . . that's crazy."

"Aren't you tired?" Rebecca says. "Aren't we all tired of running?"

Another silence, full of conflicting tensions.

"*If* we were to leave," Georgie says, "where would we go?"

The attempt to veer the discussion away from a Waco situation is valiant but in vain. No one is having a change of subject. There's more arguing about the right course of action until Laina interrupts everyone: "Let's take a vote. *In the morning.*"

Ridley looks at Laina, trying to communicate something with his eyes. Laina shakes her head.

What Alex wouldn't give for some mind powers right now. "What about me?" she says. "I won't be around in the morning. For obvious reasons."

"Dragon can pass along your vote," Georgie says. And of course this has some underlying message behind it that Alex can't decipher.

"So," Laina says. "Morning?"

"Fine," Ridley says.

More nods of agreement. Still, it takes another ten minutes before the crowd begins to dissipate.

As they finally leave, Ossi gestures at Sondra's house. "So who is going to talk to her?"

A short silence before Dragon sighs and starts walking. Moments later, he is at the stairs, knocking. The door opens. Dragon steps into the thick darkness, and the door closes behind him.

Alex turns to find Georgie on the path, waiting for her.

Ossi and Alex share a look, Ossi holding her gaze. "Need me to . . ."

Alex shakes her head.

"I'll get going, then," Ossi says.

Ossi and Georgie pass each other with curt nods, and then Georgie stalks over.

"I understand you've lived a hard life before this," Georgie says. "I know you must've done some things. But that boy—"

Oh. That's what this is about.

"He shouldn't be the first person going off to kill people."

Alex nods minutely. "He wasn't the *first* person."

"Are you really going to do that? Pretend you don't know what I'm talking about?"

"Georgie, he's had to do things before this."

"Does that mean he has to do them *now*? We came here to live peacefully."

The first time Alex met Georgie, Alex had marveled at those big eyes and her easy smile. The meeting was by happenstance. They both had been at the same hotel in Arlington, Virginia, and ended up on the same flight out. Alex had just completed interviews for the CIA. Georgie had attended a co-op conference at the hotel. At the terminal gate, Georgie had recognized her and struck up a conversation. Georgie was beautiful, and Alex was sure there was some flirtation between them. It might have gone further if Alex allowed herself to want things, to have them.

If there is anything left of that initial interest, the signs are hidden under Georgie's self-righteousness. Even with Georgie squinting into a glare, her eyes still look too big for her face.

"Do you even care about what I'm saying to you?"

"Georgie," Alex says. She really should stop using her name this way, as if trying to placate a child.

"This isn't some silly concern you can dismiss. The boy is going through . . . something. He doesn't need this now. We can't use him this way. It's a terrible thing to do, given his history."

"Given his history of what?"

Something in Alex's tone makes Georgie step back.

Later, Alex will blame it on the woods, the killing, the blood-lust setting her on edge. But now, in the moment, she doesn't notice how she steps forward just as Georgie steps back.

"That boy," Alex says, "has never had anything like what we've had. Anything close to a childhood. Or family. And the closest things he's had to those things, he's lost. Yes, it's unfortunate. But it has made him stronger than either of us."

"He shouldn't have t—"

"And I'd be careful treating him like a child. It doesn't go well for those who do."

Georgie's eyes are bigger now.

Alex is close enough to feel Georgie's breath, sink her teeth into Georgie's neck. "Unless you have what it takes to protect him and yourself, I'd stay clear."

The words hit their mark, freeing tears from Georgie's eyes.

Alex knows she has gone too far. "I'm sorry. I don't know why I said that."

Georgie wipes away the tears, but it does little to hide her distress. "This is not who we are."

Alex's nod is solemn, capitulating. "Let us hope it's not who we *need* to be."

13

REBECCA VÁSQUEZ

All forty-eight residents of Moon are packed into the community center.

Tables have been folded and pushed to the side, chairs laid out in neat rows, a line of chairs at the front where the council sits facing the waiting audience. In Rebecca's head, quotation marks surround the word "council." There really wasn't a council before this morning, and they barely qualify for the designation now.

"Well, we're all here," says Ridley. "We should get to it."

The room isn't exactly silent. Pockets of hushed conversation carry in the cavernous barn. But at Ridley's words, voices lower and attention shifts to the front.

"Most of you must have heard already," Ridley continues. "We were attacked last night."

That gets the rest to quiet down.

"As a result of the attack, one of the houses on the south side of Moon received some fire damage. Don't worry—the ants put it out quickly enough. And no one was inside the house. But . . ." Ridley pauses for an appropriate time. "The people who attacked us were Black Hand. By the time most of us got there, one of the attackers had already been killed."

A buzz of whispered discussion.

"It was a defensive act, but that made things complicated when it came to the seven other Black Hand. Some of us decided to pursue them. In the pursuit, all but one of the other Hands were killed."

A flurry of low voices begins to rise. Collective fear settles over the room.

Rebecca is looking at Ridley, who has paused again to allow for the uproar. She can't help but notice that despite the situation, he looks better, more present. Ridley wasn't eager to facilitate the discussion, but he didn't shy away from it either. When no one volunteered, he raised his hand, and his *I can handle it* energy did the rest.

Fred, from the front row, stands. "Who killed them? Why weren't we consulted?"

Ridley opens his mouth to speak, but Ossi answers first. "And when were we going to consult you, Fred? Were we supposed to come and wake you up to receive your wisdom?"

Fred sputters. "That's not what I'm saying. You know what I'm saying."

"There was no time," Ossi says. "It was act and hopefully protect our location, or do nothing and risk everything."

No one has a good rejoinder for this. Except possibly Rebecca, though she won't say it out loud. She agrees with Ossi, at least in principle. But it is just as likely that their location was already broadcast before the Black Hand came. It was the right response regardless. Still, right or wrong, it may not matter.

Ridley says, "Let's move on. Since one of the Black Hand got away, we have to decide what we'll do next. Abandon Moon or try to protect it from whoever shows up."

"Do you think more Black Hand will show up?" Tash asks.

Next to Tash, Leti is sobbing into Espeth's shoulder. Espeth's kids, June and Nat, are holding hands. June is shaking.

Rebecca looks to Ridley. He nods, and she drops the final bomb: "The Black Hand are already talking about attacking again tonight."

This destroys the last shred of calm in the room.

We've found them, the heading on the forum had read. And late in the night, there was an update. A small group of Black Hand had engaged. "They all were murdered," wrote the poster—perhaps the one who escaped. He provided an address. "Help me avenge our people." And then a flurry of responses followed, outrage turning to frenzy over the next several hours. By the end of it, a plan had emerged. Dozens of armed Black Hand within a few hundred miles of their location had answered the call. They would gather today and attack tonight.

Rebecca explains all this as calmly and succinctly as she can. "We're already out of time."

The clamor is deafening.

"Okay," Ridley says, trying to get everyone back on task. "We still need to—"

"Everyone. Shut. Up. Now." What Ossi does could not be called yelling, but the low growl in her voice is more than effective.

The room falls silent.

"Okay," Ridley says again. "So we vote. Leave or stay."

"How about we leave *and* stay," someone says. She stands for all to see. It is Karuna. "I'm not the only person here who wouldn't survive out in the world. This isn't a vote between two viable options—not for all of us."

Murmurs of agreement pass through the gathered Moonites.

"But I have a better option," Karuna says.

"And what is that?" Ridley asks.

Karuna is calm when she says it: "Shock and awe."

• • •

An hour later, the decision has been made. As people are leaving the community center, a hand stops Rebecca.

"Can we talk?"

Rebecca blinks. "Look, Mom, if you're going to try to talk me out of this—"

"I'm not."

"Or if you're trying to volunteer yourself for this counter-assault—"

"Not in a million years."

"Oh," Rebecca says. "So you're just worried, then." She catches the eye of Laina, who is standing at the entrance, and waves her off. This may take a while. "I'll be careful, Mom. I promise."

"Girl, if you don't stop trying to predict what I'm trying to say . . ."

"Sorry. Okay, what is it, then?"

Her mother takes a breath. "Yes, of course I want you to be careful. I know better than to try to talk you out of anything.

And I've lived my whole life without killing anyone"—she pauses—"purposely, anyway. So I'm not about to start now.

"I just want you to know that I love you and I'm proud of you. And"—she puts up a hand to stop Rebecca from speaking—"your brother does too. Even if he's terrible at saying it. We've been talking a lot lately about him leaving. He wants to, as you've surely figured out by now. But he isn't just staying here to protect me. As if I need protecting. He's here because he respects you and loves you, and he understands—in his more lucid moments—that what you are helping to build here, this community, is important."

Her mother comes closer. "Now, he might leave in the end." She places her hands on Rebecca's shoulders. "But whatever he does, you haven't robbed him of anything. You haven't robbed me either. You did some things the wrong way early on. We should've talked before you decided to change me. But! Girl, don't you start. Listen.

"None of this is your fault. We're here because of how the world is, not who you are. You're not cursed. We're not cursed. This is life. Just how it is. So don't you go out there with any thought of punishing yourself or sacrificing your life or who you are to protect us. Do what you need to do. Do it as safely as you can. Then come back to us, alive.

"Okay, that's what I wanted to say."

Rebecca realizes that her mouth is agape only when her mother nudges it closed, gently lifting her chin with a curled finger. Just as gently, her mother wipes a fallen tear away.

"You don't have to say anything." Her mother looks her right in the eyes. "Just come back."

"I love you."

"I love you too."

She knows better than to make any promises. But she will accept her mother's wish for her to survive. If belief can somehow remake reality, she won't weaken it with doubt.

Forty Black Hand come to the road north of Moon. Around them, gently rolling meadowlands border the patch of woods where they know Moon to be hidden.

Over the course of hours, a dozen cars, trucks, SUVs, several RVs, and a school bus arrive at the precise coordinates left to them by the sole survivor of the earlier incursion into the monster settlement. They wait until everyone has arrived and then follow the dirt road leading off from the main one, and when they reach the fence, the sign saying *Posted. No Trespassing*, they walk through it, just as instructed by the online thread, each of them squeezing their eyes shut as they pass through the mirage, the buzz of magic like static on their skin.

These Black Hand have come heavily armed: handguns, assault rifles, grenades, a grenade launcher, a flamethrower (because why not?), and every description of knife, for up-close work or carving off trophies.

The dirt road leads into the dense woods beyond the mirage.

No light. They make their way silently down this road as it snakes through the forest, pulling off the path when they get close to the true entrance, the first set of houses. It looks to them like a toy town, as if someone had just set houses on a large square of land. They know that something else used to exist here, but what sits here now looks more like a Hollywood set than a real town.

They come in from the sides of the settlement, onto the grid streets from the surrounding woods. None of them has made a conscious decision not to attack right away. It is the eerie silence that stops them. No sound from anywhere in the settlement. No music or conversation. Even the wind is absent here. Dead air. And the sense that if they are the first to make noise, they'll be the ones to suffer for it.

All the bravado on the way to Moon, the whispered promises of retribution on the sides of the main road, the anticipation as they passed through the false fence—gone. Now they are starting to feel fear. They thread through the streets of Moon, feeling their heartbeats, conscious of each breath, guns pointed ahead but eyes darting everywhere, searching, waiting for something to happen and dreading what it might be.

"Maybe they left," someone dares to say, trying to fill that dread with a reassuring thought. Now he wants them to leave too. Better to return to the road, to the forums, with the story that they've driven the monsters out, than never to return at all.

But one of the women in the Black Hand points ahead. "See that? Lights."

And so they all carry on. Not one of them turns back. They converge on a large barn, all the lights on inside, streams of light coming through the windows. Like a barn from outer

space, someone thinks. Nervous, they are drawn to the streams
of light. Like moths, they huddle.

A brave Hand steps forward to push at one of the barn
doors. It swings open, revealing the emptiness within. The signs
of a community, but no community. Through the windows, the
same sight, the same emptiness.

Hackles on the backs of necks stand up as something primal,
something ancient within their blood and sinew, tells them to
run. But the timing is bad. Their hatred has brought them too
close to get out now.

And right on time, chaos. A dozen portals open up around
them, leading elsewhere, from other elsewheres. And out from
those holes in reality spring a large black jaguar or panther,
several wolves, a teenage boy with wings and scaled flesh, and
four women, three chanting strange words and one moving
impossibly fast.

The Black Hand are shooting, but the creatures are too
fast, appearing and disappearing into the shadows, falling into
and out of rents in reality that have appeared on the sides of
houses, on the streets, on rooftops. Too much movement, too
fast. Impossible movement. And the intruders are starting to
fall, struck down or dragged into the dark, or dropped through
the ground, or pulled into the dirt by green tangles of vines,
unable to breathe. Or set on fire. Or pulled into the sky only to
drop like clipped birds. The Black Hand with the flamethrower
is down early, his hands turned to ice before shattering like
glass. One falls, then a half dozen, then a dozen. One by one,
dying screams are cut off as if with an axe. And now they have
started to run, eyes wide in the dark, tears falling. How could
they ever have been prepared for *this*? What could they have

done against this level of monstrousness? They have lost their bearing; any direction is out. They run for the cover of trees, but the woman is there, running up on them and snapping their necks. One Black Hand could swear that he shot her, but the bullet goes through her, not even slowing her down. She bites into his neck. The panther is in the trees, springing down on them. The trees themselves are eating them, pulling them into their bark, burying them in wood. Wolves are hunting them, snapping at their ankles, clawing at their backs. Five more fall to writhing masses of fur. Talons reach down from above, and one of them is swept up into the sky. He falls back through the canopy, breaking branches and bones on the way down.

For those who make it back to cars, it doesn't matter how they came. They scramble for the keys left behind and drive off, waiting for no one. Others wander the woods, looking for a place to hide, where they are sniffed out.

The one mercy is that they are killed quickly.

In less than an hour, it is over. Twenty-five Black Hand dead, and many more wounded.

Only a handful of the Black Hand escape without physical scars. None escape without marks on their souls.

Valter doesn't return to see Sonya for another three weeks. This lag is deliberate, Sonya guesses. All these conversations when he drops tantalizing bits of information, when he "confides" in her about his life and history—who he was before he became a vampire and member of the Order of the Zsouvox, who he was immediately after he became a member, who he is now. Who he will become once their orders collapse—and they will, he has reassured her.

For a while, Sonya keeps her silence, doesn't offer a single thing. But when she realizes that he isn't interested in any information in particular and that he is being forthright when she asks him questions (all except for who he was before he was turned), she decides that it might be worth conversing with him. She assumes, of course, that this is an elaborate ruse to gain her trust, but the silence and the loneliness are driving her mad—which, she suspects, he knew would happen.

"I've been thinking about what you said last time," Valter says. "About the Zsouvox. You said you don't know what they are. That Melku knows. And Damsel. And Cassandra. But not you. Why is that?"

Sonya shifts in her chair. She watches him through the glass, his big gray hair. "I don't need to know." She is careful not to mention that not knowing is part of her contract.

Her contract is different from the others. Melku brought it to her, written on actual paper. She took five days, reading it over and over before she signed it. The contract said she could make one request to the universe. And she did, wishing that all her family would live and one day be together again. She was unsure whether the second part was even possible, but the universe agreed.

There was one caveat: All her family would live and they would be together again—*if* the universe wasn't destroyed. And if she did her part, perhaps it wouldn't be.

"I have a theory about the Zsouvox," Valter says. "Do you want to hear it?"

"No," Sonya says. "I don't think I should know."

Valter stares at the spot where he thinks she is. As usual these days, he is correct. "I want to go against your wishes here. But your adamance has actually frightened me. And I am not easily frightened."

Sonya smiles at that, not that anyone can see. Her unguarded reaction represents a breaking open of her will. She has become fond of this unassuming man almost without knowing it. Which means she has fallen under his spell a little. She reels back from the revelation. It is like touching a rose stem and sticking her finger on a thorn.

"You know," he says, "it is just a theory. My own personal one. Not confirmed truth. Could a theory really do any harm?"

Sonya considers. She supposes he is right. Hearing his theory doesn't mean she will violate her contract with the universe. It is just another point of view on a matter she herself has speculated about.

"Okay," she says, even as another part of herself warns her not to proceed.

He hesitates a moment—a quirk of a smile. He is amused at himself, or at what he is about to say. An exhalation whistles through his teeth. "In the early years—more like centuries—Asha was worshipped as a god. Until she disappeared. Then she was still worshipped as a god, but it became abstract over time. She was a force, no longer a cat, and the stories of her became fables. I could never make up my mind if that was intentional. Monsters are long-lived, and not so much time elapsed between Asha as the cat god, physical and real, and Asha as the cosmic force, the alternative power to the Zsouvox, which is the force of darkness and oblivion. The Zsouvox was always described as a force, and the prophecy that it would one day take human form wasn't treated seriously."

Sonya understands where he is going with this.

He says it anyway. "But we see now that the Zsouvox is human—two humans, in fact. Or as close to human as it can be. The fact that there are two is the clue. I don't think it is a force given human form. I believe it is a god. A god *made* of gods."

And as soon as Sonya hears the theory, she knows that it makes sense. And that this conversation was a mistake.

"My suspicion is that these two Zsouvoxes are parts of the same being, and they are separate because there is a disagreement between them."

Sonya is holding herself tight. Now that she has allowed this to happen, she can't stop it, not without giving away her fear. She expects, in this moment, that the universe itself will show up and snatch the words from his tongue.

The universe does not.

"What is the disagreement?" Sonya asks him.

"That is where I am at a loss. The Zsouvox has mentioned a world above, and I suppose the disagreement stems from there. When I try to picture that place—a world above, a world beyond this universe—my imagination fails me. But the question I keep asking myself is, Why are they here? Why aren't the Zsouvoxes up there, settling their dispute? My best guess, they are something like the fallen angels. Beings thrown out of heaven and trapped on earth.

"My theory: This place, our world, is their prison," he replies. "What's happening now *is*?"

"The Zsouvox trying to break out," Sonya says.

"Only there is no way out, only through. To get out, they'll have to break the prison."

Sonya has spent time watching the Order of Asha's Zsouvox at the Bordeaux compound, always without her skin. It didn't matter, because the Zsouvox always seemed to know she was there, but it never acknowledged this, though she could feel the shift of its attention, its peering awareness. The Zsouvox seemed to think it was a game, and it went right on playing with its cards or its toys, or reading, or watching television. Only once did it speak, and it seemed to be a conversation it was having with itself. It said, "This one that watches us—is it safe to talk to her? He wants to."

At the time, she had found it strange that the Zsouvox would talk about her while she was in the room. But this seemed to be its indirect way of acknowledging her without risking itself.

After that, it waited for a time, completely still. And then it said, "Not safe yet." The Zsouvox raised its hand delicately, and she felt the pull, a drawing in, and she knew that it had called the universe into the room. The Zsouvox had a brief exchange with the universe that she was blocked from accessing, and then the Zsouvox returned to playing, the child version of itself having returned.

From that moment, Sonya thought of the Zsouvox as more than one thing, and very powerful. But she had not thought about it being more than one *god*. Even though she knew that Asha was a god and that Damsel was, if not a god, something more than merely human or monster, she had not thought to fathom the same of the Zsouvox. But then what else could the Zsouvox be but a god?

Sonya watches the man sitting outside her glass cage. She understands that this man does not limit his imagination. A terrifying thought. If she ever gets out of this cage, the best action will be to kill him.

"But you're not sure of any of this," she says.

"No," he admits. "Both orders must have had records on the origins of the Zsouvox. If the records ever did exist, they are lost. I suspect this is not the true kind of loss, but a deliberate erasure of institutional memory. Most of the time, it is internal politics that leads to erasure—one faction or the other trying to assume control of the whole—but other times, it is forethought, burying a trail so that later members can't glean the whole truth about something important, blurring a place where ignorance might be salvation.

"But I am very patient," he says. "I have the stamina to re-trieve lost things." He smiles. "We are alike in that way. I wonder how much you managed to gather before we knew of you, before we knew to guard ourselves. How many secrets about us, about the world, do you hold in that head of yours?"

Sonya holds her silence. If he knew the half of it, he would kill her now.

"The answer," he says, "is yes. I have been protecting you. The reason the Bone Witch hasn't been in here is because I've convinced them that you're cooperating. Well," he says with a little sigh, "I am giving myself perhaps too much credit. They're also afraid of that tattooed witch of yours. They don't want to risk our prized witch becoming ensnared in a hex trap hidden in your head or on your person. But I did convince them that containment and conversation is the best strategy."

"And then?"

"And then nothing. We hold you until we're sure you're safe, or we figure out a way to turn you to our side, or you die. Any outcome is fine, as far as we're concerned. And in any event, we have the time."

"Why not just kill me?"

He chuckles. "That's the least useful outcome. We can't use you if you're dead."

Silence.

"I am only telling you how we think, not how *I* think. The differentiation is important."

Sonya sits with that for a moment. "Because you're not really with them."

He smiles. "So you're considering it? Trusting me?"

"I am . . ." There is a rumbling from somewhere outside. "What's that?" Sonya says.

Thirty-Two stands, looking toward the door. He is hearing it too: an eruption of frenzied noises. He goes out into the hall and sees that in the other cells, the ones with bars instead of doors, everyone is banging themselves against the bars and yelling.

By the time Thirty-Two looks out into the hallway, Melku has already closed the rent in reality. What Thirty-Two does see is even stranger: Melku astride—or within—what can only be described as a twelve-foot-tall suit of mechanical armor. The armor has no helm, and its too-large chest is an open cockpit where Melku looks out. Below Melku's head and their extravagant mane of hair, the mage's entire body is sheathed in a shimmering black bodysuit. In the open cockpit, Melku does not stand but hovers. Around Melku, like Saturn's rings, is a hoop made from the same shimmery black material, which, whether by gravity or magnetism, seems to be keeping the tech mage suspended and centered.

As Melku moves their limbs within the mech-suit's chest, so do the mech-suit's limbs move. Exactly the same, dexterous despite the thing's massive bulk. There is a touch of strain in the mechanical limbs, though, mirrored in Melku's own movements.

Thirty-Two notes all this in the moments it takes Melku to take three steps, stop, and reach behind to draw two blades from the mech-suit's back. The blades glow, their heat rippling the air.

Melku pauses for only a moment. They extend their arms outward. Melku's and the mech-suit's legs move as one, advancing down the space between the two rows of cells, using the blades to cut through the bars. The monsters behind the bars step back from certain death before surging out of their prison.

Behind Melku, one of the monsters, a giant, slips through the press of newly freed bodies and ambles toward the tech mage. The piloted mech-suit could be anything, but it is big enough and formidable enough for the giant to consider it an adversary. Melku doesn't spare a glance behind him the entire time, but a sensor lights up in the cockpit of the mech-suit, which triggers the top part of the mech-suit to spin from the waist. The burning blades are even hotter now, their sizzle audible. The giant doesn't seem to care, swinging a heavy fist at Melku. With one quick and graceful move, Melku arcs a blade up, slicing through the giant's arm at the wrist. Cleanly separated, the hand falls to the giant's feet just as he howls in pain. He still doesn't stop, reaching for Melku with his other hand. Melku uses the other blade. A moment of surprise for the giant before the blade slices through his neck. Melku spins back around as the head falls away and the rest of the giant crumples.

Thirty-Two watches all this. Now Melku strides toward him. Thirty-Two wastes only a moment to calculate his odds before he steps back, turns, and runs the other way at preternatural speed. Leaving Sonya alone in her cell, free for the taking.

Once Melku reaches the door to Sonya's cell (an actual door, not cell bars), they swing their swords, cutting a clean X in the door and the surrounding wall. Then they cock one machine leg to kick the door down. The explosion of door bits leaves a nice hole for Melku to stoop through. And this is what Sonya sees: Melku, like something out of her dreams, piloting a twelve-foot-tall robot.

Relief spreads across Melku's face. "Step back," they say.

Sonya backs away from the walls of the cage, and Melku cuts through it, nice and clean, with one of their red-hot swords. Melku sheaths both swords quickly and gracefully, which looks very strange given the size and heft of the thing Melku is piloting. Melku reaches into that slice in Sonya's cage with both mechanical arms, machine fingers prying the slit wider. That happens quickly too—the prying, the slit spreading and cracking the cage apart until Sonya can slip through.

"My father is here," Sonya says. "A couple floors below this one."

"No time," Melku says. "Need me to carry you?"

"I can walk."

"All right," Melku says.

Already the ants are forming a portal beneath their feet. As it opens, they both start to fall. And Sonya does fall, easily, landing on the warehouse floor with the dull echo of noise that happens in a very empty space.

Melku does not fall.

Sonya looks up, waiting for Melku and their machine to obey gravity, and after long moments when it doesn't, she looks closer. A hand is there—a regular-size forearm and hand, holding Melku up by the neck, Melku wriggling like a fish on a hook. Around that forearm and hand, a cloud of gnats, which forms the outline of a face, and as it does, the face speaks.

"I got you," Smoke says. "And everything you love."

The gnats begin to stir, moving toward the still-open portal between realities.

Sonya doesn't see Melku's face, but she hears their voice: clear, authoritative, without a note of hesitation: "Close the portal."

There's a moment of stutter, as if the ants are having trouble processing the request. But then the portal closes, Sonya's pro-test caught in her throat. So fast. The machine falling. Sonya moving out of the way.

She makes herself look, see what remains of the machine. And most of it does remain. Not so for Melku.

Retching punctuated by sobs. When she has no more bile or tears, she screams. The retching and sobbing are relatively short; the screaming lasts quite a bit longer.

The only thing that quiets her are the eyes, two swirling neb-ulae staring down from the ceiling, as large as the ceiling itself.

There you are, Abyssia says, but Sonya doesn't hear it. The words are not for her.

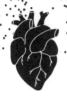

A VISIT WITH CHAOS, AND THE ARRIVAL OF THE MULTIGOD

I am sitting on asphalt, a man cradled in my arms.

I am sitting on asphalt alone.

I am underwater.

I am in space.

The sun is hot above my head.

The man has an open head wound, skin stained red.

I am crying.

I am not crying.

I am angry.

His eyes are open. I have to close his eyes!

I am reaching out and touching the seed and it is so cold, like ice, like the soft caress of deep space.

I am on the asphalt, a man cradled in my arms. Three men stand before me, holding guns.

There is a ship piercing the membrane of the world, the skin of that ship burning.

My skin is burning.

I am touching the seed and seeing . . . *myself.*

I am on the asphalt, a man cradled in my arms. Three men standing before me, and I am going to kill them.

I am at the Pits of Yn, open-mouthed, staring at all those bones.

"So we could be safe," my mother says, nails digging deep into my back. "To continue. Because if we hadn't done what we did, we would be in those pits, with purple vines choking our bones."

I don't know what to say, but I understand.

I am in the ocean and there is so much blood in the water, a congregation of dead bodies below me, swaying together like stalks of seaweed.

Three men are standing before me, holding guns, and I am going to kill them. I take one in my hands and press his face into the negative space of my chest, the window of my soul. He screams into the void, his lungs exploding.

I rip the others in half.

I try to revive him. I fail.

I try to revive him. I fail.

I fail and fail and fail and . . .

I clone his body, but he is not the same. He can never be the same. The universe splits.

I save him, arriving right before they shoot him, and a whole universe is born where he lives. But the universe still exists where he dies.

I save him and save him and SAVE HIM, and yet he dies. It cannot be undone. It has already happened. The universe splits, and splits, and . . .

Nothing ends.

The sky is cloudless. And a ship hovers over Water Island. It explodes and does not explode.

I am that ship, laid barren, an empty ship filled with ghosts.

"We had no choice," my mother says, a lie whispered over the pit of corpses made from the lie. "The universe understands only strength."

Centuries later, I am touching the seed and I see . . . myself. But not just one. All selves. All pain. I hurt and hurt. I am filled with it to bursting.

I burst.

A self is a lie you commit yourself to. "I had no choice," says the lie.

I pick up the three men and throw them into the sun.

I kick the earth into the sun.

The earth burns and doesn't burn. Ten billion human beings, dead. Ten billion alive. The universe splits.

Does it happen if it also doesn't happen? Does it matter?

Is it a dream?

I am at the bone pits, turning to my mother. "The universe lives," I say.

"Then we must kill it."

I shudder away from her.

I am sitting on the asphalt, every version of me, every era of me, all at once, sitting, waiting for him to die.

If a self is a lie committed to, what is a self that experiences every self, bright as all suns, in a land with no shade?

What is a mind that experiences everything? Every single thing, happening and not happening. Every moment, every permutation of every moment, sitting on the head of a needle.

What do *you* think? What is a mind that is pierced by infinity?

Yes. Chaos.

17

I'm going to tell you a story.
No. Let me *show* you.

18

SSASMERAN, THE TRAITOR

Mera has been sitting in the holding cell for hours. Dee is there too, but at the moment, he isn't much of a conversationalist. He sits in the corner, a thin shadow around his hunched body, the lights hot and white against his skin.

She knows why he is angry with her, knows they will have to talk later about this and everything else, all the things that have been building between them for so long. But she can't have that conversation here, not without giving away her plan. Dee knows this too, she suspects. Nonetheless, he remains too angry to make small talk. Probably better that way.

Dee hears the footsteps first, lifting his head and cueing Mera to perk up as well. It doesn't take long before they both see the source of those measured steps.

Mera recognizes Huren at once. It isn't just the purple and orange streaks on his face, as distinctly patterned as a fingerprint.

It is in the tight, slow movement of his limbs, reflexes even more controlled than those of most Ynaa. Old power radiates off him, undeniable and fierce.

Huren is immortal. This is no different from any other Ynaa in this era. But Huren was already several thousand years old by the time the Ynaa discovered how to extend their lives indefinitely. And because of his age, he has a particular Ynaa trait, developed to its extreme: the ability to move his limbs very slowly while simultaneously seeming to glide across any distance as if he existed in a bubble of space-time all his own.

Mera had once cultivated that trait too, but that was in another life.

Huren walks through the force field that keeps Mera and Dee imprisoned, the hum of electricity halting before activating again. He smiles, thin lips curling.

"You call yourself Mera now, right, traitor?"

Huren asks the question in Old Ynaa. *Shelrek* is their word for *traitor*, and he says it with the hiss appropriate to someone of her status. It is the worst word in the Ynaa language, but Mera has lost any trepidation the word once gave her.

"The Manejrish sent me to discuss terms," Mera says calmly.

"They should have done that themselves. *They*"—he pauses for emphasis—"should have known that *you*"—another pause—"would get them nowhere with us."

"They were afraid you would hurt them."

"That is not our way. We only require that ten percent of their population be exterminated. But we wouldn't kill during a discussion of terms."

"You wouldn't have changed your terms either."

"No," Huren admits. "Ten percent is a kindness. There was a time when we would have responded to an attack on our people with total extermination."

"Yes," Mera says. "Your brutality is remembered on every world you step on."

Huren smiles, revealing a mouth cramped with serrated teeth. The blue-gray tentacles on his head squirm lazily. "I see you brought your pet." Huren slowly turns his head to look at Dee. "It looks healthy. Too bad about the original."

Mera's fists clench, but her expression doesn't change.

"I am no one's pet," Dee says in Ynaa.

Huren manages a subtle expression of surprise, a slight rise of the ridge above his beady black eyes and the faint glow of his orange and purple face streaks. "You taught him Old Ynaa?" The laugh is a slow growl that vibrates the entire cell. "How interesting. You still wear their skin, you keep them as *pets*"—a pause, a deliberate extended look at Dee—"and now you teach one our language? You have truly lowered yourself, Mera."

Mera ignores the provocation. "You will kill none of the Manejrish," she says. "Those are the terms."

Another low tremble of laughter. This one lasts much longer—a maintained display of his derision. "And what will you do if we don't accept these terms?"

Mera finally allows herself to smile, just as Dee grabs at his chest.

"What did you do?" is all that Dee has time to ask Mera. In seconds, Huren has reached Dee, is lifting Dee off the ground, is puncturing the soft flesh of Dee's chest with expert force, pinpointing the source of Dee's discomfort. Dee screams in agony and horror before going limp. And then Huren pulls out Dee's beating heart, the blood dyeing the Ynaa's blue-gray skin a deep red.

The heart starts to glow, the light at its center beginning to shine through. The veins look like dark roots writhing along the surface of a setting sun.

Huren turns to look at Mera slowly. He has returned to the careful movements he used just moments before. He knows there is no time for escape, no point in warning anyone of what is about to happen. Only enough time to say the old words that all Ynaa say when they know their end has arrived.

"Orunaa mesh. Orunim cintaar."

My old enemy. My new friend. It is a message to Death herself. Mera doesn't repeat the words back as any Ynaa should. She is no longer Ynaa. She just watches as the explosion engulfs everything in a searing white light.

• • •

Mera's second sight fades to black when her clone link is severed. Her first sight observes as the firework of debris from the destroyed Ynaa ship blooms from the blast's center. All but one of her reef drones are already on their way back to the ship. The remaining one, feeding her the image of the explosion, will stay in the system, watching for the arrival of any Ynaa and sending back any details to Eno, the ship's AI.

Each drone sings a series of notes as it attaches to the skin of the ship. When the last one sings, the ship instantly leaves the Manej System at superluminal speed.

"I'm going to bed," Mera says, the shock of her clone's death making her own body ache. "Maintain course."

Eno sings a note in confirmation.

The Ynaa think body links are a sign of weakness. They also think it wise to consolidate their power in massive interstellar ships spread thinly across the galaxy, which means an attack done fast enough hopefully won't give a ship the chance to send a distress call. All facts that Mera exploits in her plan. She leaves a probe in the system to take responsibility for the attack, hoping that she alone will incur the ire of the Ynaa, hoping Ynaa hatred of her will keep the Manejrish safe.

Mera finds the original Dee in the short corridor, on the way to his own cabin. He slows as she gets close, so she does as well. She waits for him to speak, but he doesn't.

"You can avoid me, or we can talk," Mera says. "Your choice."

"Do I have choices now?" Dee asks.

Mera meets his gaze pleadingly. "Look, I thought it would be better if only I knew the plan."

"How long was the bomb in there?" Dee asks, his voice sharp, arms crossed defensively.

"I put it in when I made the clone," Mera confesses.

"It's so easy for you, isn't it? To keep secrets."

"Sorry," Mera says. And she is sorry. A little.

"My body is not a thing you can destroy and then apologize for later."

"Your clone body," Mera corrects. She realizes her error immediately and redirects. "There was a bomb in my clone heart too. I was being thorough in case they detected—"

"You're missing the point entirely."

Mera sighs. She remembers the confusion in his eyes when she let their clones get captured by the Ynaa warship. She knew he'd be angry once he found out the reason she let them get caught. But actually seeing it—all this hatred in his eyes . . .

"What did you want me to do?" Mera asks. "The Ynaa were going to kill a tenth of the Manej population."

"They might do that anyway," Dee says, almost yelling. "Or worse. Stop lying to yourself. This was about vengeance."

Mera says nothing.

"You could have told me," Dee says. "You should have told me."

"I already explained why I didn't. Stop being a child."

Dee's expression darkens. He takes a step back, unfolding his arms. Mera notes his ragged breath, how his chest heaves with each inhalation.

"If I am a child, whose fault is it?" he asks. There are tears in his eyes now.

Mera steps back. She tries to say something, but the words catch.

"Whose fault is it!"

"Derrick, I . . ." She stops.

Dee's expression changes instantly to something almost unrecognizable. But Mera *has* seen it before. When?

Dee is quiet for a long time before speaking. "You know I love you." There is no warmth in the words. It is a cold statement of fact. "I was too young to guard myself against it." Dee begins walking again, away from her, toward his cabin. "I didn't know then what I know now," he says—barely above a whisper, though it vibrates with rage—"that loving you is a prison."

Dee walks to his room and shuts the door quickly behind him.

Mera won't see him again until the Zsouvox comes.

Mera goes to her cabin. She takes off her battlesuit and slips into sleep clothes. She puts her dreadlocks in a single neat braid and slides into bed, covering herself all the way up to her chin, the soft nanofiber sheets doing little to soothe her anxious mind.

She tries to sleep but can't, rolling around in bed in a futile attempt to find comfort. She finally settles on her back and closes her eyes. Time passes like this, stuck behind her closed eyelids, trying to empty her mind of Dee in the hallway, that wounded look on his face. He is overreacting, surely.

He will leave you.

Mera sits up in bed. "Eno?"

"Yes," says the ship's AI in a gentle voice. It is not the voice Mera has just heard.

"Did you say something a second ago?" Mera asks anyway.

A pause. "No. Did you hear something?"

Mera looks around the room. No one. "Eno, do a scan of the surrounding area."

A longer pause. "There is a large object about fifteen light minutes away. An orphan planet, I believe, though the shape is somewhat irregular. It isn't giving off any readings."

Mera keeps looking around the room.

"Is there something wrong?" Eno asks.

"No. Forget it."

"Having trouble sleeping?"

Mera sighs. "Yes."

"Dee is having trouble sleeping too."

Mera doesn't respond to that. And she has no idea why Eno has even chosen to share this information. "What about the Ynaa?"

A few seconds pass while Eno corresponds with all the stealth reef drones in the surrounding systems.

"An Ynaa intergalactic ship is in the Manej System," Eno says. "There has been no action so far. They're angry, but all of it seems to be directed toward you."

"Better than decimating the Manejrish," Mera says. "Should we attempt the Ples system?"

"No," Eno says. "We're safer here."

"Why's that?"

"Founder ships are in all nearby systems. Ples system is crawling with Ynaa."

"Shit. Any ideas?"

"Wait."

That was the plan after blowing up the Ynaa warship: Wait out the initial search in deep space. And she can wait. Forever, in fact: She is immortal. But how long will her mind last out here? And Dee is still so young. He'll go crazy in this purgatory.

Mera heaves one more sigh. "We'll give it another week. If nothing changes, we'll hibernate."

"Okay," Eno says. "I will share this with Dee."

"No, not yet."

"Are you sure?"

What is with Eno today? "Yes, I'm sure. That's a direct order."

"Okay," Eno says in her usual soft voice, though Mera is sure she detects a slight edge.

"And track whatever is out there," Mera continues. "Make sure it really is nothing to worry about."

"Okay," Eno says again. The edge is gone. Was it ever there?

Maybe I am going crazy, Mera thinks. She lies back down and closes her eyes, trying again to get some sleep.

• • •

When Mera finally told Dee about Derrick, they were in bed, his head on her chest, her hand slowly stroking the short nap of his hair.

It was not her idea to tell him. They had just come back from a mission to inform the Azri of a potential Ynaa arrival in their system, to warn them off from any acts of aggression. Usually, she did these things by herself—he was still so young—but she had decided to take him along. He saw a world filled with Azri. The wonder in his eyes: For so long, it was just the two of them. She knew he would ask.

"Why don't we ever visit our home world?"

His breathing was even. He was so secure. And now she was going to end that for him.

Before the Ynaa became the dominant force in this galaxy, Mera explained, they would send scouts to infiltrate other worlds. Scouts typically manipulated their own DNA to make themselves look like the people of these worlds. And when the scouts found a world that was both interesting and vulnerable, they recommended a period of occupation.

Interesting always meant the same thing to the Ynaa: diverse biological information. The Ynaa were looking for one thing in particular: a biological answer to mortality.

"Your people didn't know they had it," Mera said. "And they never found out that this was why the Ynaa had chosen them for occupation."

Dee had been quiet for a moment. His head was resting on her chest, so she couldn't see his face. "What happened?" he asked finally.

Good, Mera thought. He understood the subtext: *your* people, not *our* people.

"The humans were smart," she said. "They recognized that they couldn't kill the Ynaa, so they accepted occupation. The Ynaa offered technology, and they took the offer."

Dee's breathing had intensified. Mera's breathing was still a slow current in an icy lake. This trait of hers, this slowness, didn't seem to bother Dee. He accepted it without rebellion.

"The occupation went badly?" he asked.

"Not especially. The Ynaa killed several people for their 'insolence.' Back then, the Ynaa responded to any threat with murder; they were still that cautious. The human governments did nothing. They didn't want to upset the peace. And the people the Ynaa killed were dark-skinned, like you and me. On Earth, that made their lives less valuable for reasons . . . *difficult* to explain.

"But one got himself a gun. It was luck more than anything.

The Ynaa are hard to kill. But he managed. And in retaliation, the Ynaa killed over twenty-five thousand souls."

She could feel Dee's heartbeat on her chest. It was fast and hard. She remembered Derrick's heartbeat, how it thumped anxiously against hers, how his skin felt so soft, so vulnerable, how it made her feel safe.

"Why don't I remember any of this?" Dee asked.

He was greatly confused, as he had been when he first opened his eyes in the growth chamber, already a man, not knowing when the growing had happened. "You weren't there," Mera said.

"Where was I?"

She couldn't protect him. She couldn't protect any of them. She had landed in the Caribbean, surrounded by islands and by people with skin accustomed to the sun. She had been attracted to the water. It reminded her so much of Sa, her beautiful ocean planet. It took her some time, but she found what they wanted, and her people came. When they arrived, a blue-green world awaited them. When they left, the ocean was still blue, but the land was red.

"Where was I?" he asked again.

She could have lied, but what good would it do? He would have to know eventually. "I cloned you from a man who died on that planet. I made you."

Dee lifted his head to look at her. His expression was guarded, eyebrows slightly knitted, mouth tight. She had no clue what he was thinking, which made her feel anxious. (Yes. That was where she remembered that facial expression. Derrick used to make that face when he was trying to hide his feelings.)

She had thought about what his response would be when

she told him. She had expected him to ask to go back. And she would have to tell him that Earth was on the other side of the galaxy. Space equals time: The world he returned to would not be the one she had left. And that part of the galaxy had been quiet ever since. Who knows what happened to the humans.

But he didn't ask about going back. He didn't even seem upset. Not then. He just looked into her eyes for a long time. "What was his name?" he asked.

And she told him, feeling the old ache in her heart.

"How did he die?" Dee asked.

Mera didn't want to answer. The facts of it mattered so much less than her own culpability. She said, "On the night the Ynaa massacred all the men on St. Thomas, Derrick went to help some friends get off the island. They were met by three men outside his friend's house. One of them had a gun. These men knew who Derrick was. As ambassador to the Ynaa, he was my assistant. And he was killed for that affiliation."

She wouldn't say he was seen as a traitor. Like Mera is now.

"Ambassador?" Dee repeated.

"It means a representative of a people. That's who I was back then. His death is why I left the Ynaa behind."

"What about the other twenty-five thousand men?"

"What?" Mera said, to buy herself time because she didn't know how to answer the question.

Dee sat up in bed so he could look her in the eyes. He repeated himself.

The truth was that Derrick's death had been the final straw. It made the Ynaa, what they truly were, real to her in a way that nothing else had. How many people had died because she was late to make that decision within herself? How awful that

Derrick was the sacrifice needed to precipitate that change of heart.

"I can't explain to you what I was then. How selfish I was." It wasn't a direct answer, but the same terrible truth lay beneath it. That was the same Mera who created Dee, gave him a life that served only her and her grief.

He looked at her. He was still so young. Could he see her? Did he know who she really was?

He said, "We've saved more lives since then."

"Doesn't balance all the loss."

"Nothing can. Loss can't be undone."

How right he was, and neither of them really knew it. Not yet.

He has to leave you. You have to let him.

Mera opens her eyes. This time, she doesn't panic. She lifts her head and casually surveys her room. Once again, no one.

"Who are you?" Mera asks.

I've had many names. Someone calls me the Night Lady. I like that one.

Mera has never heard the name before. "Why are you here?"

As she asks this, Mera curves the fingers of her right hand. Under the sheets, reefs detach from the fiber on her sleeve, forming the grip of a gun. Mera places her index finger on the trigger as it forms. Her eyes dart about the room, but she keeps the gun at her side.

It is not an orphan planet.

"What are you talking about?"

"Mera," Eno cuts in. "There's a problem."

She sits up in the bed, the gun still in her right hand but resting on her thigh. "It's that thing nearby, isn't it?"

"Yes. It's right outside the ship."

Did the Ynaa discover some new form of cloaking technology? Mera gets out of bed, slips out of her sleep clothes and into battlewear, which is slightly more difficult to do because her right hand is still firmly wrapped around the grip of her gun. As she leaves the room, she keeps the gun at her side while carefully surveying everything around her.

"You still there?" she asks.

No answer.

Mera goes to ship control. Dee is already there. He averts his eyes from her, staring deliberately at the feed of images being produced by the ship's reef drones. They are observing the mass from several angles, getting as close as possible.

The thing is much larger than this small ship. It has no discernible shape, appearing as a blotch of ink on the void, tendrils wafting back and forth as if on a gentle tide. At the moment, it is unresponsive to the presence of the probes or the ship.

What is alarming to Mera is that it appears darker than the black of space surrounding it. And even stranger, it hurts to look at the thing, as if she were staring into an exploding star.

This is not Ynaa.

"I don't know how it got here so fast," Eno says.

"Have you been hearing a voice?" Mera asks Eno.

"No," Eno says.

"What voice?" Dee asks, rubbing his eyes as he stares at the feed.

"I'll explain later," Mera says. "Eno, I need you to plot a course for Ples system."

"The Ynaa are there."

"Let's deal with that when we need to. Do it quickly."

A pause. "It's not working."

"Fuck!" Dee says. "What is going on?"

It is the Zsouvox.

Dee turns, looking past Mera. His eyes go wide.

Mera whirls around. To their eyes, I am almost equally as strange as the swaying black blotch outside their ship.

No one speaks for a long moment. Then Dee lifts his gun. "Mera," Dee says. There is so much care in his voice that it almost makes Mera turn to look at him. "Please come here."

"No," Mera says. "And stay where you are."

Dee fires his weapon. The blast hits me, but the beam shrinks as it makes contact with my body, as if it were traveling a great distance, and then it disappears. He fires again, with the same result.

Dee is going to fire again, but Mera says, "Lower your weapon."

"But—"

Mera cuts him off. "Have you been paying attention? We're outmatched. Now, lower your weapon."

Dee glares at her but obeys.

"Are you a threat?" Mera asks.

No.

"Okay, *friend*," Mera says, adjusting to this new situation. She lowers her gun and disassembles the reefs. "What does this thing want?"

I could have said a lot of things then. I could have tried to explain what the Zsouvox truly was, that it had been made by the gods in a place called Akasha, that it was made because the gods were obsessed with questions they could not answer and so tried to make the answer themselves. And with such things, done out of obsession and ignorance, with no purpose other than to test limits, the thing they made had tried to destroy them.

But I did not say any of this. I did not say it, because in my memory no iteration of this moment had those words in it, and this version of me, who had regained her sanity, was careful not to create another, branching reality.

Instead, I said, *It is a being from outside your universe—a being that eats universes.*

Which was the part of the truth that I thought could fit easily inside their heads.

"That is the most terrifying thing I've ever heard," Dee says in a tone that is equal parts terror and awe. He is still so young, Mera thinks, still so interested in the mysteries of the universe. He does not understand that the universe is the enemy. This is the one thing the Ynaa believed that Mera maintains. The universe is nothing to gawk at. It will tantalize you as it annihilates you.

"What does this have to do with us?" Mera asks me. "Why are you telling us any of this?"

Because I will need a favor when this is over. But first, please step away.

Before she can ask why, I push her away.

Mera falls backward to the floor.

"What the . . ." But Mera is looking up now as a hand wraps around my neck. It is just a hand at first, but an arm is growing out of that hand, and then a body.

"Are you all right?" Dee asks, already kneeling next to Mera, one hand on her shoulder, the other around the grip of his gun aimed at the Zsouvox. Its complete body has formed, so black it seems to burn the light around it into a dark gray halo. Its head isn't a head at all, only a gaping mouth with long, irregular teeth the color of deepest shadow. Mera can hear the Zsouvox buzzing in her brain. One word over and over again: *Devour.*

The Zsouvox lifts me off the ground and slams me into the wall of the ship. The impact is soundless, the ship unharmed by the force—neither the Zsouvox nor I obey the conventionally understood laws of physics.

Mera watches me, can see my freckle of stars sparkle. As the Zsouvox's mouth comes closer to my head, my spiraling nebulae dim, and the stars blur into streaks.

Devour, it says again and again in Mera's mind. She feels dizzy. Next to her, Dee is groaning, his lifted arm shaking, his finger still on the trigger of his gun. Mera gently pulls his hand down.

"There is nothing you can do," she says hoarsely, her voice not sounding like her own.

She watches me struggle against the grip of the Zsouvox. Inside my body, Mera can see a star growing rapidly. Soon it is a glowing red sun. A solar flare bursts from the sun's surface and licks at the Zsouvox, slicing at its side. The Zsouvox cries out in Mera's mind. The gash is a long streak of white, surrounded by a gray outline that quickly fades to black. Already the gash is shrinking, the Zsouvox mending the wound.

The sun shrinks and spins away from its position in the center of my chest. Another sun replaces it, moments before going supernova. The light is so bright Mera has to look away. When she looks back up, the Zsouvox is on the other side of the room, its back pressed up against the far wall, shrieking.

Dee is on the floor next to her now. He is still alive, but he looks fatigued.

"I'm sorry," he says—she can only guess at what he means—and then he loses consciousness.

Devour, it says in her mind. DEVOUR. DEVOUR!

Mera pulls Dee's body toward her. She is weak and he is heavy, so it takes all her effort. She wraps her arms around him and presses one side of his head to her chest. She can feel his breath, weak and erratic against her. She can also feel his heartbeat, which makes her remember when she placed the bomb in his clone's heart. She has been so careless. So callous. So Ynaa. He is right. This was always about vengeance.

DEVOUR! yells the Zsouvox, pulling Mera from her thoughts.

Not over yet.

The Zsouvox unmoors their body from the wall and glides deliberately toward me. As it approaches, I conjure forward a cluster of stars. The cluster spreads, and each star grows. Mera watches as two new copies of me crawl out of the center of my body. One immediately sinks into the floor of the ship, disappearing from view. The other dashes out to meet the Zsouvox.

The Zsouvox grabs the new me by the neck and brings me to their mouth. I fight against them, limbs swinging wildly. Then I stop. A whole galaxy rushes forward within my body, so large that only part of it is visible. It zooms in farther until all that remains is a dark absence of light at the center of the galaxy inside me, a supermassive black hole.

It pulls at the Zsouvox. Simultaneously, the other me appears behind the Zsouvox. Inside that me is a supernova even larger than the first.

Close your eyes.

Pale light explodes out from me. Mera closes her eyes, but

even then she can still see my light from behind her eyelids. She expects it to hurt, but I make it cool against her skin.

Then my light dims, and Mera opens her eyes to see only me standing there, having taken the Zsouvox into myself.

Mera takes a deep breath of relief. She feels the tension in her body ease.

All over this multiverse, I am battling the Zsouvox. It will soon be over for me, but it won't seem that way for those who experience time as a straight line. The remnants of this moment will be seen and felt through all time, space, and dimensions.

"What are you?" Mera asks.

Yun is everything. I am an aspect of Yun.

Mera is clearly unsatisfied with the answer. As she should be. She looks down at Dee, unconscious in her arms, his breathing regular. "What do you want from me?" she asks.

You know what's the most frightening thing in creation? Something is growing in the window of my body that Mera can't yet make out—a small brown speck in a pitch-black sea. *Loss. You understand, don't you?*

Mera nods.

It is visible now: a human child curled up as if in the womb. It is slender and androgynous, tendrils of long, inky hair draping over dark skin so smooth and radiant it is hard for Mera to look at.

Loss can be counteracted only by gain. I push the body out of me and into reality in the form of a black egg. *The Zsouvox will need you now. To gain something new in exchange for what it has lost.*

"And what makes you so sure I will accept this request of yours?"

I smile. Mera doesn't know how she knows I am smiling—I have no mouth—but she can feel it, wholly obvious and strangely familiar.

Because time isn't a straight line. I take a few steps closer so she can see the little bursts of orange in my unblinking, nebulous eyes. *And because you will be stuck out here in deep space for a very long time if you don't.*

Yes, Mera agrees. The Ynaa live forever, just like her. And they can keep a grudge. They'll stay in the surrounding systems indefinitely and dispatch new ships to search out other systems. Her plan was always fatally flawed. She was just too stubborn to see it.

I will make it so the Ynaa never find you again. Make it so they cannot even see you.

"An ultimatum."

No. A deal.

Mera is angry, but she won't be forever. Her adoption of the Zsouvox is not just a favor. It is a gift. Loss must be counteracted by gain.

Mera ponders deeply before speaking. "Okay," she says. "I accept."

Dee stirs in Mera's arms. She slides her fingers along the short bristles of his head. Like Derrick, Dee likes his hair short. But Dee has a muscular body, unlike the scrawny island boy she grew to love. They have the same face, but they are different men.

He will leave you within a decade.

Mera nods. She is slightly relieved. A decade is longer than she expected.

When she took Dee out of the growth chamber, he couldn't even speak. Over the next twenty years, she took care of him, comforted him. She gave him what he needed so that his mind could catch up with his body. She gave him language, both human and Ynaa. She taught him about the known universe. She gave him immortality.

She understands why he has to leave. She made him to love her. There is nothing he is that he doesn't owe to her. And all of it rests on a fundamental betrayal. She has made him to be something to her, not to himself.

Dee will die in a love like that. They both will. She has to give him a choice. And herself.

He will be gone a long time. In many timelines, he comes back, but you have already changed. Wait for him, if you can.

"In these timelines, what do I change into?"

I smile again then. This time, I let her see my smile, the truth dancing at the edge of her consciousness. My voice, my smile—she knows them as intimately as her own.

The short answer, you now know. The long one, you will see for yourself. Eventually, all roads lead there.

Then I am gone. There is no sign of my leaving; I am simply not there anymore.

Though I've haunted this moment many times—and now visit it with *you* as my phantom companion—this was never my story, not as I am now. It is hers, as I was.

In the ship, Mera still sits, Dee in her arms, waiting for him to open his eyes, for her strength to return, for the Zsouvox to wake up and find that it can no longer devour worlds.

These two lives. She will be responsible for them both, responsible for the clone of a dead lover, and a shard of oblivion. One for another ten years. The other for a time she does not yet know. The Zsouvox will have to learn the importance of life again. She will have to teach it. Has she learned enough to teach it? Has she learned enough to teach herself?

"Where shall we go?" Eno asks.

Right, she thinks. *The whole universe is open to them now.* "I don't know," Mera says. Then she has another thought. "Where do you want to go?"

For a time, Eno doesn't respond. When Eno finally does, her voice is soft, with an edge of bewilderment and glee. "You've never asked me before."

Mera continues to stroke Dee's hair. Someday he will want to return to Earth. Someday she will help him get there.

"I've always wanted to go to Halar in the Sitre system," Eno says finally. "I want to see the schools of vollu fish leap across the Winnard Sea."

"That's beautiful," Mera says, smiling. "Let's go there."

THE BEAST UNDER THE WORLD: PART THREE

THE BEAST UNDER THE WORLD
PART THREE

SMOKE
WATERTOWN, MASSACHUSETTS

EARTH 0539

JUNE 10, 2028

NINETEEN MONTHS AFTER THE BOSTON RIOTS

The sight mage is at her desk when Smoke enters.

Verily closes the book slowly, her face empty, eyes focused on him as he approaches.

As always, Smoke looks at the closed book, wishing he could understand its contents. But everything in those pages is written in an unbreakable code. Even the Bone Witch, with her spellwork, has been unable to render the pages legible. This book predates the young girl, but with each sight mage, the written pages grow in number. As far as the Order can tell, all the sight mages use the same code. The Order tried to forbid the books at first, Smoke was told. But that ban led to a rejection of divination. Not even torture or the threat of death could force a sight mage to do what it refused to do.

There is only one way to speak to a seer. And so, he begins with a question she might answer. "How are you today?"

"I'm well," Verily says. "And you?"

"I'm . . . hopeful."

This one is younger than the last one, awakened to her power at just five years old. Verily is twelve now. The only other one to gain sight so young was Cassandra. He also would love to know why Verily and Cassandra achieved sight so early. But all the sight mages are locked boxes. That's a secret she will not tell.

"Where is Dragon?" Smoke asks.

Verily says, "He is in Moon."

No surprise there. She's answered this question before. "And where is Moon?"

"I have never answered that question."

Smoke bridles his frustration. "Is there a way for us to find its location?"

"Soon there will be news from the Black Hand."

Smoke fails to conceal his astonishment. This is a different answer from the times he's asked about Moon's location before. "When?"

"Soon," she repeats.

Smoke could have found Dragon before, when the boy was in the city, working at the New Era co-op association. He held back this information from his masters, convincing himself that he could retrieve the boy anytime. But then Dragon disappeared completely, out of reach, and Smoke knew the decision for what it was: weakness. Sometime over the years while the boy was away, once the initial grief at the loss passed, Smoke had begun to pity the child. He wished for Dragon the same thing he had received: a chance to make up his own mind. That he thought Dragon would simply come back to him was his own error.

Smoke had been Dragon's minder. He had tried to train all the softness out of the child so that he could be their weapon and kill anyone or anything that might threaten the Order. The same job that Smoke himself was trained to do. At some point, he realized that Dragon had begun to see him as a father figure. But at the time, his job within the Order, his purpose to the Order, was more important than care, more important than love.

He doesn't know what he'll do if he finds Dragon now. "Is he all right?" Smoke asks. He's never asked this before.

Verily stares at him for a moment. Amused? Surprised? Her pupils are wider, that's all he can tell.

"He is *not* all right?" Smoke asks.

"He's fine."

Good to know. Perhaps, once the Zsouvox is done with this realm and once Thirty-Two takes over, Smoke can persuade Dragon back to their side. Perhaps they can secure the future of the world together.

"Once the Zsouvox is made whole, what will happen?" Smoke asks the young sight mage.

For a moment, Verily looks as though she will give him the more typical response—that she has never answered that question—but then she closes her eyes and says, "They will likely leave this universe. Whether or not they destroy it as they leave is the question."

"Can it, really?" he asks. "Destroy the universe?"

She opens her eyes. "You are actively working to make the integration happen. That is the gamble you must accept. One does not play with fire without getting burned."

An apocalypse is exactly what the Cult, the renegade organization within the Order that now controls the Order, wants. Twenty-Nine, religious zealot that he is, loves the Zsouvox so much that he would welcome the obliteration of everything. But Thirty-Two wants something else, something more. If only . . .

"You know, don't you?" Smoke asks Verily. "Will the universe be destroyed? Tell me."

"I have never answered that question."

Smoke's edges begin to dance, bits of him peeling off. If he kills her now, then maybe—

"You don't need to worry," says a voice behind him. It is the absolute last voice Smoke wants to hear.

Smoke draws his power back into himself before he turns. The unfathomable god is standing in the corner of the room, a pale child's body with the face of something ancient. Smoke pushes down any surprise, projecting, as always, only mild, unthreatening annoyance.

The Zsouvox says, "There are other places than your multiverse, you know. Outside it. Beyond it. Within me." The eyes of the child rest on Smoke, searching. "If you maintain faith, there are many places I can put you while I finish my work. A lifetime is nothing to me. I can give you a hundred years. Two hundred."

Smoke keeps his mouth closed. One thing he has always known how to do is shut up.

"But if you break faith with me, stand between me and my work, your life is nothing to me."

Smoke nods, head lowered in obedience. He also knows better than to ask any specifics of what the Zsouvox's work might be. He has his guesses. For a creature zealous enough to believe that its duty is to end all things, surely this plane of existence will not be enough.

Eventually, all things will be surrendered to oblivion.

22

From the beginning, Smoke had not been like the other children at the orphanage. For one, he came from Haiti, farther afield than the other children at Saint Ash. He was small and skinny and spoke a strange language, and that only haltingly. He was still very young—almost three and not sufficiently verbal, according to Inness, who took one look at him and said, "He will do. Like clay, this one—easily shaped."

He was taught English, his native language quickly forgotten, and as soon as he could read well enough, he was given the Book of Shadow. He spent long hours reading, the elderly tutor behind him striking him with a rod when he mispronounced a word. After readings, he was lectured by the tutor, who also struck him when his attention seemed to wander or he couldn't answer a question she asked. Martha was a failed shadow mage herself, able to move around only a small room by manipulating the absence of light.

Smoke proved himself quickly, which infuriated Martha

even more. The beatings intensified. At the time, Smoke did not understand why he was being abused. He went to Mother Inness to complain, struggling to explain his feelings. He was so engrossed in the Book of Shadow he had learned little else, and he had no words for the anger burning inside him.

"She beats me," he said. "For no reason."

"How is your study?" Inness asked.

Smoke stared at her, confused. "I am strong."

"Then she is doing her job," Inness said.

"She is hurting me," he said with a defiant glare.

Inness was like the other sight mages, as he would learn later—all emotion under tight control, unmoved by anything, even the abuse of a child. But seeing his glare, she narrowed her eyes ever so slightly and looked at him with what he took for mild disgust—even, perhaps, guarded fear.

She said, "You will do worse to many more people. You will be a plague."

Smoke doesn't remember what his response was. He had no idea what she meant, so he no doubt went right ahead expressing his indignation until he was asked to leave.

But he was certain that this moment, Inness's prediction, had haunted his life, led him down the road he took. Indeed, it was a path revealed without being sought, a path toward power. It didn't matter that the prediction was dark, negative. He would be powerful; he would be great. Later, he would find the means to pursue that path. If he was to be a plague, he would be a righteous one. If he was to be a blade, he would cut deep for his side.

His powers grew over the next five years. He was one of three gifted children of his generation. One was a sight mage like Inness, the other a defective light mage who turned their defect into something useful. Smoke believed himself to be the most powerful of the three.

Secretly, he trained himself to go anywhere he could see. The first time he went to the moon, he was foolish enough to materialize fully there, and he bore the consequences. Smoke returned, curled in a ball at the foot of his bed, looking as if he'd been dipped in acid. He healed himself by use of shadow magic, cleaving away the outer layers of his flesh until the skin was raw but unblemished. All this he did in the minutes after his return, by himself. Alone. And when he emerged from his room, pinkish with bloodshot eyes, the children recoiled from him and the staff ignored him. Martha beat him again, sensing that he had done something reckless—something that she herself could not do.

Smoke wishes the Order had found him before he did what he did. If they had, he could have justified it beforehand as a blow to the enemy. That would have saved him some inner turmoil. But they had not found him until almost a year later, and so only he bore the blame for what happened.

It started with a fight—three of the other kids making fun of him, calling him a loser, a loner, unwanted. None of the other kids intervened on his behalf. Everyone watched it happen. Melku didn't even look up from their book. Smoke didn't touch them. Instead, he called them weak. One of them, a fire mage, punched him, his hand hot, burning Smoke's face. Smoke's response was measured. He had only separated a finger from the boy's hand. There was screaming and lots of blood. The other two boys had backed away, which was a relief. If they kept on, he could have hurt them badly.

The short-lived fight was interrupted by Martha. Unsurprisingly, Smoke was beaten, blamed for all of it despite the burn on his face.

Infuriated, he went again to Inness to complain.

Inness, behind her desk, watched Smoke impassively. "I had a child," she said. "A boy. I left him when he was a baby. Do you know why?"

She had said this with so little modulation in her voice that Smoke didn't realize she was asking a question. It took him a moment to reassemble the words, derive meaning, and then shrug. How the hell could he know why she left her son?

"As a sight mage, I know what will happen. Can you imagine knowing how your child will die, before he is even born?"

Smoke was ten at the time. He could not imagine.

"A bullet to the head. During a hurricane. Perpetrated by the Black Hand, an organization that you will help create."

Smoke's face was hurting, but for a moment he forgot the pain.

"Do I resent you? Yes. It helps that I am supposed to. But not enough that I should try to stop you from becoming what you become. Nor can I kill you. I cannot pull you out of the earth, watch you die like a weed on asphalt. I can do nothing."

All this without even a stirring of emotion. Just the words spoken without passion, stagnant as a windless day.

"Sometimes the thought occurs to kill you. It floats up from the ether beneath my mind. I swear, I do nothing to conjure it. Many people believe that all a sight mage can do is foretell, but our emotions are knives. Even now I protect you by not letting you see what I actually feel."

"So you won't help me," Smoke said. Even to his child's

mind, he understood that what was happening, what she was saying, was tragically unfair.

"Help you how?" she said. "It has already happened. Shadow mages as strong as you will eventually go mad with power. It was a mistake to make you to begin with. Too late now. No. It was always too late." Inness closed her eyes then. "I can see it. The hurricane overhead. The two men. A woman. And my Matthew. Dead. But that's not why I left. I left because I have always left my son. That is who I am."

Smoke did not feel pity. Her lack of feeling did not inspire that complex emotion or ask it of him. Instead, all he could feel was anger.

"You should go," Inness said. "Before you do something before its time."

Smoke did leave. The edges of his skin were beginning to stir.

Could he have proved her wrong? Probably not—destiny and all that. But the thought hadn't even occurred to him at the time. Only rage followed him—that and the desire eventually to go beyond Inness's imagining, to prove her wrong by shocking even her. If he was to be evil, he would surpass expectations.

It took two weeks and two more beatings from Martha before he finally took hold of his destiny.

He started with his teacher, coming upon her in her rooms. Seeing the determined look in his eyes, Martha had tried to flee. She dismantled herself and then reassembled outside the orphanage doors—where he was waiting for her. She tried again, but he could feel her trying, could feel where she would end up if he allowed her to move. He did not allow her. He put his hand against her stomach and started disassembling her. She screamed out, just a little, until the power claimed her throat.

In less than a second, in less than a tenth of a second, they both were on the moon.

He released her there, though not fully assembled himself, and returned to Earth.

He went looking for Inness after. He found her in her office.

"Well, then," she said. "Today is the day." In answer to Smoke's unasked question, she said, "Of course I knew. But there is no escape for me. Neither will there be for you. The thrust of death is perfection. The blade always pierces."

Smoke did not understand. Neither did he care. He took her to the moon.

It was nighttime, so one by one, he visited the sleeping children. He managed to dismantle them all without them waking. Each time he returned to the moon, he would assemble himself enough to catch a glimpse of the work he had done. He wished he could say that he didn't feel satisfied. He wished he could say that he wanted to stop. That place, the orphanage, was evil, and he had visited evil on it.

In the end, he couldn't find two of his orphanage siblings. Melku and Cassandra, the prodigies. Secretly, he was happy he didn't find them. The damage he had done was enough. There was more remorse later, after some time had passed, but not enough for him to rewrite the story he had built in his own head. What he had done was judgment.

He spent the next two years wandering the world, doing what he wanted, occasionally killing people he thought deserving of death. In those final months before the Order of the Zsouvox found him, his justification for killing had become as thin as a strand of hair. It was probably what finally brought him to their awareness. The Bone Witch had to restrict his powers so that the Order could "reeducate" him. If they had asked, he would have told them that he didn't really need to be compelled to serve. Those years on his own had started to make him afraid of himself. For a while, he was a resident of the lower dungeons, but little by little, the Bone Witch lifted the restrictions on him.

The Order offered Smoke a purpose—something he hadn't known he needed until it was given to him. And then, eventually, Valter gave him something even greater than purpose. A father. Love.

•••

There is a knock at Smoke's dormitory-room door. The creak of the door opening. Footsteps.

"I've heard."

Smoke doesn't turn at this. He continues writing in his journal.

"How long until it happens?"

Smoke puts down his pen. "Two days."

"Why not now?"

"Our sight mage was very specific. Two days from now, the battle might go in our favor."

"Might." A pause. "Where did you get this?"

When Smoke turns, Valter is holding up a varnished wooden figurine in his palm: three turtles of decreasing size perched one atop the next, the smallest on top.

Smoke shrugs at first. "A market somewhere." But he tries to attach a memory to the object. "A street vendor in Kathmandu."

"That must seem like nothing to you. To name a place so far away. Anywhere in the world is yours at a thought."

"A little bit more than a thought."

Valter chuckles wryly. "You've even been to the moon."

This isn't the first time he's made this joke. Smoke turns back to his desk and begins writing again.

The dormitory is modest, but it is the best living quarters in the Trapp dungeon. For a monster who isn't a vampire to have risen so high within the Order is no small feat. Smoke reminds himself of his good fortune by filling the room with trinkets from places he's visited, so that it feels like something more. Every shelf, every surface—even the drawer next to his bed—is covered with tchotchkes of wood or ceramic, like the turtles. At some point, they meant something to him. But Valter is right. Over time, they have decreased steadily in sentimental value.

Valter's footsteps draw closer. "So, you've started keeping a journal."

Smoke nods. "Seems like a good habit."

"What are you writing in it?"

"Events, my feelings, questions I have about my life, about the world."

"You have feelings. Questions."

By his inflection, Valter is inviting Smoke to continue, to share his feelings, his questions.

Smoke puts his pen down again and turns. "I have worries. In two days, the world might end." He pauses, decides to be a little more direct: "This thing we serve wants to end the world."

"You sound . . ."

"Terrified?" Smoke scoffs. "And you're *not*?"

Valter's face is all paternal sympathy—a mask that's usually quite effective with Smoke. Not this time. When he sees the lack of effect, he changes tack, sobering. "Nothing has changed.

This part is above us. We can't stop it. But if the world doesn't end—if, say, the Zsouvox loses—we will be an organization without a head. It's a position I can step into."

"What about Twenty-Nine?"

The quirk of Valter's lip is barely noticeable, but Smoke can see it. Smoke has always been able to see who this man is underneath.

Valter doesn't have to say it, but when he touches Smoke's shoulder, the reassuring paternal mask slipping back on, he does say the words: "I will kill Twenty-Nine, and the rest will applaud me for guiding them away from ruin."

"If the world doesn't end."

"Right. If the world doesn't end." Valter steps away, placing the little wooden pyramid of turtles back on the top shelf. Smoke hadn't realized he was still holding the thing. After that, Valter gives a wary exhalation. "Well, I'll leave you to it. Try to get some sleep at some point."

Smoke wants to say something to keep Valter in the room a little longer. He knows this is a childish response on his part, like wanting a bedtime story, like wanting to be tucked in safe and sound from the monsters outside. There are no monsters outside. *He* is the monster. And the other monsters are inside these walls.

"I want to see the world you will build," Smoke says. "After."

Valter is at the doorway. "Survive and you will," he says. "Play your part for a little while longer and we will take over this world together."

"I will play my part," Smoke says after Valter has already left. "We will build a better world together."

23

JUNE 13, 2028

"What now?" Georgie asks.

No answer comes.

With all the community center's lights still on, it is easy to see everyone's shell-shocked expressions. They have all survived the attack on Moon. To accomplish this, they have killed at least two dozen people. Somewhere out in the dark, the ants are disposing of the slain Black Hands. Ridley tries not to think about that. Instead, he goes from face to face, looking for signs of what he is also feeling. The terror and self-loathing. The relief and the guilt that come with it.

Ossi, sitting on the couch, a blanket draped over her, is the only one who looks as though she'll get good sleep tonight.

"I'm serious," Georgie says. "Now that we've killed another group of intruders, what are we supposed to do? Go back to our lives?"

Laina is lying on the rug at Ossi's feet, staring up at the ceiling, barely blinking. "That's what I want to do. Wake up tomorrow as if nothing had happened."

"But we can't," Georgie says.

"No." Rebecca is by a window, staring out at the lightless town.

Most of the nonfighting residents were sent through the portals to vacant apartments all over the country. A temporary solution. But now that the attack is over, Ridley isn't sure they should be called back.

"You all can sit around feeling sorry for yourselves," Ossi says. "I prefer realism. There was no way we were going to live here forever without having to do this. Anything worth having has to be fought for if you plan on keeping it."

"Okay, fine," Georgie says. "But I can't do *that* again. I have only one mass murder in me."

Connor says, "I wouldn't have said I had even one in me if you asked this morning."

"I don't think we should be calling it mass murder," Ridley says.

"Then what would we call it!" Georgie's voice cracks, the words coming out as if they were strangling her. Georgie has been sitting in a fold-out chair, head lowered, but now Ridley can see she's shaking, her entire body convulsing.

Connor draws his chair closer, puts a hand on her back. "You're okay," he says. "I'm right here."

The tension in the room has grown even thicker.

"*We* did this," Espeth says. "By leaving the settlement." Tash and Espeth are sitting on the couch, drawn close together. Espeth's eyes are red from crying, and Tash is staring into the middle distance. It is clear that neither of them has ever had to do anything remotely like this.

"What happened is because people hate what they don't understand," Ridley says. "You're not wrong for wanting to have normal lives, for wanting your children to have normal lives."

Espeth doesn't say anything, but the look on her face tells Ridley that Nat and June were also out that day. How can anyone blame her for wanting her kids to have a normal day outside Moon?

"There's a bright side to all this." Jesmeen is sitting on the arm of the couch, opposite Espeth and Tash, arms folded. Her glamour has slipped, so her hair falls to her back in green ringlets like lush vines. She looks reluctant to finish her thought.

A nod of encouragement from Connor helps her.

"If Karuna's plan works," Jesmeen says, "we may not need to do this again."

"It won't work," Ossi says.

Still looking out the window, Rebecca says, "Without some greater lever of protection, Moon won't be safe. How long will it take before they persuade law enforcement to come out here? Or the military?"

"Oh God," Jesmeen says.

"Shock and awe gets those Black Hand shitkickers off our backs," Rebecca says. "It doesn't stop real power from crushing us eventually."

An awful silence. Dragon, standing by the door, lifts his head, and for a moment he locks eyes with Ridley before looking away.

Laina repeats, "A greater lever of protection," but doesn't add anything.

"If Karuna's plan doesn't work," Ridley starts. "If we can't stop future attacks . . ." He really doesn't want to say it, but they all know the only option left. "Then we abandon Moon. We take our chances in the real world."

"I'm not going anywhere," Ossi says.

"Maybe we can find a new place," Jesmeen suggests. "We've saved a lot of money from our businesses. We just need to purchase enough land for all of us."

"I am *not* going anywhere," says Ossi.

Rebecca shakes her head. "This place was special. We had protection, an escape route if we needed it, a way for our businesses to stay hidden. The world outside isn't like it was. People will notice. And we will be back where we started."

"She's right," Ridley says.

"It is our best option, though," Laina says. "We should try."

"But we might be able to stay indefinitely without anything happening," Connor says, still stroking Georgie's back. "Right?"

"Haven't you been listening?" This from Georgie, her voice barely above a whisper. "We are screwed no matter what we do."

Ridley says nothing. No one speaks for a long time.

"Well," Georgie says, "this was the plan we gave to the residents. It'll buy us time at least." She is no longer shaking, and her voice has regained its strength. "We should talk to the others—prepare them for what might come. I can do that."

"I'll help," Connor says.

Ridley nods. "The rest of us can start discussing an escape plan."

"I told you," Ossi says. "I am not—"

Ridley stamps his foot. "If you say it again . . ."

"You'll do what?"

"Your position is not a position. We stay here and, what? Die?"

"I'm not dying."

"Oh, so you're going to fight the United States, huh?" Ridley is yelling now. "The entire fucking military?"

A quiet chime interrupts the next volley of useless bickering. One of the portals has just shut down, which means someone has just come through.

Everyone stops, waiting for the outer door to open and reveal who it is. No one speaks. The unease is palpable.

Footsteps on the inside, between the inner portal and the outer door. Multiple footsteps. The doorknob starts to turn and—

Just then I feel my heart start to pound in my chest, and my breath grows heavy. Sweat beads on my forehead. It's as if I were trying to pull myself out of a well and really feeling the exertion. I get a sudden urge to fall backward—an unmooring, a sense that gravity has shifted ninety degrees. And then I *am* falling backward, through the floor as it gives around me like Jell-O that has only begun to set. I fall down through the cold, past flashes of color, auroras, gas clouds, and stardust.

And then I'm rushing up, as if I were being pulled from the water, or more as if my body were filled with air, and the water rejecting me, pushing me up out of it.

As I break the surface, I feel my physical body shiver, a deep cold rattling through me. And then my eyes are open, staring up at a ceiling.

ST. THOMAS, USVI
EARTH 001

Someone shifts in the chair beside me. I try to turn, but my neck feels wrong.

"Uncle Cal," she says. "You awake?"

A hospital room. I try to speak, but it feels as if something has settled in my throat, or something was there but isn't now, having pushed aside everything I would use for speech. I groan and cough.

"It's okay. Wait, wait. Slow down."

I'm pushing myself up in the bed, but I'm not doing such a good job of it, flashes of bright, hot pain erupting from every corner of my body. I am a house on fire.

She's at my side, hand on my chest. "Wait. Stop!"

That gets me to quit moving. I settle back onto the bed and try to speak again. "What . . ."

"You were in an accident. You fractured some bones, cut yourself up pretty good. And cracked your skull. You been out." She rubs my chest affectionately, with concern. "Tanya's here," she adds. "She went to the bathroom."

"How long has it been?"

"A little over a week."

I hear her distress in the way she answers, but she looks down into her lap to hide her face, her shoulders slumping. She says, barely above a whisper, "Are you hurting?"

I don't answer right away. I breathe in and bring myself closer to my body, closer to the pain. I am hurting all over, all at once, but it isn't as bad as I expected. Mostly, I feel tired, as if I could pass out again right now. A dull ache throbs in my side—not particularly painful, but insistent.

Finally, I answer: "It isn't so bad. I'm okay, don't worry."

She looks at me again and I can see the inner conflict on her face. She wants to say something.

"What is it?"

She hesitates, but the anger returns. I don't know how, but I can sense that the anger isn't directed exclusively at me. What she wants to say, she is already regretting before saying it, angry at herself for having to say it.

"It's all right. Tell me."

"Why did you crash?" she asks.

I pause for a beat, considering how honest I'm going to be. "I was tired. I drank a little too much. Promise me you'll never drink and drive. I'm lucky I didn't hurt anyone."

"You're lying," she says. "Something happened."

I watch her. She is about to speak, and suddenly I know what she will say. All there is to do is wait.

"You have to stop," she says.

"Stop what?" I ask, feigning ignorance.

Anger flares in her eyes. All at me. "Stop visiting the monsterverse. Stop visiting other universes. It's dangerous."

"It hasn't been. You've read all my accounts."

"It's different now. There are people who can see you. Who can hurt you."

At that moment, happily, a burst of clarity takes over and I understand the fear beneath the fear, the complicated emotion behind Gina's words. She has lost so much already, and I am the closest thing she has to her dead father. And here I am in this hospital bed. And it can't be just an accident. The universe, she believes now, is malevolent. And I have stirred it awake, drawn its attention entirely to me. I can say nothing, offer nothing, to convince her otherwise. This isn't logic, and even though she is right—sort of, anyway—this plea is based on pure feeling.

I smile and nod, saying, "I'll stop. I promise I'll stop." The lie comes out of me smooth, and I don't try to shore it up with any more words. I look her in the eye with as much reassurance as I can muster.

Something in her calms. She wants to believe me. She wants to hope.

"Oh my god." Tanya is at the doorway. We lock eyes. "You're awake. Let me call the doctor in." And she disappears again.

Gina says, "She loves you, you know. Like, really loves you." I try to laugh it off, but Gina gives me that fierce look I'm now so familiar with. "You have a chance with this. Don't fuck it up."

As the doctor is checking on me, Tanya is out in the hall on the phone with my mother. "Yes, he is talking and everything," Tanya is saying, pacing in tight circles outside the door. "Yes. Yes. Don't worry. I'll talk to the doctor."

I seem fine, the doctor explains, but she wants me to stay one more night for observation.

When the doctor leaves, Gina says, "Remember your promise."

"I will," I say. A sense of déjà vu comes over me, as if I had been in this bed many times before, making promises and breaking them.

Gina doesn't look satisfied, but she's at least decided that there is nothing else she can do. She's said the thing. She has performed "concerned parent"—a role she shouldn't have to play—to a sufficient degree. I shouldn't have put her in a situation where she had to try to save me. I shouldn't be so far gone, so past saving. But how can I explain? How can I know better and still know that I can't stop? Not now. Not yet.

Tanya is back at the door. "Your mother says she is coming down. Day after tomorrow. Just her. Your sisters are going to try to come on the weekend."

I shake my head. "It's fine. I'm fine. I don't want them to come."

Tanya makes a face—half amusement, half motherly sternness. "I don't think you have much of a choice, mister."

I don't reply. There's no use. I just let the silence fall over all of us, wincing through the throbbing pain that flares up inside me like a beacon.

Gina looks to Tanya, then back to me. "I'm going to get something from the vending machine. Want anything?"

I shake my head, wonder how they've been feeding me, then note the scratch in my throat. A feeding tube. Not there now. Then I wonder who is going to pay for all this, and that fresh horror sends me spiraling long enough to miss Gina slipping out of the room and Tanya slowly approaching the bed.

When she sits down, I snap back to the moment, to this woman staring at me as if I might break apart.

"You scared me," she says. "I didn't know I could be so scared. Never been so scared in my life."

That can't be true, I think. I know not to say it.

"You're a mess. You're a goddamn mess, Calvin."

I could tell the truth here, say what really happened the night of my accident, but I know she won't believe me. And I know it doesn't matter anyway. What happened was my fault. I could apologize, and I really want to, but I also know that I am not done making this mistake. I could say—

"So, you're just going to stare at me?"

"I love you. And I think you love me too."

Now Tanya is the one staring.

"I think the question is, what are we going to do about it?"

She's shaking her head. "I can't get involved with you. I'm not going to try to fix you, Calvin."

"Since when did you start using my real name?"

She glares at me.

"Fine. Don't fix me. Let's say I fix myself. What then?"

"This isn't the time for a conversation about us."

"What, then?"

She's blinking at me. I think the expression on my face is what causes the shift. I can see several thoughts come and go just by the way she's looking at me. I don't know what they are, but I can guess. She's never seen me so intense before—or not in a long time, anyway. I'm being serious. Not distracted. Not confused. I look like I know what I want.

Maybe that's what she's thinking, but she's shaking her head again. "I can't."

"Tanya, I came to you before because I wanted to stop running from what this could be. And, if anything, the accident has solidified my decision. If you want me—if you would have me—I wouldn't waste your time. I promise."

The words are what make me decide. No matter what, after this last leap into the multiverse, I am going to stop. I don't know how yet, but I am at least going to try. Ask Abyssia to take the power back. Whatever.

A voice in the back of my head asks, "Why not now?" But I ignore it. I need to finish what I started. And then I'll stop. I promise. I promise.

Tanya is looking at me. "You need to talk to someone."

"I know."

"You need to do the work. Get better. Stop scaring everyone who cares about you."

"I know. I will."

She is biting her lower lip. "Don't promise me. Don't do it for me. Do it for yourself."

"I am doing it for myself. But is it wrong if I'm also doing it for you?"

She wants to smile and does, just a little. Hope swells in my chest, and for a moment, all the pain I'm in is erased.

One more time. I promise. Just one more.

"We'll talk after," Tanya says.

"After what?"

"I don't know yet. After I know you're serious and not just making promises."

"I can do that."

She is biting her lip again.

"What about that guy you were seeing?"

She folds her arms. "None of your business, is what. Ask me about that later too."

I think I get the message. She's not waiting around for me. She's not giving me false hope. Too late.

"How are you feeling?" she asks me. We talk for a while about that, about other things. She updates me about work. She had to cancel some classes to be here, take some of them virtually. She won't be able to stay forever. I try to make it clear that she doesn't have to. I'll be fine.

And then Gina is at the door, eating from a half-empty bag of Ruffles. "A'you dating now, or what?"

We laugh, both Tanya and I at the same time, a little awkwardly.

I don't dare say anything. I just look at Tanya.

"The boy needs therapy," she says. "But I don't know. He's growing on me."

I'm not sure what that means, but I decide to shut up so I don't spoil anything.

We're all talking now, Gina pulling up a chair. She wants to know what therapy is like. Tanya is the only one of us with experience, so she explains. Lots of talking, like a Q and A, but almost exclusively about trauma. If it's working, crying's involved. Gina thinks that sounds awful. I agree, but I do my best to back Tanya up. Therapy sucks, I say, but get the right kind and it could be life-changing. The backing her up convinces me that I do need therapy. I'm surprised the thought hasn't occurred before.

Just one more time, I think. One more, and I'll put all this craziness behind me.

After an hour passes, I find that I'm spent. All the energy of waking up, of having serious conversations, has been sapped. I'm starting to nod off.

"Look at him," Tanya is saying. "Eyes drooping and shit."

"Like a baby," Gina says.

They both laugh. Tanya says, "Don't try to stay up on our account."

And it's as if my body were just waiting for permission. Eyes heavy, body heavy, I'm slipping back into dreams . . .

25

EARTH 0539

When the outer door opens, three people step through.

Ridley recognizes one of them: the sight mage. The second woman, the one to Cassandra's right, is a mystery: tall, with a long cloak, the hood pulled back to reveal a head shaved clean. Striking. But Ridley's eyes have already moved on, breath catching at the sight of the third woman, standing a few steps back from the other two. And he isn't the only one. Ridley is certain that no one could ever look at this woman and not react; she is that stunning.

"Right," says the cloaked woman. "Before we begin, I'm Damsel." She performs a mock curtsy, fingers pinching the hem of her cloak and lifting it just so. "To my left is Cassandra. And to my right—"

"Sonya," she says. "None of you have seen me before, but I suspect my voice is familiar."

Ridley looks to Laina, whose eyes confirm the truth. The invisible woman.

"To business," Damsel says, affecting primness. "We're here to warn you that the Cult of the Zsouvox knows your location. They're planning an attack." She puts up a finger before Ridley can speak. "Please save your comments. Anyway, you've probably already discussed running, correct? Don't answer. I don't really care. The point is, we will need you to stay right here. And when the Cult of the Zsouvox comes, we'll need you to help us fight them." She laughs and it is light, melodic, like birdsong. "Sorry. We'll need you to fight them *first*. And then we'll step in to help at the right time." Damsel pauses, a slow smile rising to her lips. "Okay. Now you can ask questions."

For a moment, everyone stares dumbly at the woman. Connor's mouth is actually hanging open. Then, finally:

"Yes," Ossi says, the word almost a snarl. "I'm not one to run from a good fight, but—and forgive my rudeness—why in the fuck would we help you fight a cult? Also, who the fuck are you?"

"They are the Order of Asha," Ridley answers, which, he is sure, helps only a little.

Damsel nods approvingly. "Glad someone's been paying attention."

"Well, I try to mind my own business," Ossi says. "And you still haven't answered my first question."

"Because you have no choice," Damsel says.

"Hell I don't."

Considering that mere minutes ago they were at each other's throats, Ridley is almost glad he and Ossi are on the same page about *not* helping the Order of Asha. "You were right," Ridley says to Damsel. "We were discussing getting out of here. And given the information you've just shared, we'll be stepping right through that portal and joining the other residents who have already left."

The smile Damsel gives him is all teeth. "You're not listening. And I don't repeat myself. Dragon, please explain the situation."

Dragon, still standing by the door, looks just as startled by this as everyone else.

This is when Sonya steps forward. "I'm sorry," she says. "Damsel can be . . . theatrical."

Damsel rolls her eyes.

Sonya continues: "We can't make you do this. But we know you will."

"And why is that?" Ridley asks.

Cassandra finally speaks. "Because it is ordained."

"*And*," Sonya quickly adds, "because we can help you protect this place once this is all over. Protect this place indefinitely."

"How?" Laina asks.

"Secrets," Sonya says. "Enough to buy your safety and the safety of every other hidden settlement. And perhaps even enough to remake the world. If played right."

Everyone is staring at Sonya, suspicion warring with a dawning awareness of the many implications of what she has just said.

When Ridley and Laina lived in Boston, the invisible woman was in their house any number of times without their knowing. How many powerful people could she have visited while invisible? And what was it that Melku had once said? Information buys protection. How much information could the Order of Asha be sitting on?

"Trust me," Sonya says. "Help us now, and we will help you survive after."

These three women. Not particularly similar in appearance—Damsel with her tall, lean frame and sharp features, Cassandra with her light skin and freckled cheeks and mess of curly hair, and Sonya with her stocky, muscled figure and dark skin (a shade darker than Damsel's) and hair braided back away from her face like a nuisance to be subdued—but they are similar in one specific regard that is hard to name. Ridley can name it only because he's been seeing it more lately—in Ossi certainly, but also increasingly in Rebecca. A hard casing of mental fortitude. It's there in the eyes, in the way the battle-tested hold themselves. *I can handle what comes. Put it in front of me, and I will stare it down without flinching.*

The Moonites will need the same mental toughness if they are to survive and keep Moon.

"Your offer is not enough," Ridley says.

Sonya doesn't speak. She waits. But on her face, Ridley can see pain, annoyance, frustration, desperation, rage—all unvarnished, all unconcealed. He has never seen a face so expressive.

Ridley says, "We want more than your help. We want the means to help ourselves. If we agree to help, you'll give us full control of Moon. You'll open communication between settlements. And you will give us all your secrets. Every single one. We'll figure out what to do with them."

Damsel laughs. "You really think you can—"

"Deal," Sonya says. She meets Damsel's incredulous stare. "The Order of Asha will eventually die. We have one important goal to fulfill before that happens. And the fulfillment of that goal is worth any price."

Cassandra is silent through all this, unsurprised as ever. Her eyes are on Ridley's. He doesn't know what to make of that. But the only words she's spoken since arriving here are bouncing around inside his skull. *It is ordained.*

"How much time do we have?" Laina asks. "You may not know this, but we just fended off an attack from the Black Hand."

"We know," Damsel says blithely. "You have a day. They'll be here by tomorrow evening. Any more questions?"

"Dozens," Ridley says, shifting his attention from Cassandra back to Damsel. "But I figure this is as forthcoming as you're going to be."

Damsel smirks, which is as good as an answer.

Ridley really doesn't like this woman. He can recognize her superficial attractiveness. Not as beautiful as Sonya, but no one he's ever met possesses Sonya's absurd physical beauty. (She is so striking, in fact, that there must be some magic in it.) But Damsel's superficial attractiveness is matched by her speech, which is solid all the way through. An effortless confidence. Easy to bend under the pressure of such vocal command. Damsel doesn't ask or defer. She declares.

None of these qualities are bad, in isolation or together. But Ridley knows that all these things are distractions from Damsel's one important quality, present in her voice, in her eyes, in the subtle curl of her mouth when she speaks. The way she turns on everyone with precisely the same withering gaze. With every glance, with every remark, it's as if she's saying, *Please. Surprise me. Make this worth my time.* But at the same time, equally present is her certainty that nothing could ever be worth her time.

Ridley has been discounted many times in his life. He has witnessed other people's condescension more times than he can count. When your politics are radical enough to be considered delusional, it sort of comes with the territory. But he has never seen anyone look at another person the way Damsel looks at everyone, as if they were worms she had decided to tolerate—worms she had deigned *not* to crush beneath her feet.

"All we need is for you to follow our instructions," Damsel says. "Hold them off until a particular time, and then we'll step in. Be smart and you might make it out of this."

"Okay, then." Ridley lets every bit of his hostility toward them show on his face. "We'll be good pawns. You can leave now."

Damsel seems amused by his sudden rudeness. Strange but not surprising.

Expression blank, Cassandra turns, heading back to the portal room. Damsel does another mock curtsy, this time with a deeper dip, before following Cassandra.

Sonya stays. "Where is my sister? Sondra."

"Out the front and to the left," Ridley says. "The house at the northernmost point of Moon. You can't miss it."

She nods and heads to the main entrance, stopping to tousle Dragon's head.

"Where's Melku?" Dragon asks.

Sonya's face is full of emotion. "Gone."

She's out the door before anyone can process the words.

26

Sonya finds her sister exactly where Ridley told her she would. Last house on the north side of the settlement, in an area overgrown with weeds. The house itself looks well kept, but somehow, incongruously, there's a desolation to the place, an aura of sadness.

Sonya sets her shoulders and knocks on the door.

She hears a noise come from inside—a dragging, and very light footsteps. The door opens, and Sondra is standing before her, darkness hanging heavy around her like a physical presence. She doesn't meet Sonya's eyes, just leaves the door open and disappears back into the dark interior.

Sonya enters and resists reaching for the light. She walks into the spare living room, finds a chair—again, even its niceness somehow suggests desolation—and sits there. Sondra is already on the long couch across, curled up under a heavy quilt.

There's a musk in the air that Sonya notes and then puts out of her mind.

"How are you?" Sonya asks.

"Better," Sondra says. "Today was a good day."

Sonya doesn't know what she expected her sister to say, her very first words after all this time, but it wasn't this. There is no kindness in the tone, but it isn't hostile either. And the words themselves are polite, open.

Sonya isn't the first to speak again.

"How are you?" Sondra asks.

Sonya weighs that question and also opts for open, though a little direct. "Melku is dead."

This earns a stirring from her sister, not exactly a sitting up, but she lifts her head from under the quilt, props up on the arm of the couch so she can look at Sonya in the dark.

"Dead? How?"

"After I left you that day, I went looking for Father. And I found him in one of the Order of the Zsouvox's compounds. But it was a trap, and they held me there for months. Melku came to rescue me. They didn't make it out."

Sondra is very quiet.

Sonya supposes this is a lot to take in. So much has happened since the last time they spoke. But she has lived all of it, so it all feels like a summary of pain that could never be summed up in words. An inadequate recounting of the feeling in her chest.

"I'm sorry," Sondra says.

Again, not what Sonya expects. "I'm not here to say we're the same. Melku and I weren't together when they passed. I loved them, but we were something in between. Not quite friends. Not quite colleagues. A relationship . . . interrupted. Not like what you had with your husband."

Sondra remains silent, waiting for Sonya to find her words—a kindness Sonya never expected.

Sonya says, "I'm here because I talked to Cassandra, and she said I can go to you, that you can ask any question you want, and if I know the answer, I can answer it."

Finally, a response she expected: "Why now?"

Sonya answers honestly. "Because nothing you do now can change the path we are on. And everything to come after this, you'll do willingly, without being manipulated."

"So, you finally say it, after all this time. You all were manipulating me."

"We all were being manipulated," Sonya says. "I had no idea Melku would die." She decides to go further. "Though I have a feeling Melku knew."

"Why manipulate anyone?"

"The sight mages serve their own ends. Who knows what they're doing or why? But for us, we dared not go against their advice. We manipulated each other, ourselves, everyone, because we feared a worse fate. You know this. You pretended not to all this time, but you knew."

Sondra sits up then, draws the quilt over her knees. "I did. I've had a lot of time to think, to grieve, to throw my anger at you in your absence. I realized you were just as trapped as I was, just on the other side of a wall. We couldn't really see each other."

"I saw you," Sonya says, tears welling in her eyes.

"No, you didn't," Sondra says, but it isn't with anger, only sadness. "No one really sees anyone else."

Sonya doesn't argue, mostly because the words surprise any argument out of her.

"I can ask you anything, right?" Sondra says.

Sonya nods, a rock in her throat.

Somehow, in the dark, Sondra sees her nodding. "Why did he have to die?" Sondra asks.

She expected this. Now all that's left is the awful truth. "Because his death brought you here."

Sondra's voice is shaking when she says, "That's all?"

"No. His death has also galvanized a movement back home. Which will be good for you after, if you accept your place in it."

"I won't ask."

"You don't have to. If we survive tomorrow night, it'll all happen without any manipulation from anyone."

"What's happening tomorrow night?"

That's when there comes a knock at the door, as if ordained.

It's Ridley: "Tell me how it happened. Tell me how Melku was killed."

When Dragon walks into the house, Alex looks up from the living room couch, quickly reading the distress on his face.

Alex finishes wrapping her wet hair up in a towel. "Join me?" she asks.

"Okay." But he doesn't move right away.

"What happened?"

Finally, he comes over and sits. Everything comes out all at once. Alex doesn't interrupt.

There are a lot of questions she could ask. It is a lot to take in. But her first question is out of concern: "Were you close to Melku?"

"No." He pauses, thinking. "But I liked Melku. They were nice to me."

"Oh," Alex says. "I'm so sorry."

"It's fine. I'm fine."

She watches him, noting the truth he's trying to hide. "You

must be worried about seeing Smoke tomorrow," she says, trying to draw him out.

He sits there for a long moment, unable to speak. Or choosing not to.

"You don't have to talk about it."

"Are *you* worried?" he asks. "Mister might be there."

This stops her short. The same question. Now she has to acknowledge the power of it. Is she worried about seeing him? In her heart, she doesn't think he'll be there. Mister isn't a fighter, not in that way. So why would he show up to a battle?

Alex is worried about something, a nameless thing aside from her anxiety over the coming battle. But she says, "I don't think he'll be there."

"Smoke will."

"Yes, if anything is sure in the universe, it is that bastard showing up to relish in people dying."

"He'll stay back at first," Dragon says. "Smoke will show up when he can do the most damage."

The words come out flat. Dragon is so drawn into himself—she can't tell what he's thinking or feeling.

"I think Karuna should be able to help," Alex says. "Or the Order of Asha, if they really want to win this thing."

"Yeah."

"Let's just hope he doesn't try to talk to you," Alex says. *Or capture you*, she leaves unsaid.

Dragon falls silent. Alex doesn't want to push him too much, so she flicks on the television. She is busy flipping through channels when the knock comes.

She gets up to answer it.

The person standing there, averting his eyes, isn't anyone

she expected. Alex hasn't really talked to Harry, but there are a lot of people in this little community she hasn't had the pleasure of talking to.

"Good evening," Harry says. "Is, uh, Dragon home?"

When she opened the door, she flung it wide. Harry is being polite, asking if Dragon is home. He clearly is. And when Alex looks back to see if Dragon has heard the request for his presence, she finds him staring at her, past her, to the man at the door. Dragon has a bewildered expression on his face. And something else. Discomfort? Frustration?

"Come in," Alex says. Even if she wanted to cover for him, it's too late now.

Hesitantly, Harry steps over the threshold, looking in every direction but where Dragon still sits.

"I'll leave you both to it," she says.

"No!"

The sudden exclamation from Dragon startles Alex.

"I don't want to be alone with him," he says softly but boldly, because no diminution of volume could stop Harry from hearing the words.

Harry, for his part, takes the insult well. With a sheepish look, he runs his hand through his hair. His other arm, missing the hand and most of the forearm, rests at his side. He catches Alex looking at it, and this is what undoes him. A blotchy, brickish red spreading across his face. Harry tries to smile, but it looks awkward, and his eye has begun to twitch.

Alex looks to Dragon to save her, but now he is just glowering at the man.

Harry looks down at the floor, looks back up, a mask of determination suddenly there amid the nerves, the worry. "I know an apology won't do much. I've treated you terribly. I have no excuse for it or for not coming to you sooner to apologize. Not just accept you being around, not just tolerate your presence, but *apologize* to you, like to another person. Because you are a person. Sorry." Harry's blush spreads again, all the way down to where his neck reaches his collar. "I know you know you are a person. I'm just acknowledging that I haven't always treated you as one." He pauses. "I mean, I've *never* treated you as one."

Here he stops, if only for a moment, daring to look at Dragon, trying to see how his speech is being received.

Dragon, arms folded, still glowering.

"Well, as I said, I know an apology will do next to nothing." Alex has to give it to him for not breaking eye contact. "And I don't think we'll be friends or anything. But I promise to treat you better in the future. Do my very best to treat you better. You've always been the better person. I want to try to earn, at the very least, a genuine . . ." He trails off.

Alex wonders if he was going to say "friendship," which would be the wrong move in this situation.

"A genuine end to the enmity between us."

Good try at a save. But he sounds as if he were about to ask Dragon to take a walk around the promenade.

Dragon stops glowering to say, "Your timing is bad. We may all be dead tomorrow."

Alex notes the sweat that has beaded on Harry's forehead.

"Well, yes," he says. "But it would be worse to hold off. I'm sorry, is what I wanted to say, in case I haven't yet. I am very sorry for how I've treated you over the years. I regret it deeply."

"Do you?" Dragon says. By the tone, it isn't a question he wants Harry to answer. "You seemed to enjoy it. I find it hard to believe you've suddenly had a change of heart."

"It wasn't sudden. I've been feeling this way for a while."

If Mister ever apologized to her, would she forgive him? Alex wonders. No. She wouldn't. But this feels different from that. What Mister did was a violation on every level. She doesn't know what Harry did, at least not in any detail, but she assumes he mistreated Dragon, particularly when they lived together after the Boston Massacre. It must have been very bad for Harry to come apologizing like this after so much time, and for Dragon to respond so coldly. But Alex can at least understand both sides, whereas, when it comes to Mister, she doesn't understand, will not understand, and no justification will ever suffice.

"You should've come sooner," Dragon says.

"I was worried I was too late. And I know—this is even later. But I needed to say it."

"For yourself."

"Because it was the right thing to do."

"Okay. Fine. You can go now."

"If I may," Alex says. "Dragon, I love you, and I could never in my life understand what it could possibly be like to have had the experiences you've had. I come from a background of immense privilege, and the trauma I've experienced—most of it—came from my own decisions. Or close to it. I preface with all this because I have to tell you that you're being a brat, and I don't want it to come across as if I am taking Harry's side."

Seven blinks. That's how long it takes Dragon to close his mouth, for his anger to flare in Alex's direction. "What the fuck would *you* know?"

Alex almost says, "Language," but she knows this is the wrong time to treat Dragon like a child. "Dragon, you . . . hurt this man, and then he spent the next several months in an underground dungeon being tortured."

"I was forced to do it!"

"Yes, and he knows that, which is why he's apologizing. And, yes, he is responsible for his actions. But he also was traumatized beyond belief, and imprinted much of that trauma onto you. It was wrong. It wasn't fair. But it was a very human response."

"And I tolerated him for years, thinking I deserved it! But I deserved none of the things that happened to me. He *came* to the Trapp compound. I was forced to live there all my life. Before, I put up with him blaming me for what happened to both of us. I don't have to accept his apology now!"

Alex has seen Dragon angry, sad, even despairing, but she has never seen him *this* angry. She backs away from him because his skin has started to change.

Harry does not back away. "He is right. I've said what I needed to say. He said his piece. I'll go."

Alex holds her tongue. Any more, and she really will be taking a side. She feels a little bit stupid now for butting in this much.

"I wanted to ask you something," Harry says. "I wanted to know what your first memory was. Down there. I don't know, it seems foolish now. And I'm asking for selfish reasons. But it must've been awful. And very personal. It has taken years for me to work through the fear of that place. I'm still afraid. But I hope you can someday leave it behind you and never have to worry about returning there."

With that, Harry turns to walk out, not waiting for any response.

But he does get one: "Smoke wiping my forehead with a washcloth."

Harry turns back to look at Dragon.

"I was sick. He wiped my head with a cool cloth, fed me soup. I remember thinking that I had a body, that it could . . . shut down, and that he was trying to keep me from doing that, shutting down. I was grateful. Scared, but grateful."

Harry smiles. "It is a better memory than I imagined."

"Does it help you?" Dragon asks, toneless.

"Not in the way I intended," Harry says. "But I'm glad you told me."

Dragon nods, his face a hard mask.

Harry nods back. "I'll leave. I'm sorry for disturbing you both."

Alex is about to say that it's all right, but he's already out the door.

"That was interesting," she says.

Dragon keeps looking at the door, now closed.

"So that's really your first memory?"

"No," Dragon says. "That memory is from after I ate my first hands." He looks at her, and he seems old—a glimpse of the full-grown man he is becoming. "My first memory was the hands."

Alex wants to reach out to him. She wants to hold him in her arms and try to comfort him, though she knows that no words could possibly make this any better. Still, she reaches for him and isn't surprised when he pulls free of her.

Dragon goes to the door, and at first she thinks he is going to catch up with Harry, even as she thinks that's the last thing he would want to do. But she doesn't have to wait long. As soon as he opens the door, as soon as he steps free of the porch, he is unfolding his wings and shooting up into the sky.

When Harry enters the house, Karuna is on the couch, her phone to her ear.

"I know it's late," Karuna says. "It'll only be a moment."

A beat of silence as someone—Karuna's sister, Harry guesses—considers what Karuna is asking.

Harry closes the door softly and stands by it. Karuna looks up and smiles at him, and it looks almost like how a normal person might smile. In a flash, Harry imagines a whole alternate scenario for them both, he the husband coming home from work, Karuna already home from her midafternoon class, checking up on her . . . dad? No, her mom, who injured her leg but is otherwise doing fine, and Karuna should really stop worrying. But Karuna insisted on speaking with her. After this call, they'll have dinner, go to bed, cuddle, even make love.

The reality pierces the fiction. "Hey, baby," Karuna says. Not to him. And her voice is tender, again like a normal person's, nothing like Karuna's usual detachment. "I know, I know. I wanted to hear your voice. How are you?"

Another beat of silence while Karuna's daughter says something—likely recounting her day, and slowly falling back to sleep as she does so.

"That's wonderful, baby girl. I wish I could've seen it." Another silence that causes Karuna to frown. "I'm sorry."

Harry knows that the next pause can't be anything good, because of how wounded Karuna looks. A small, terrible part of him relishes the vulnerability before concern takes over.

Karuna's eyes are watering. "I'm really, really sorry, baby girl. Maybe next week."

Her eyes widen, and suddenly Harry can hear another voice on the phone, though it's faint.

Karuna says, "I didn't mean to upset her." She says, "That's not my fault." She says, "I'm trying here. I didn't ask for this." She says, "Something happened, so she can't come visit after all."

Harry considers that this perhaps isn't a conversation he should be privy to, but now he's been standing by the door too long and doesn't want to move and make things more uncomfortable.

The person on the other side of the phone—Karuna's adoptive sister, Harry is certain now—is saying a lot of things, Karuna nodding, until abruptly, she stops. And then no one is talking, and Karuna is wearing her thinking face, stump to chin, while tears fall from her eyes. The combination of details feels incongruous, and it would be if it weren't Karuna.

Karuna says, "You're right. And since I'm presumed dead, you don't need my permission. You've been taking care of her all this time. Thank you. I mean it. She's yours." Karuna hangs up.

Blinking away tears and wiping her face, she looks up at Harry. "You're in late. Where were you?"

Harry blinks at her.

But Karuna's face is a mask. She does not want to talk about what has just happened, no matter what Harry does or says.

He considers asking anyway.

Karuna prevents him with a question of her own. "Did you finally talk to Dragon?"

Harry nods. "Nothing useful."

"But you've reconciled."

Harry shrugs, settling into whatever they're doing, certainly not talking about what just happened with her daughter. "As reconciled as we're going to be."

Karuna is satisfied with this information. "Proud of you," she says.

"Do you have a plan for tomorrow?" Harry asks.

"I do," Karuna says. "Same plan as last time, with some extra tricks mixed in."

She means the portals. "Have you shared the plan with anyone yet?"

"Ridley came over," she says. "We discussed it. Tomorrow morning, we're going to meet up again."

"To do what?"

"To figure out as much as we can about tomorrow night," she says with an edge of exasperation. Clearly, he should have known the answer already.

"Okay," Harry says. "You going to bed anytime soon?"

"Can't sleep," Karuna says. "Too much on my mind."

Harry is still standing by the door, thinking through whether this is an invitation to keep her company or dismissal to go to bed and leave her alone. Well, he has to decide something. He leaves his shoes at the door and joins her on the couch.

She looks at him for a moment, and then she does something he could never have imagined in a million years. She stretches out on the couch next to him, resting her head in his lap.

"This okay?" she asks.

Harry nods, then realizes she can't see him nodding from her position on his lap. "Yes," he says. "It's fine."

She shudders a little, but Harry can't see why. He can't decide what he should do in response. Is she crying? Is she cold?

"Thank you," Karuna says.

"For what?"

"For not asking."

He nods. "No problem."

A silence descends that Harry is too terrified to break. His body isn't doing anything . . . inappropriate. He's grateful for that.

Finally, she says, "I've been having a dream lately."

"Oh?"

"Too real to be a normal dream."

Harry doesn't quite understand what she means, but he isn't going to break the spell. Whatever this is, he doesn't want it to end. "Tell me about it."

"I'm a child again, in Ireland. I'm sitting up in a tree, two stable branches beneath me. A king's chair. My dogs are barking in the distance, which is normal. Everything just the way I remember it—night sky and a diamond dusting of stars above me. Perfect. From here, I have a view of everything in existence.

"I hear something beneath me, and I look down and someone is there. I can't see their face, but I know they are watching me, waiting.

"I ask, 'What do you want.' And they say, 'I'm sorry. I didn't mean to frighten you.' I tell them that I'm not frightened, though child-me is a little frightened, which makes no sense, but anyway, they smile at me, and though I can't see their face, I know they're smiling. It's as if I am smiling back at myself. They say, 'Things are going to be different now. I'm sorry you have to do this part alone. But you're not really alone. I am here. Always. Me and all you've ever been or will be.' They say, 'You and me, we're a tangled web.'

"And then I feel something on my hands, on my legs, and I look down and I see that I'm covered in ants, and child-me is startled—which doesn't make sense; it's just ants—and I stand up from the king's chair. I lose my balance. I fall. But suddenly, nothing is beneath me, or everything is beneath me—the whole yawning sky."

"Sounds terrifying," Harry says. He touches her head with the hand left to him, waits.

She doesn't shrink away. "No, it was beautiful. It felt like the opposite of a dream. It felt like waking up."

Harry nods, for himself this time. "I'm sorry we're trapped here," he says. "I'm sorry there's nowhere else we can go."

"Perhaps that won't be the case forever."

"What do you mean?"

"I have the power now to go anywhere," she says. And there's so much passion in Karuna's voice, she sounds like a different person entirely. "I could go home."

"To your daughter," he says.

She doesn't answer right away. Then: "I think it's best she stay where she is. She has a life."

Harry is confused by this. If that's not home, then where?

Suddenly, Karuna is sitting up. Suddenly, Karuna is leaning toward him. She kisses him on the cheek before he can process what's happened.

And before he can ask any questions, she's standing up, walking away.

"Good night," she says.

He fights to settle his defiant heart. "Good night," he says, and watches her go down the hall.

He sits there on the couch, thinking it all through, what just happened. Around and around in circles he goes. It's too much. After minutes of this—a half hour?—he decides that nothing has changed. Whether this is an aberration or not, he's not going anywhere. Home, for him, is here. His decision. His reasons. The only thing he can control.

Now he's the one stretching out on the couch, and it reminds him of the cabin where he stayed for years before coming here. He slept on that stiff couch often. This one is better. He'll sleep here tonight.

29

Later, minutes before one in the morning, Rebecca, Ridley, and Laina return to their house. They briefly discuss sleep, but none of them are tired, the adrenaline of so many events running through them.

They settle in the living room, and Ridley pulls out his box of Settlers of Catan, with pieces he himself carved. Rebecca doesn't really like the game, but it is a perfectly fine way to pass the time, to wait out all this excess energy.

It is strange, because she was tired a couple of hours ago, but now she has turned a corner and will have to find her tiredness again.

"You have any sheep?" Ridley asks her.

She looks at her hand, sees that she does have sheep, but shakes her head anyway. "I don't want to lose this place," she says. "I don't want them to take Moon from us."

Her "them" is meant to encapsulate many people, many obstacles in their way.

Ridley ends his turn. He says, "If we don't die tomorrow, I think we'll be able to keep it."

The equivocated hope isn't particularly reassuring.

Rebecca plays her turn, building a few roads to the nearest shore, where she can trade in any resource at a lesser cost. She wishes there were some metaphor in how this game is playing out that she could use, some lesson.

Laina is falling asleep, right there leaning against the couch. Neither of them tells her that it's her turn. In silence, they wait to see if she will open her eyes.

After a minute or two, Ridley whispers, "If we make the sanctuary towns legal somehow, the government could protect us."

"You really believe that can happen? And would you want that? You're an anarchist."

Ridley shrugs. "I don't know."

Rebecca can see that he is withholding something. "What is it?" she asks.

"This used to be a ghost town. The Order of Asha, in collaboration with New Era and who knows what other organizations, bought it and then turned it into this. So far, no one has made that connection, but eventually the Black Hand will, and the next thing they'll look for are other ghost towns. They won't find all of them, but it is clear we can't hide forever."

Rebecca lets the weight of this information settle.

"After tomorrow," Ridley continues, "if we get access to the other towns, I'm going to try to unite all of us under a single banner. Every secret monster settlement in the world."

"That's crazy ambitious," Rebecca says.

"But worth trying."

Laina stirs. "What are you two talking about?"

They look at each other.

"Going to bed," Rebecca says.

• • •

A few hours later, Laina wakes to use the bathroom. After, she can't go back to sleep. She knows better than to grab her phone and flick through Instagram Reels. But her mind is buzzing with the worries of the coming conflict and the residual stress of the past week.

She gets up and starts pacing the halls of the second floor and realizes that it has been a long time since she paced like this. For over a year, she hasn't had a good reason, and through this realization she recognizes that this is a stress response—has always been, and it had gone away without her noticing. Strange to learn this about herself now, to mourn the loss of a very specific kind of peace just as it slips away from her.

Since she can't stop pacing now—silly to fight the coping mechanism—she decides to check Ridley's room. She opens the door gently, looks inside, and sees the empty bed. She hasn't slept in his room in a while. Rebecca is more of a cuddler, and with recent events she's been asked to fill that role. But the empty bed is evidence that Ridley is also struggling—something she already knew from before the threats to Moon. And so she feels a special terribleness for having neglected to check in on him.

She expects he'll be downstairs, so that's where she goes. She also expected him to be in the back room of the small bookshop, sorting and labeling outgoing book shipments, but she doesn't find him there. Instead, after a hectic search of the interior downstairs, she finds Ridley sitting on the porch, the outside light casting a soft glow on his hunched form. He looks up as she opens the door, and they lock eyes: hers bleary from sleep, his a little bloodshot from the lack of it.

"You haven't slept at all?" she asks him.

He doesn't answer, the truth seemingly obvious and not worth remarking on. She goes to lean on the porch railing, and only then does she see that the thing he is hunched over is a bird of happiness, half completed.

"You haven't done one of those in a long time," she says.

"Yeah," he says. "I was starting to think I'd lost interest in the hobby entirely. But suddenly, with death threatening for the third time this week, the impulse came over me." He lets out a breath that sounds more like acceptance than exasperation. "This is my second one."

And sure enough, there's the first attempt lying beside him on the bench. From a glance, she can see that it isn't his best work. Probably why he has opted for a second attempt. The carved wooden bird in his hands looks a lot better: smooth curves, unblemished by stray nicks or unintentional slips of the gouge.

"Want to talk about what's bothering you?" Laina says, tilting her head back past the eave of the roof to see the night sky.

"What *isn't* bothering me? The world is on fire. *Our* world is on fire."

"And Melku," Laina says.

The sky is truly breathtaking at this hour, in this place sequestered from the light pollution of the city, the stars shining in all their glory. In this sliver of present, nothing is on fire that she can see. The quiet remains—a pocket of safety, an eye of tranquility within the roiling mess.

"I was so angry at Melku," Ridley says. "And now I don't know how I feel." He puts down his second bird of happiness beside the first, and they look like two siblings that have lived radically different lives.

"It'll come to you," Laina says, thinking about those first hours after seeing her brother's body—that limbo of mute grief.

Ridley says, "All this time, we've been stumbling like the blind into each new situation. Every time I think I'm making a choice for myself, when I think about it too long, I realize that the choice was made for me. I am on a path. It's like . . . Well, it's like I've been fired from a gun, but I don't remember who or what fired me or where I'm headed. I'm just careering toward something that will annihilate me, and I can't see it. I can't divert myself either."

We're all like that, Laina thinks. The whole of history is like that—human beings stumbling toward annihilation. But she doesn't think this is a helpful thing to say—to *think*, even—and what if she helps bring it about by voicing it? What she chooses to say is a little more hopeful. "We've found each other. If life aimed me toward you, I'm glad it did."

He looks at her, and the internal war is clear on his face. "Do you think Melku knew they'd die that way?"

"I don't know," Laina says. "I know one thing, though. If we can't control the big things, at least we can control the little ones. Our little pack has done more to define me than any of the other mess we've been through. I'm still sane because I found you and Rebecca."

"You're right," Ridley says. "I should be more grateful."

She comes to sit beside him, the two little wooden birds of happiness between them. "I am not trying to invalidate your feelings. You're grieving. This situation fucking sucks. But . . ." Laina picks up the first bird of happiness, running her fingers along its bruised breast. "Maybe pick a metaphor where you aren't a bullet, my love."

Ridley laughs at this. "How many times have I been shot now?"

"Damn it, Riddle! Don't go bringing that up. I'm hoping no one gets shot this time."

"You're right. Sorry."

"For the record, twice. And that's all it is going to be."

Ridley nods. "I'll make sure of it."

"Come to bed," Laina says, standing up. She takes one last look at the night sky. It will be morning soon. "Let's try to find sleep together."

"I'd like that."

A VISIT WITH A DAUGHTER
OF THE SISTERHOOD OF SIGHT

30

I have never answered that question.

I have never answered that question.

I have never answered that question.

The first time, I am sitting on a bed. It is late afternoon. And one of them speaks to me. Far away. Hundreds of years past. The sister asks me a question, and I answer. She flits away. It is like a fly against the ear—a buzzing that holds secrets. So many secrets: of past and present and future. Things to come and things that might come. Myself, staring back at me. I am frightened, so I shut my ears to it, close my eyes.

I have never answered that question.

I have never answered that question.

The fourth time, I am eating lunch, and she comes. The sister asks me two questions.

I have never answered that question.

She asks me about a lynching in the 1930s. A schoolboy accused of kissing a young white girl against her permission. She wants to know what happened to the girl. I do not know what happened to her. I've never met her. And I do not know how to ask another. So I tell her to ask someone else. She is annoyed by this, and I laugh out of nervousness. One of my brothers—one who turned to ice on the moon—looks at me from across the table, curious. I stop laughing and stick out my tongue at him. I remember he will die. It is the first time I remember what hasn't happened yet. I remember and I start to cry. Something starts dying inside me, a *chip, chip, chip* away at my soul.

I have never answered that question.

The fifth time, I am in bed, and the shout of her mind wakes me from my sleep. She is everywhere at once and then gone again. When she comes back minutes later but years older, she apologizes to me. She had just woken to her power. But she is better now. I know immediately that she is the strongest of us. Sister Inness, reaching out to me from the past even as she raises me in the present. She tells me what I must do. It takes her all night, and when she is finished, I am very tired, but she is not. Sometime within the night, I have learned to hear them all, our entire Sisterhood.

She is impressed by me, tells me I am very strong. And though I know of her far greater power, the words are without falsehood. She tells me I'll grow stronger still. She tells me not to love anyone and, in the same breath, says that she knows I won't listen. She knows because I did not listen. And now she remembers the loss, the heartbreak, even though it hasn't happened yet.

She also tells me another secret, warns me to prepare because the day is coming soon.

I have never answered that question.

The next day, in class, we share a look before she begins the day's lessons. Her expression does not change, but it is as if I had crossed into a different country. I can read a mountain of meaning in her face. I can hear her voice in my mind, and in her voice, not just words. Memories. A knotted braid of experiences witnessed first-, second-, and thirdhand.

Reflexively, I look around me to see if anyone else can see what I'm seeing. As always, Melku has their head in a book, their pencil writing without their touching it. Smoke returns my gaze, smiles shyly. I almost return it. But then I remember what he has done—no, what he will do—and I can't will away the terror that comes to my face.

He shrinks back from me in nameless shame.

It is that look, that deep sadness, that has never allowed me to hate Smoke. When you know the fate of everyone you've met, no matter what they've done or will do, it dulls hatred.

I can feel Inness's own pain, mixing with mine. She tells me this is the price.

I have never answered that question.

There are many of us. We all manifest differently. I cannot push my awareness out. Sister Ilianna does that for all of us. Through her we see the world, and not just what we see with our own eyes. Sister Evelyn and Sister Wren hold the splitting. Just glimpses across what you call the fractal sea. My special gift is called "carry." It is the power to turn all our emotion into pure energy, hold that energy, and push it out once it can cause no harm. The Sisterhood uses my power to keep our true selves hidden. But I must carry our collective pain. A burden I must always bear, even after we complete the task.

I have never answered that question.

Astra can speak to the universe. She holds the contract with Yun, and by extension, we all hold the contract.

Inness's gift is visitation. Yes, like yours. She can transmit her consciousness across all of us. She is what allows us to mediate with each other, share memories, see across time and space. Together with splitting, visitation also allows us to communicate with our parallel selves.

Among us, there is no hierarchy. We are all equals under the gift.

When I was at last initiated fully into the Sisterhood, I felt them celebrate inside my mind. Inness stood behind them, quiet. Evelyn and Wren celebrated with the others, but it was soft, mournful. I felt them, and so I asked, and they showed me myself. I opened up and took the truth in. I had to stand under the stars and send the emotions out into space, or it would destroy me. The sisters told me that this was the other price beyond knowing the end of things: carrying the weight of emotions that come with knowing the future. But in the Sisterhood, I would be eternal. The sisters would feel my offering in the past, present, and future. I would be of use. It comforted me for a time, but sometimes it can feel like a prison.

I have never answered that question. But another will when the time comes.

I am the one who will bear witness, they tell me. I am the one who will have to choose. They tell me more things I have never told you, but believe me, you're better off for it.

They say that I am a great power, and it is good fortune that I was made in this era. They show me their own eyes. They share their own minds.

I am naked, as they are, standing in a circle, all our tender parts exposed. I shake under it: all that we are, laid bare for each other. I see their ugly, and they see my beauty. I see their beauty, and they witness every dark corner of me, embracing it all with love.

None of us are perfect, they say. But we have each other. There is no one else, they tell me. No one but us.

I feel the chill as they all have. I know what they mean, the darkness in it. I do not have the luxury of closed eyes.

No one matters but us, I say, stepping through.

Their sounds are joyous. One laughs, and it is nothing but sharp teeth and cracked bones. Her name is Lassu. I do not like her, and I love her still. She presses a rusted knife into me. I feel the pinch.

I can explain it no other way.

Some of them, I can see, are insane, their minds cracked open and weeping.

I love them too. Their gifts are strong, and we all are of use.

There are no conditions here, they tell me. Our love is forever, no matter what. Nothing can be done against the Sisterhood, because everything is for the Sisterhood. Even if I betray the whole world, it is for them. Because we know all there is to know. Our purpose is to be the arrow and the bow. We feast on the meat and the marrow and throw the leavings to everyone else.

How can I ever lie to them? The tree grows as it should because no one can lie. We all exist inside the circle because there is nothing outside the circle. We are a nest of serpents devouring each other and ourselves.

I have never answered that question.

I have never answered that question.

No, we do not answer to her. She serves us all, and we serve her.

Our goals are our own. We serve greater wills than the universe.

Sometimes, when I am alone in bed, I allow myself to feel all the things I have ever felt. My heart swells until the room is full of my emotions. The walls crack crack crack. It takes practice to keep yourself together, to not split apart.

I have never answered that question.

On Water Island, Melku asks me why I didn't save them. Because it has to be, I say. I cannot cry, not in front of Melku. I must do it alone. I must cry where no one sees, let it all swell into the open sky, push the clouds away, the summer rain. I must water the earth.

Melku asks me why it has to be. And I say, I have never answered that question. It is a secret I can't tell. The truth is, I could not. The truth is, I never could. The truth is, something is eating the world. And secrets keep it from eating more of the world. But sometimes it must eat a little. Our brothers and sisters were mostly bone, little bodies but so much inside—churning, delicious energy. They are on the moon still, their energy . . . dispersed. Dead matter. My mind is also dispersed, but spread out across the whole of the Sisterhood, living within the web of reverberations, my being stretched out forever and ever.

I cannot, but you're not really here. You're an absence. I am too. Though I burn. A body in this chair. A body. A body that cannot touch, that cannot be touched, lest I destroy the world. I am to be used. The sisters use me. We use each other. We are nothing but the using. I should not cry. But you are not really here. I am cracking the walls. Please don't look up. It is too much of myself, too naked. I don't want you to see.

It is my burden to want things I can't have. To want and to know I won't have them.

You have never told her how you felt, Inness tells me. The one who sheds her skin. It is your burden. We all have one. Mine is to abandon my son.

Mine is to kill the person I love, Evelyn says.

Wren does not speak. Her burden is to not speak.

The terror is in knowing that it is better this way: the Order of Asha diminished, the Cult in ascendancy. The terror is in knowing that to save everything, we must risk everything. To save everything, many things must be lost.

I have never answered that question.

To exist, what else? And when we are no more, it will be according to our will just the same. We do not care for the gods. We do not care for the monsters. We do not care for human beings. We care for ourselves and the arrow of time. There is no falsehood in this.

And yet I can never stop burning.

Each of us is different. The whole of us is the same. We are a murmuration. We are what emergence becomes when it is mature and steady as a storm. We are the eyes of entropy.

Don't be frightened. The universe has allowed it. Though I don't think she could get rid of the Sisterhood if she tried.

I have never answered that question.

I have never answered that question.

I have never answered that question.

Soon.

A RUIN, GREAT AND FREE

Laina wakes a little later than usual. The sun is already up, shining through the window at full glare. Subdued noises from the kitchen are the only thing piercing the quiet, the smell of coffee wafting into the room.

Ridley isn't there beside her. She sits up on the bed, stretches, calls for him. No answer. She slips some shorts over her bare thighs and then has the sensation that she needs to pee. She's done this all backward. She'll go to the bathroom first.

Instead of Ridley, she finds Rebecca in the kitchen, pouring herself coffee from an already half-empty pot. "Needed something stronger today," she says.

"Where's Ridley?"

"Good morning to you too." Rebecca puts her mug down, picks up another one, and crosses the distance between them. The mug placed in Laina's hands is still warm. "Milk tea," Rebecca says. "See, *I* was thinking of you."

Laina gives Rebecca a kiss on the cheek. "I didn't mean to hurt your feelings."

"You didn't," she says, poking Laina in the side.

Laina almost spills the tea laughing. "You're in a mood."

Rebecca grins.

"He's downstairs, then?"

Rebecca shakes her head. "Karuna came by to get him."

"What? Why?"

"Their little project, I'm guessing. Tomorrow isn't promised, and all that."

Rebecca says this without even a hint of worry—surprising because the words reignite last night's terror for Laina. Valiantly, Laina tries to shove it down, not let it show on her face.

Rebecca notices anyway. "I'm sorry. I'm making jokes because, well, that's what I do when worrying won't do anything."

"What I love about you. I just worry." Laina takes a sip of her tea and sighs. "It's perfect."

"I know my girl," Rebecca says. "They're in the community center. We head over after breakfast?"

Laina dips her chin in agreement.

Breakfast is a slice of toast with cream cheese and onion jam, accompanied by small talk that isn't about what will happen once the sun sets. Laina pours her anxiety into her chewing, and more than once she has to concentrate on her breathing to slow her heart down. But the light meal helps—the company, the casual bursts of affection shared between them. On the walk to the community center, she is as good as she's going to be.

She's fine until she steps inside.

Because there, filling up an impossible amount of space, is

Ridley and Karuna's little project. Which isn't little at all. Four—
no, five—whiteboards curved into a semicircle and filled with
neat script, papers and note cards spilled out on every table surface, the tables in a mirrored semicircle, like a procession, or an
audience, with Ridley and Karuna standing in the open space
within the whiteboards and tables. Wordless, they are both just
staring at their work in depthless concentration.

And if Laina wanted to be triggered, wanted to worry about
what is ahead of them, a more perfect instigator could not be
designed than what is in front of her. At a glance, she knows
that two of the whiteboards are a timeline of all the bad things
that have happened to her for the past six years.

"My god," Rebecca says, verbalizing Laina's inner thoughts.

They had done something similar to this back in Boston,
gathering all known evidence so that they could look at it and
think through everything. But what's before them is greater by
orders of magnitude, a more complete picture than they ever
managed to amass in the basement of the former bookstore.

Ridley looks at them, saying, "This is as good as we're going
to get before . . . tonight."

"Everything we've gathered from research, our own experiences, and talking to everyone in Moon," Karuna says.

Laina gulps. She wants to run. But where?

"Any new conclusions?" Rebecca asks.

They both look back to the boards. "Well, the conversation
last night gave us a little more to go on," Ridley says. "The talk
about tonight's battle being ordained. Reminded me of the barn,
when we were attacked by Smoke. Melku kept asking Cassandra
questions about what to do next or what would happen next.
Sometimes she answered. Sometimes she didn't."

"Before now," Karuna says, "we didn't connect it to anything larger . . ."

"But now?" Rebecca asks.

"We think . . ." He turns again to look at Rebecca and Laina, his eyes moving between them. "We think the Order of Asha and the Cult of the Zsouvox are engaged in a war of causation." Seeing Laina's and Rebecca's expressions, he clarifies: "A war between two timelines."

"I still don't know what that means," Rebecca says.

"A war between two potential futures," Karuna says. "In one timeline, the Order of Asha wins. In the other . . ."

It is the only time Laina has ever seen Karuna show even a hint of worry. And her current expression is more than worry.

"Something bad happens," Laina says. "To us."

"To more than us," Karuna answers. "To the world. To more than the world." She tilts her head to one side, squinting at one of the whiteboards. "We think."

Ridley sighs in exasperation. "And that's where we're stuck. The what. The why."

Rebecca isn't unnerved by any of this. She has already slipped between two long tables to survey the whiteboard, nodding and pressing a thumb to her lips as if to trap something inside.

Slowly, reluctantly, Laina follows, approaching the leftmost whiteboard as if she were coming up on a wild animal. The tight, cramped script is still very legible, and Laina has the thought that they must have used a fine-tipped marker for this. The differences in the script tell her that the board was written on by two people, both with careful, beautiful handwriting. She recognizes Ridley's and knows that the other must be Karuna's. Laina's own chicken scratch would not have looked like this.

On the first whiteboard is a timeline: the attacks on Rebecca's first pack, Lincoln included, by the strange wolf they fought in the meadow. The next thing in the timeline is Laina's video, the one of her brother's death. She released that video the first time, only for it to be erased from existence, along with the video of the protest by Rebecca and her pack on the highway, where they blocked traffic in their wolf forms before changing back into humans. At the time, both videos were all over the internet, shared on national and worldwide news. And then they were gone. This is on the timeline too, under the popular name for what followed: the Fracture.

During the Fracture, people were split over whether the videos existed at all and whether monsters were real. The loss of evidence, and the obvious terror spawned by that inexplicable loss, created a rift in the collective consciousness, the contract of shared reality. Some people chose not to believe—to put the monster back into the shadows, so to speak. Some became obsessed. Some simply ignored it. To Laina, all responses seemed reasonable. At the same time, people were killing one another, hurting people they suspected of being monsters, losing their minds. Ridley went to a SEN Collective meeting where Melku introduced everyone to a sight mage named Cassandra. At that same meeting, Ridley was attacked by a monster who could turn himself into dust. That would have been crazy enough, but a literal *god* also made an appearance. All this on the whiteboards.

The Fracture ended with a series of massacres at pro-monster protests nationwide, the biggest one being the Boston Massacre. Laina was there. Ridley and Rebecca were both shot, and Lincoln's ex-girlfriend was killed. Karuna Flood and Harold Shiner were also there, bewitched into being shooters themselves.

Luckily, Dragon had intervened, saved Harry and Karuna, and helped them escape.

Years passed as a human-supremacist group slowly rose to power. This is chronicled on the second and third whiteboard. A Boston married couple was murdered. A local monster retaliated. A riot resulted: Anarres Books burned, a local cooperative association bombed, a St. Thomian senator assassinated. Laina, Ridley, and Rebecca were spirited away to a secret intentional community for monsters, one of several. And there they found Harry, Karuna, Alex, and Dragon. And others Laina didn't know, all their disparate timelines presented as bulleted entries on the whiteboards.

The first attack on Moon. The second attack on Moon. And now what awaited them: an attack by the Cult of the Zsouvox. Looking at it all together, taking it in, the actual details seem absurd, a garbled mess of strange events.

"This looks like chaos," Rebecca says.

And because this is exactly what Laina is thinking, a terrible shudder goes through her.

Ridley seems ready for that response. "But look at the connections. More than could just be coincidence, right? Look at the way events always seem to follow us around. You might think it's our personal biases. But how do you explain Laina receiving the video, the surveillance, Melku's secret apartment in our building, the ants saving us in the nick of time? It's like we were being guided here."

"Why us?" Rebecca asks.

"We don't know," Ridley says. "Perhaps it could've been anyone and just *happened* to be us."

"Or it had to be us specifically," Karuna says. "Destiny."

"I don't like either answer," Laina says. "My brother died

for this. I refuse to accept that he died for no reason. I refuse to accept that he had to die at all."

They all look at her, silent.

If they die tonight, will that also be for no reason? Or destiny? Either answer only makes Laina angry. Even if the world doesn't end, why should they be sacrificed? And why should they be sacrificed without knowing why it was happening?

That's why Ridley is doing all this, she thinks. That's why knowing matters to him. There's also something else. She can see it in Ridley's entire body, but especially in his eyes. Ridley has found purpose in trying to understand what's happening to them. He is searching for a way out of the cage in his own mind, and through it finding a way back to himself, the way he was before being trapped in Moon.

For Ridley's sake, Laina decides to swallow her anger and fear. "Talk it through with me again," she says.

The following discussion lasts the rest of the morning, through lunch and midafternoon. By late afternoon, Dragon, Georgie, Connor, Tash, Espeth, and Jesmeen are also here. After sunset, Alex rolls in at full energy while everyone else is starting to flag.

But the puzzle keeps everyone invested, keeps them staring at the boards, picking up papers, throwing intermittent questions at each other.

An hour after sunset, they hit something.

Connor: "Wait. How do we know that the Order of the Shoebox—"

Ridley: "*Zsouvox.*"

Connor: "Yeah, right. How do we know that they have a sight mage?"

Dragon: "They have one. I've seen her. A young girl."

Connor: "Yeah, but how do we know the sight mages are on opposing sides and not working together?"

Ridley: "You got a better idea, then?"

Connor: "I'm just saying . . ."

Ridley: "None of this makes sense if they're not in opposition."

Georgie: "So two opposing sight mages."

Dragon: "And two opposing Zsouvoxes."

They all look at Dragon.

Karuna: "You never brought up another Zsouvox before."

Dragon, after a pause: "I didn't remember."

Karuna, unconvinced: "You didn't remember . . ."

Dragon, softly: "No. Damsel told me not to tell anyone. She threatened to erase my mind if I did."

Ridley: "That woman."

Karuna: "If you're comfortable taking the risk, what can you tell us about it now?"

Dragon, after a short pause: "Damsel had it at the Bordeaux Compound on St. Thomas. She said it was a Zsouvox. I think she was hiding it."

Connor: "Wait, do we know what Zooboxes are?"

Ridley and Karuna (at the same time, respectively): "We don't." "Did Damsel tell you what a Zsouvox is?"

Dragon: "No."

Laina: "Wouldn't it be a god? I mean, if Asha is one, it stands to reason . . ."

Connor, overwhelmed: "Anyone want a beer from the fridge?"

Jesmeen: "Get me one."

Espeth, to herself: "I'm going to need something stronger than a beer."

Karuna: "Assuming it's a god might be a mistake."

Rebecca: "That's all we're doing here, making assumptions."

Karuna: "*Informed* assumptions."

Laina: "I'd say that it is safe to assume that the Cult of the Zsouvox worships its own god."

Karuna: "Then why would the Order of Asha also have one?"

"Because they're the same god."

This voice comes from the air next to Georgie, who is standing beside a whiteboard, startling her and almost causing her to fall over one of the long tables.

Sonya—not wearing her skin and thus invisible to everyone in attendance—clarifies: "The same god split in two."

Everyone is looking at the spot where Sonya should be, wondering how long she's been there, wondering if they can ask follow-up questions, wondering if she is even still there. Laina, for her part, wouldn't be surprised if this is all they get. When "the voice" used to visit her, she was all ominous revelations and quick exits. This is what the voice has always been like.

Karuna: "How do you know they're the same god split in two?"

Sonya: "I don't. It's just a theory."

In that moment, Laina has a terrible thought: No one knows what's going on. Because up until this point, she expected the voice to have more than theories—expected it without knowing for certain. She had thought the voice knew everything and was choosing not to tell them, because of, well, who knows? But she was wrong, *is* wrong. Sonya doesn't know. And where does that end? Laina thinks: *Never.* If the right question is asked, not even Asha would know the answer. Even the Zsouvox— no, the Zsouvoxes—wouldn't know all the answers. And this is so much worse than Laina not knowing. If even the gods don't know, if they're all lost, both the high and the low, grasping at shadows, then . . .

Ridley: "So what do we think? The Order of Asha is trying to keep these two, uh, Zsouvoxes apart. And the Cult of the Zsouvox is trying to bring them together. If the Cult succeeds, it will, what . . . end the world?"

Karuna: "If we're fine with great leaps of conjecture, then sure."

Georgie: "But why? Why would a god want to end everything? And if everything ends, what's left?"

Silence.

Ridley: "Well. We've hit another wall."

Laina, toneless: "There is nothing but walls. Walls on every side. And beneath us, a black sea."

Everyone is staring at Laina. Everyone except Connor, who has just returned from the kitchen with two longnecks in hand.

Connor: "Guys . . ."

They all turn to him, and then from him to where he's looking: the open doorway.

A naked man stands there, face and body gaunt, skin pale, watching them through sunken, all-black eyes.

Ridley: "I think our time is up."

In a solemn procession, the warriors of Moon follow the creature through the woods. As they enter deeper into the forest, Laina has the thought that they'll pass some threshold into a forest so oppressively dark, so shrouded in fog, they won't be able to see in front of them, with only this pale creature to guide them through that deeper dark.

Almost as if she's thinking something similar herself, Rebecca whispers, "What do you think it is?"

"A vampire," Alex answers. "It's hexed. And starving."

The light of the moon through the trees is glinting off the vampire, making his skin appear to glow. Laina tries to keep her eyes on the head, which is shaven clean—so clean that she wonders if hair even grows there anymore. Though she tries not to look, her eyes keep wandering down to the emaciated back, the skinny legs, the withered buttocks.

Rebecca tsks. "The poor thing."

Ossi says, "We might be grateful later that we're healthy and they're not."

It's the first thing she has said for a while, and this, what she's saying now, is perfectly on-brand for the stern-faced woman. Laina knows that Ossi isn't really interested in where they're going or why, and she doesn't care a fig about the enemy, hexed or not. Her only interest is surviving. It isn't a perspective Laina could manage, even on her worst day, but she is grateful for it, grateful to have Ossi on their side.

"Why do you think they're not attacking Moon itself?" Laina whispers.

Ridley, standing next to her, considers the question. In front of him, Ossi tilts her ear to them as if listening. "My best guess?" he says. "They don't want us to use the portals." He looks at Laina, communicating the rest with his eyes.

Laina understands. They think the portals are an automated defense. They don't know about Karuna's ability to direct Melku's insects. Which makes sense. None of them knew she could do that until yesterday.

"But why send this thing?" Ossi asks, referring to the naked vampire leading them away from Moon.

It is Alex who answers. "Because this guy here," she says, "is the bait."

"Just like us," Ridley says.

Again Laina has to swallow the fear. They will die today.

Within thirty minutes, they are at the large clearing where Laina, Rebecca, and Ridley have picnicked before. At night, the place carries an aura of menace that is not present in the daytime. The vampire carries on, crossing the clearing to join the monsters standing motionless on the other side.

Laina takes a good look at them. "They're all emaciated."

By their ashen pallor, Laina guesses most of them are vampires. But they all look severely malnourished, ribs protruding beneath their skin. None of them are wearing proper clothing, though some have bits of rags to barely conceal them. A handful of shifters, already in their animal form, look even worse: patched and mangy fur, skin and bones beneath. Even from across the meadow, she can smell the stench of their unwashed bodies. Laina would be relieved, if not for the two giants—one male, one female—towering over their brethren. They are just as emaciated as the other monsters, but they'll still be a problem, Laina is sure of it. She hopes Karuna understands this too.

"I count thirty-seven."

Thirty-seven to their dozen. They are going to die here. She pushes the thought out of her mind, but it remains just beneath the surface, playing on repeat.

"Thirty-eight," Dragon corrects. "The Bone Witch." He points to the tree line, and he's right—a frail woman is standing under the cover of the darkness, staring impassively out at them.

"Well, they're not charging us, at least," Alex says. "Looks like we got a moment to discuss strategy."

"We'll get one of the giants," Jesmeen says, Georgie and Espeth nodding.

"What about the other giant?" Dragon asks.

"We ignore it," Ridley says.

"Yes, we need to ignore it," Laina says, interrupting Dragon's protest before it can begin.

She sees when he puts it together.

"Move fast," Ridley adds. "Incapacitate and move forward." Then he starts taking off his clothes.

The other shifters follow, one by one flinging themselves into the change.

Now what? Laina thinks. But she doesn't have to wait long before it happens. Suddenly, the giantess drops through the earth. As soon as she does, the portal closes over her.

With that, the calm ends. The other giant pushes himself free of the spell that was holding him back. Laina can actually see the moment the magic snaps—a rippling in the air, whipping out from the giant's back like a cut tether. As he lumbers forward, the other tethers binding the monsters together go taut. This pulls the Cult's vampires and shifters forward until all the tethers snap free, and it is as if they all awoke from a dream, their dazed expressions suggesting a sort of confused madness. All at once, their gazes fall on the warriors of Moon. And then every last monster charges.

"Here we go," Alex says, and sprints forward.

The shifters take off.

Dragon releases his wings and launches into the sky.

Jesmeen puts out her hands, Georgie and Espeth joining her in a chant of power. Tree roots spring from the earth, weaving around the giant's ankles, and the giant pitches forward and crashes to the ground like a felled tree. More roots shoot up around him. They swarm and constrict. Like a hand of many fingers, they grasp his body and begin to pull him down beneath the earth. The soil around the giant roils, almost liquid pliant, turning the churned earth to quick mud. His eyes are wide with astonishment as the earth begins to swallow him. Bit by bit, he sinks, thrashing in vain. Moments later, he is gone, a few bubbles rising through the mud to mark his passing.

Alex and the shifters sprint over the freshly upturned earth.

Laina pulls herself down into her wolf, feeling almost as if she were riding her wolf self. This sensation amplifies, and through the effort her wolf grows, marginally at first, then dramatically. She is at least a tenth larger than her normal wolf size, her paws digging into the grass and soil beneath her, steam coming from her nose. Around her, much is happening. The other shifters are running next to her, ahead, behind. She sees Connor's brown coat loping beside her, Ridley's gray coat just ahead. Rebecca is to her right but behind. Another wolf is running farther off: Tash. The moon is a soft, bright beacon above them, lighting the meadow, shimmering against their fur.

Suddenly, Dragon is swooping down, releasing a torrent of fire from his wide mouth, setting the whole front rank of the Cult's monsters ablaze. Alex leaps over the front line. The shifters weave around the torched and screaming monsters, pressing forward. Like a dancer, Ossi sets herself spinning through the air, swiping and clawing at a group of vampires. She leaps off the chest of one vampire and onto the back of a wolf shifter, biting down on her neck before moving on. She swipes at the legs of another vampire, sending him careering sideways, where Ridley intercepts, catching the vampire's neck in his open mouth.

Rebecca and Connor are pulling another vampire apart as Laina passes.

In the sky, she can see the outline of Dragon's wings as he makes another swoop ahead, setting the rear rank of monsters ablaze. If Laina feels any terror at this spectacle, it is subsumed by the bloodlust of the wolf, a bloodlust she is encouraging now, freeing it to do the damage it intends, wants, has always wanted, the human finally not holding the wolf back.

Laina is biting into the neck of a vampire, claws digging deep into his chest. How did she get here? One minute she is running, and the next she is on top of this stranger, biting down. He is strong and trying to buck her off him, but she sinks in deeper, blood filling her mouth, gushing out from his flesh. All around her, the sounds of screaming, of tearing, of blows landing. All around her, the terrible noises of violence and death. Her wolf is delighting in this. She lets it delight, lets herself. To survive.

The vampire is dead, and she is on another. This one bats her off, Laina tumbling until she is upright again, paws in damp grass. She charges once more, and the vampire is waiting for her. He throws a fist. But Laina opens her mouth around it, letting the fist pass between her teeth, canines lifting flesh from the vampire's knuckles. Laina bites down with a growl. Again the hot spurt of blood as she grinds flesh and bones into potted meat. The vampire tries to swing himself free, but Laina doesn't stop until the hand and forearm tear away. The vampire screams, eyes wide in pained surprise. Laina leaps again, bringing the vampire down, teeth in neck, tearing. The vampire goes silent. Up through the vampire's damaged neck, blood spurts into Laina's wide-open mouth.

As she releases the vampire, Laina hears something approaching from behind with terrible speed. But then the ground beneath her opens. She falls, down through a rent in reality. Below her: starlight, wisps of gray-white cloud, the bright bloom of the half-moon. Here, where she is falling, the air is cooler than where she was, the din of battle far away. She is aware of trees in her periphery, rattling in the wind. A moment passes where she stops midfall, and it is as if time has slowed down— Laina weightless, hovering before the force of gravity presses down on her, the ground above her head, the sky below her feet.

And then she is back through the portal, back into the noise of the battle. She halts again in midair, feeling the press of gravity against her back, as it should be. Her paws soon find purchase on the grass below her feet. She has arrived, but not in the place she just left. It is a strange feeling, as if she has just returned from a long journey even though only moments have passed.

Laina takes stock of her immediate surroundings. She is behind enemy lines, watching the battle play out before her. At the moment, the Moonites are winning, doing damage and being transported by Karuna before damage can be done to them. Throughout the battlefield, portals are opening, dropping her allies down into the earth before spitting them out again elsewhere. Laina understands the assignment; she flings herself ahead and into another vampire, trusting that if things get out of hand, Karuna will be there to save her. This one doesn't see her coming, and she is on his back before he can respond. Her teeth around his head, his neck snapping as she pulls the head back beyond its natural limits. Not enough to incapacitate a vampire. She grips that same head and tosses him around like a rag doll, until the rag-doll body separates from the crushed head.

A small part of Laina wishes this weren't so satisfying. But this is what she is here to do. Kill. And survive.

Two vampires turn to her at once, charging. Laina stands, waits. A hole opens beneath her, and she hurtles through a series of portals before falling from the sky, flying ants dispersing as soon as she clears the portal's opening. She lands on a mountain-lion shifter, making short work of the poor, unhealthy creature, who is probably guiltless in all this.

But then Laina falters at seeing her next antagonist.

Mason stops too, holding Tash up by the neck. "Look who

it is." On Mason's own neck, there is not even the slightest evidence that Laina once ripped her head off.

Happily, Tash is still alive, writhing in the vampire's grasp, making desperate noises through bared teeth.

Deciding not to hesitate, Laina launches herself at this vampire. Luckily for Tash, the vampire is more interested in Laina. Mason tosses Tash away with little effort and turns to face Laina head-on. And Laina is already airborne, but just as she is about to connect with this vampire, mouth open and claws ready, Mason weaves out of the way, catching Laina by the leg in midair. Before Laina can think to respond, Mason whirls her through the air and brings her down hard. The impact as her body makes contact with the ground steals the air from Laina's lungs.

"Not this time, little wolf," Mason says, grinning wickedly.

Laina can only watch, stunned, as the vampire's foot comes down on her rib cage. There is a crack and a sharp stab of pain. Mason does it again and again. "Do you know . . . how long it took . . . for my neck to heal?" Each word she spits out is punctuated by another stomp to Laina's rib cage.

Laina gasping, trying to scramble away. Mason grabs her by the tail and pulls her back in range of another kick. "I'm not done." Two more kicks, the latter so powerful it sends Laina skidding across the wet grass. And somehow Mason is right there as Laina slides to a stop, wedging both her hands into Laina's mouth, pulling Laina's jaw apart, unfazed by Laina's teeth stabbing into her hands. Mason continues single-mindedly, wrenching Laina's jaw open wider and wider. The pain is unbearable as the corners of her mouth begin to tear.

"When I'm done with you, they won't be able to stitch you back together," Mason says.

Laina can hear her wolf screaming, and she can feel herself as separate again, her human part trying to run from the violence, from the pain. She feels the moment the wolf begins to give up, and this is when her self-preservation kicks in. Somehow she reaches down into some deep reservoir of magic. Her wolf grows in size and power, and with a sudden burst of force, she snaps her mouth shut, catching a few of Mason's fingers before she is able to pull away.

Reeling back, Mason lets out a frustrated scream.

Laina takes advantage of the moment to put some space between them.

"You'll pay for that, little wolf," Mason says.

Laina's wolf makes a sound near enough to a cackle.

Expression cold, Mason lunges.

But suddenly, a portal opens between them, and Alex falls upward through the portal, naturally—gracefully—catching Mason with a roundhouse kick that sends the vampire spinning.

Alex turns. "You're all right?" she asks.

Laina makes a soft noise, moves her head up and down—a wolf's nod.

"Take a moment," she says. "Let yourself heal up."

Footsteps approach. "You've grown so much."

Laina looks past Alex and growls.

Alex turns to see Mason wiping blood from her mouth.

The vampire is smiling, the sharp canines revealed, but the smile itself is all warmth.

Alex's eyes widen. "Mother?"

"My little Amethyst."

Alex looks at her mother. As she looks, a part of herself is transported to when she was a child, lying on that basement floor, slick with blood. Her mother standing over her. Her mother telling her that they must go. Her mother telling her to come with her. Her father dead on the floor, emptied of blood. She is the only family left to Alex—to *Amethyst* then, in that time. But why won't she stand up. Why won't Alex go with this woman?

Because she isn't her mother, not truly. This creature killed her father and wants to be free to do the same to others.

Like this woman in front of Alex now. Not her mother. Though she looks superficially like her mother, the years having changed nothing, this woman smiles as if it is a performance. And the soft fondness she has fixed to her face also a performance, painfully familiar.

"Won't you step aside, dear?" Alex's pretend-mother says.

Not once in Alex's memory did her mother ever use the word *dear* with anyone.

"I have some business to complete, and then we can catch up."

Alex is still too stunned to speak. Surely, her mother can't think that Alex will do such a thing—step aside and watch her kill Laina? Surely, she doesn't believe they'll just "catch up."

"You're in the way," her mother says.

And just so, this woman, this creature, lets go of any semblance of humanity. The kindness leaves her eyes. Only frustration is left, like a child being kept from a prize, a predator being kept from its kill.

Still, the child in Alex does not want to believe it. "Where have you been?" Alex asks.

Her mother shrugs. "In a dungeon mostly. Sometimes they let me out for a capture or kill."

Alex doesn't need to ask what dungeon. She is filling in all the years, all the time that she was living in her adoptive father's compound while, downstairs, her mother languished in a cell. Right beneath her feet all that time.

"Why didn't you come to me?" Alex asks. "Why didn't you let me know you were alive?"

Her mother looks confused by this, running a hand through the short spikes of her hair. A terrible haircut, like that of a hip TV mom from the early 2000s. "Well, as I said, they had me locked up mostly. Look, Amie, we can catch up on everything in a minute. Let me just—"

"No," Alex says. "It is crazy that you think I'd just let you kill my friend."

"Your friend?"

Well, that might be a slight exaggeration. Laina and Alex are *friendly*, at best. Still: "Walk away. I don't want to have to hurt you."

This tips something in her mother. Some internal mechanism whirs to a stop and changes direction. Any show of motherly interest disappears. There is a cliff for every vampire—a precipice that, once fallen from, is difficult to regain. The pull toward that cliff edge makes a vampire dangerous. Sometimes the pull is so strong that the person can't be blamed for leaping from it. Sometimes it is a gradual thing—a pull that can be ignored or even stepped toward. A million small instances of accepting that pull until there is nothing to do but jump. Sometimes the pull is fierce, and it feels as if there's wind at your back, and you have to use force to stay rooted where you are. At different moments in her time as a vampire, Alex has felt all three. But no matter the pull, no matter the *way* one falls off a cliff, once it happens, it is the same. A vampire who has done so sees everything in front of them as food to eat or a toy to play with. Any opposition to those goals is a challenge to be pushed aside. All life is shrunk down to what can keep the vampire alive or what is in the way of that life. For a vampire more than for any other monster, it seems, there is a compelling path toward abandoning humanity. Her mother, or the woman who was once her mother, has fallen off the cliff. And Alex is staring down at her.

"Stop," Alex says. "Stop this."

Her mother lets something like remorse show. A lie. "I was content in knowing you were out there somewhere, alive. I figured, as long as we didn't run into each other, we could avoid certain messes."

She leaves the last part unsaid. But Alex understands. She disagrees on one point: What is coming could *not* be avoided.

When her mother comes at her, Alex lets her combat training take over. Her mother throws wild flurries of punches and kicks at Alex, like a berserker on a battlefield. Alex deflects them easily, stepping back, letting her mother pursue. Taking advantage of an opening, she hits her mother in the face. Another punch to the ribs, another to the liver. All without much heat behind them, all warnings. But her mother persists, landing an open hand across Alex's face before she can back out of reach, dragging nails down her cheek. Blood drips down the right side of Alex's face, pooling stickily in the curve of her neck before staining Alex's shirt. Vampire blood isn't appetizing to other vampires, but her mother's eyes go wild at the sight of it all the same. Again she comes at Alex, and again Alex parries the blow. Through all this, everything has slowed, the noise around Alex turning soft, muffled, her perception narrowing to what is in front of her.

Alex is at the cliff edge, the wind at her back trying to push her over. She forces herself back from the precipice. If she does this, she must do it with her full mind. She has to do it without abandoning her humanity. The tears mix with the blood on her face. She is a canvas dripping with fresh paint—a ruin, great and free.

Her mother is surprised by Alex's sudden quickness. One fast, hard blow to her neck, and then Alex jams a foot down into her mother's shin, shattering the bone there. Unsteadied, the older vampire stumbles, falling against Alex, choking and gasping. And Alex is ready for what's next, catching her mother by the head and bringing her down onto one knee. The hard crunch of the impact contrasts with the gentleness—the almost sweetness—of the gesture. She brings her mother back up, doesn't shrink from the damage she has done, and ends it with a twist of the neck.

The sound is terrible, and Alex has to close her eyes for a moment.

Her eyes open to her mother's surprised, broken face, the rest of her body limp and hanging. She is still alive. Severing her head alone won't do. She must remove the heart.

Just a little farther, she tells herself. Alex has to look up to the sky as she does it, so she doesn't see the blackness beneath her, that beckoning abyss. She sways a little from sudden vertigo.

Until this moment, Laina has observed everything. Now she looks away to give Alex privacy.

After a time, her back turned to Laina, Alex asks, "Are you okay? Can you walk?"

Laina can't answer in this form, so she tests out her legs instead. Sharp pain erupts from various places, but she can stand, and she is limping only a little. Alex turns to look, and Laina can see the flush of exertion in her cheeks, the sparkle of tears in her eyes. Despite Alex's efforts, something of her inner anguish is slipping through.

"I'll go check if—" Alex starts to say before a portal opens up beneath her and she falls through the earth, leaving her mother's corpse behind. Laina doesn't look. She tests her legs again, and the pain is still there, the pulse of broken ribs still throbbing, but it is duller now. She is already starting to heal. She surveys the battlefield once more and sees that Rebecca, Ridley, and Connor are struggling with a creature that has an extra set of arms . . . and a tail.

Laina sets off in that direction.

33

Orchestrating all this, Karuna sits on a distant hill, watching the battle through a pair of glasses that condense space. She can see through various synthetic insects with a thought. (The impossible technology can read and translate the relevant brain waves into directives that it then fulfills.) And she can adjust angles of view by jumping into these synthsectoid eyes spread across the battlefield. Synthsects surround her too, to pick up anything that tries to approach, anything that might aim to harm her in the midst of her taxing work. Controlling all these tiny machines has her at the edge of her powers. She has no tech magic to aid her. That was Melku's power, and she is not Melku.

Or that is what she might be thinking. Or perhaps she is remembering her dream and the words the person said to her: *"I'm sorry you have to do this part alone. But you're not really alone. I am here. Always."*

An alert blasts in Karuna's mind. A synthsect in her outer perimeter. She looks through that set of eyes but sees nothing.

She sends her perception through each of her surrounding satellites, and when she is satisfied, she returns to her work.

Out of nowhere, the giant woman returns, dropping out from the sky in the center of the ongoing battle. A cloud of fine dust disappears as the giantess lands. Karuna immediately sets to work forming a portal beneath the—

Another alert screams inside her mind. Karuna sends her perception to the synthsect and she sees the same cloud of fine dust, passing through her inner perimeter. Panic sets in just as Smoke materializes in front of her.

Smoke smiles. "You were difficult to find. No matter now."

Karuna doesn't speak. She begins to draw her synthsects from the surrounding woods to her.

"I thought I'd ended these damn tricks when I killed their owner," he says. "Corrupted light magic has no place in this world."

Karuna can feel all the synthsects coming closer. Through one eye, she continues to survey the battle, opening and closing portals at half efficiency. She tries to drop the giantess through a portal, but the clever creature sidesteps the attempt. Sweat sheens on Karuna's forehead.

"You shouldn't be able to use this power. But . . ." His eyes roam her body. "You struggling, no?"

One by one, the approaching synthsects begin to flick out of her awareness. Karuna pulls her attention away from the battlefield and, in her full sight, sees Smoke's outline, still dancing like an aura of ash.

"I understand Melku's toys better than you could imagine. Which is why Melku is dead."

Karuna withdraws more machines from the battle, bringing them to her.

"You not listening," Smoke says.

"You were Dragon's guardian, weren't you?" Karuna asks.

The change of subject traps Smoke's full attention. The particles of self around him settle into him.

"He's down there now, on the battlefield. Why haven't you gone to him?"

"I was tasked with finding you. To mark you for the Bone Witch." Seeing Karuna's questioning look, Smoke regains some of his confidence. "You won't be able to hide again. Not that you gon' be alive to do so."

Her face shifts then. Resignation. One final card left in play. Karuna lights the beacon with a thought. "Finding me is the justification," she says. "I know the truth. You're a coward."

Anger flashes on Smoke's face just as a rush of air trips one of the sensors in Karuna's inner perimeter.

She can see Smoke's intent to pull her apart limb from limb. But the sword punches through his chest before he can do anything.

Blood sprays Karuna's face. Even though it's too late, Smoke tries to dismantle himself. A torrent of electricity convulses around him, setting him in place.

"Something Melku left to us," Karuna says.

"Invisible. Like its wielder," says Sonya, into Smoke's ear.

"Turns out you didn't know as much as you thought," Karuna says as Smoke burns away in a burst of electricity, never to return.

34

On the battlefield, only the twelve-foot giantess remains.

Her eyes are a sharp blue, skin pale from years without sun. The evidence of neglect is present on her body, in the strips of cloth she wears as clothes, but here, now, she looks saner than one might expect—lucid, even. Her clever eyes scan her would-be assailants with none of the mindless menace of the other, slightly larger giant. Instead, she exudes eerie calm.

On the side of Moon, only Tash has been taken out of the battle, transported back to the settlement by the ants. But the remaining Moonites understand that this is not a situation they can leap at without some caution. Each of them is hoping a portal will remove the obstacle entirely. But so far, she hasn't been sent away. Karuna might not be able to save them this time. They hope she's had the chance to at least save herself.

When the giantess finally steps forward, it is Connor who responds first. The closest to the giant, he throws himself at her. The others don't have time to reach him before he engages, but they take their cue and surge forward. They stop short when, with a casual backhand, the giantess sends Connor cartwheeling through the air.

He lands in grass several feet away and begins to rise to his feet, visibly disoriented.

Instead of advancing, the giantess waits again. She appears watchful, eyes on them, eyes on the ground around her. She's searching the grass for the ants, Laina realizes, to see if a portal will open now that she has hurt one of them.

A half minute more in this uneasy quiet before Alex says, "All at once. All together."

And then they run at her. Laina, Ridley, and Rebecca circling in. Dragon flying above. Ossi, head-on, an efficient machine. Connor, regaining himself, coming up last from her left flank. Georgie, Jesmeen, and Espeth standing back, whispering a hex they hope to throw at the giantess, at least incapacitating her long enough for the other Moonites to deal a killing blow.

The giantess watches all of them come. She shifts her stance, stooping low to the ground, and calmly waits for her first assailant.

And it's Ossi, leaping into the air, going for the giantess's neck with teeth and claws.

Too quickly, the giantess slips out of the way, spinning around delicately, and sets off in the direction of . . . Connor. He falters as she comes up on him. Too late. She grabs him and slams him down into the ground, then proceeds to hammer him with her fists.

Everyone picks up speed now. Desperate, they leap at her, biting whatever flesh they can find.

But with a determined grimace, she keeps pummeling

Connor, again and again, until the ground is soft around him, and he is soft. And wet. She spots Alex next. She whirls— so fast!—and punches Alex in the chest. The giantess follows through with the punch and Alex is brought to ground. The earth sighs beneath Alex, beneath the force of the giant's fist. When she lifts that fist, Alex is in a crater, her chest cratered, blood bubbling up from her throat. And then, almost absently, the giantess pulls Laina from her leg, tearing away the skin and muscle that Laina has in her jaws. She brings Laina up for inspection, their eyes meeting. Under her grip and her impassive gaze, Laina squirms. Rebecca and Ridley roar as one, clawing and biting their way up the giant's back, her shoulder. They just have to get there. The giantess ignores the damage they inflict. She has her prize.

Laina can feel the pressure behind her eyes when the giantess begins to squeeze. She feels her rib cage shatter.

Nothing after that.

Ridley and Rebecca watch as the giantess releases Laina; they hear her limp body hit the ground.

And then the giantess is spinning, Ridley and Rebecca flung free and airborne—just in time for the giantess to punch Ossi in midleap. The combined speed and power of the strike sends Ossi tumbling headfirst into the dirt. Calmly, the giant yanks her foot free of the vines threatening to pull her into the earth. And then she is leaping to catch Dragon by the leg. She throws him, sending him whirling at terrible speed into the coven of witches. They have only a moment to pause their hexwork before Dragon collides with them. Their bodies do little to slow Dragon's momentum, all of them fetching up in the dirt at different spots.

All this in barely a minute.

The giantess stands at full height, taking in the damage she's done. Strips of skin hang off her like tassels. Her clothes are not even a suggestion now. But she is uninterested in her wounds or nakedness. Already there are signs of healing as the bleeding from all her cuts, scratches, and bite marks slow.

Rebecca and Ridley have found Laina. They nudge her still body with their noses, keening loudly.

For the moment, Ossi is the only one still in condition to fight. She shakes off the dizziness, the shock, observing the damage around her as calmly as she can. Then she turns to the giantess with the same sort of attention, finding in her opponent's eyes a reflection of her own measuring gaze. A match, Ossi thinks. No, more than a match. But Ossi has never been in a fight she couldn't see some way out of. And over the centuries, she has found her way out of many fights.

Well. Now or never.

In a blink, Ossi closes the distance. The giantess responds, putting her hands up defensively. This time, Ossi is prepared. The giantess will swing at her or try to stamp her into the ground—both options telegraphed by the visible tension in the giant's body. When Ossi is within striking distance, instead of trying to counter either possibility, she keeps running, between the legs of the creature and then around one leg. The giantess readjusts, reaching down to scoop Ossi up in her hand, no doubt to crush Ossi in her grip. But Ossi spins back in the direction she came, circling the other leg and coming around on the creature's hamstring. She leaps, claws angled to rend flesh. The giantess tenses from pain as Ossi climbs up one leg, a trail of blood and torn flesh in her wake. She jumps onto the back and immediately feels a subtle shift of tension from the giant. *She's going to try to pin me with her body.* As she has the thought, the giantess throws herself backward. And they are both airborne, the giantess now on top, Ossi below—falling to earth. With a cat's instinct, Ossi sets her front claws deep and kicks with her legs, swinging herself onto the giant's front as the huge body hits the ground. The world quakes. The shock distracts Ossi for only a second. But it's enough. The giantess engulfs her in a bear hug, Ossi biting and clawing and squirming as the grip tightens. She is doing damage, but the giantess remains resolute. Ossi fights her own panic. She just needs to keep going, do enough damage, dig deep into the giant's chest, let the blood pool around her, get herself slick enough to squirm free. The pressure is terrible, but Ossi does not stop. Finally, and with no time to spare, she slips free. Ossi doesn't waste the moment. She goes for the giant's neck. The giant brings her hand up defensively. Ossi's teeth hit against knuckle, and the world shifts again, the giantess rolling onto her belly. Ossi flings herself off before she is crushed.

Ossi puts some space between them, making a low rumbling noise in her throat as the giantess tries to regain her bearings. *I can't let her get up.* When the giantess is on all fours, Ossi rushes at her one more time. If she can get on her back again, near the shoulders . . . if she can get access to the neck. But as Ossi gets within range, something new happens. The giantess turns her head, and those ice-blue eyes meet Ossi's before changing to a glowing amber. On instinct, Ossi skids to a stop and leaps back just as the giantess transforms with the same improbable speed as other shifters skilled at the change. And what stands before Ossi now is no longer a giant human. A monstrous bear has spun into the world.

This creature has the same calm, calculating eyes. And she knows what Ossi knows: The math has changed.

The bear ambles forward, and Ossi regains herself in time to dart out of reach of swiping claws, feeling the wind of their passing.

No time for relief. The werebear is even faster than the giantess. Already turning. Already coming at Ossi again, mouth open, long claws reaching.

"Get out of the way!"

Ossi knows the voice. And so she obeys, rolling out of the attack path. The werebear misses again, half distracted. Because someone is falling from the sky.

What they see first: a teenage boy. And then, in that quick change that no eyes, even monster eyes, can process, reality has skipped. And what's waiting on the other side of that skip is even stranger than a usual shift. This is not something either land-borne shifter has seen before. Not in the flesh. This is something large (gargantuan compared to the boy): brownish-green skin of hard plates, more than twelve feet of height, a maw large enough to swallow a person, red glowing eyes, sharp-taloned feet, and wings that blot out the sky behind him.

Dragon has held this form back, revealing it only once, when he needed to save Alex's life. The reason for holding back has always been concern for those around him. Though a dragon is a powerful form to take, it is also impractical in most settings— prone to do more damage than good. Better to change parts of himself—a gift that he uniquely possesses—than change the whole of his appearance. But now, with so much damage already done (not his doing), there is nothing left but to embrace the fullness of what he is.

Dragon comes down for the attack. With her massive claws, the werebear swipes up at him. He weaves away from the swipe, stays low to the ground, and swoops around for another approach. This is a mistake. The bear goes low and comes up beneath Dragon as he passes. She catches Dragon by the neck, bites down, pulls him out of the sky. Pinning Dragon, she claws at his sides, his wings.

The earth trembles from the violent thrashing of these colossal creatures. From Dragon's perspective, chaos. A blur of claws and teeth and fur. Dragon straining under the werebear's weight. Glimpses of the werebear's sharp eyes as she does her damage. She sinks her teeth into Dragon's neck. A quick bite that goes deep. Another bite, this time to Dragon's wing, ripping through the patagium with brutal precision.

Dragon kicks out with taloned feet and finds one of the bear's legs. The werebear falters, and Dragon's long neck snakes up to bite at her face. His jaw closes on air, her weight on him gone. She has leaped off him. Now is the moment. Dragon rights himself and gathers air into his throat, igniting the flame fueled by the special organ in his core. But again she is there, impossibly fast. She wraps her long arms around Dragon, trying to wrestle him to the ground. Dragon wriggles and undulates out from under her grasp. The escape is brief. The werebear's teeth again close on his neck.

Again he tries to eviscerate her with his talons. But this time, she is ready, pushing his leg down with a mighty arm. With deliberate calm, she goes for his other wing. This snaps him into himself, into his instincts, and he barrel-rolls until the werebear loses her grip on him. Once he is free, he flees, shaking the earth with his pounding footsteps. She immediately pursues.

Pure terror seizes Dragon, and he thinks, *I need to get away.* He looks back, and she is there. On his heels. She won't stop. She won't give up until he's dead.

And as he faces the possibility of dying, another voice arises from the back of his mind. It is the voice of his other half. *She is chasing you for a reason.* And suddenly, he understands. Why she has been so aggressive. He remembers all those moments in his life when he underestimated himself or shrank himself down for someone else's benefit or, without realizing it, placed himself in a box of someone else's making. Someone else's idea of his usefulness, of his limits. It has always been an unconscious act on his part, making himself fit neatly into what would be convenient for someone else, to play by their rules in their game.

No longer. Dragon is his name.

He spreads his wings wide. Because of the damaged wing it takes significant effort to launch himself into the air. But his will carries him upward. Dragon leaves everything behind. He surges up and up, beyond the clouds. There's no time for him to kiss the lid of the world. He has work to do. He veers, tucks his wings in, and hurtles earthward. When he breaks the cloud layer, he is already drawing heat into his core. The bear spots him. There is a moment's tension in her body, but then she relaxes. She does not move either. Maybe she can't. Maybe this is the price the Cult exacted from her: to serve at the price of her own life. Most likely, she understands that it is too late. He is falling through the air faster than she can run. The fire that has gathered in his chest rises to his throat. The heat ripples the air. Smoke streams from his nostrils. And when he is close enough, wings flared to keep him aloft, he releases a torrent of flame as large as he is. The bear faces it head-on, eyes dispassionate as the fire takes her whole. Dragon keeps spitting fire until there is none left and the giant shifter is a mound of light gray ash.

When he lands, he turns away. It is done.

The field is littered with still bodies. Many of them are the emaciated corpses of the other side. But there are other bodies as well, lying in the field.

His attention lingers on one of them. Georgie, lying motionless in the grass.

He doesn't feel when it starts: the tingling. Only when it starts to hurt does he notice. The wounds he suffered from the werebear are *burning*. He cranes his long neck to stare down at a wound on his leg and sees the thing writhing there. The body of it is long and thin—a slithering, trembling thing, disappearing beneath the open tissue. Even as it disappears, the glow remains. All over him they squirm, almost translucent, fat on his lifeblood. Soul worms.

His body goes stiff. Dragon can feel dozens of them, working their way deeper and deeper into him, taking over his body inch by inch. This is the Bone Witch's magic, transferred to him by the giantess. Convulsions heave up from inside him—a tight, wrenching sensation. The telltale warmth of building fire.

Desperate, he tries to wrest control from the worms, feeling that strange tug-of-war inside his body as it obeys his will less and less. He pushes the fire down, even as his head turns to the remaining Moonites. Somehow he is within spitting distance. *No, no, no*, he screams inside his own mind, trying and failing to push the fire down.

They are looking at him, but they're not understanding. Dragon tries to speak, but his mouth is not built for it. He tries to change back, but he can feel the worms like hands holding this form in place.

The only thing he can do is close his eyes.

He doesn't see when the sky opens up—a massive portal appearing there. Inside the portal, storm clouds around a central calm—the eye of a hurricane.

The worms release some of their hold on Dragon. He opens his eyes: *What?* He uses the moment to wrest back a little control, and he uses that control to stifle the fire inside him. The action causes the worms to redouble their efforts. No, not the worms themselves—he can feel the Bone Witch beyond them, pulling his strings through them.

Many things happen then:

Sondra, bursting from the tree line, in woo-woo form. The creature, both slender and enormous, barrels in the direction of the Bone Witch, who is standing far across the clearing, amid a thicket of trees. Sondra, bewilderingly fast, the ground giving beneath her, the sky above her an angry, many-tentacled thing around an eye of calm.

The fire builds again, Dragon's mouth opening.

The Bone Witch releases her own woo-woo, empowered by the storm even in his emaciated form. He rushes to meet Sondra.

Fire gathers in Dragon's throat, the light from it brightening in his open mouth.

Another portal gapes in the sky. Through it bounds a shrouded woman astride a gray tiger. A great gray tiger with angel's wings.

Through the soul worms, the Bone Witch redirects Dragon to the sky. Fire rips from him.

The shrouded woman weaves gracefully around the fireball

and flings her shroud free, revealing bare arms covered with tattoos, all of them glowing bright. Two spears materialize in Damsel's hands: one made of light, the other of shadow. She reels back and hurls the first spear. This one strikes the male woo-woo in the shoulder, sending him tumbling into the dirt. She tosses the other spear into her dominant right hand, cocks her arm back again, releases. The spear made of shadow sails through the air and strikes the Bone Witch at terrifying speed, impaling her where she stands. The Bone Witch slumps against the spear. The spear dissolves, and the Bone Witch crumples lifeless to the ground. The magic holding Dragon releases him, and he tumbles out of the change.

Damsel circles the battlefield. She is the only one to see when the pale Zsouvox appears out of a cloud of fine white dust behind the Bone Witch's corpse.

Dragon has returned his gaze to the heavens. He sees Damsel up there, gliding through the sky on Asha's back, Asha's eyes glowing like meteors burning up in the atmosphere. He remembers Damsel's words from years ago: "Asha is the god of everything you know."

A god, Dragon thinks. *Damsel is riding on a god.*

Following Damsel's gaze, he glances to the tree line. He sees the pale Zsouvox coming out of the woods. It is in that familiar child's form, eyes and skin pale as eggshell. The light of the moon sets its skin aglow.

One final portal opens out of Dragon's view.

Damsel's tattoos start to glow. Another black spear materializes in her right hand.

Zsouvox White doesn't seem to care. It looks past Damsel to the opened portal.

Damsel lifts her hand to throw the spear.

"Obliterate," the pale Zsouvox says.

And Damsel's right hand—and the spear she's holding—disappears in a spray of fine dust that vanishes to nothing.

Damsel looks at Dragon. She looks at me. The tattoo at her neck, a perfect circle, changes to the numeral *1*, then *2*, The numbers continue, ascending into a blur. Her tattoos dance on her skin, multiple new sets of tattoos every second, like fresh pages, all of them glowing the brightest blue.

"Obliterate," the pale Zsouvox says again.

Damsel winks at me before she—and Asha—explode into the same shimmering white dust. The fine particles dissolve into nothing before they touch the ground. Gone. Obliterated.

This is when I freeze time.

The Zsouvox goes still, like everything, like everyone.

Until suddenly, terribly, it isn't: first just the eyes, the egg-shell pupils moving in white sclera. The motion is slow, then fast, as the pupils lock on to me. And once they do, the Zsouvox's head moves as well. The expression is unambiguous, knowing. It lifts a hand, and by instinct I shut my eyes, expecting to be obliterated. But then I feel the pull and I reopen my eyes to see that I am rushing toward the pale Zsouvox. I am being pulled by some other power. I feel utter terror—complete, all-encompassing—when, to my left, something else catches my attention. The dark Zsouvox rushing toward *me*. So fast, on a path of inevitable collision. The look on the dark Zsouvox's face is serene with inexplicable acceptance. The dark Zsouvox opens its arms—a welcoming gesture, like a god reaching out to hug the earth. Somehow the moment of impact is soft, tender, the arms of the dark Zsouvox around me. I did not know I could be touched like this, in this place, away from my real body. I am somehow not terrified. The dark Zsouvox is the sun; I am the earth. We move together like dancers, spinning toward the pale Zsouvox. Surprise crosses the pale Zsouvox's face, and then . . . resolve. Time stretches and collapses, and we—the dark Zsouvox and I—complete our journey. The pale Zsouvox's arms open to receive us.

I close my eyes to shut it all out. But it doesn't matter.

On impact, we plunge into a blackness deeper than sleep.

A VISIT WITH THE
UNIVERSE HERSELF

35

Here you are again.

There was a time before I had a mind, but naturally I don't remember it. All this was here when I opened my eyes. I crawled through the muck on my own, brought myself to clarity, to language, to higher thought. And then I spread myself out across all this that you know and all that you don't. I spread myself out until I was all of it, all that you are or have ever been or will be in all your iterations.

I am the forest and the tree.

I knew when it entered. The thing. It was out of time, and then it was in it, arrived at a fixed point, all ink-black tendrils and need. Despair as a mouth, devouring. How can I explain this to you? There was time before it, but once it arrived, it had always been there.

She was there to meet it. Who you call Abyssia, but I call sister and mother and self. She was powerful even before I knew her, but I surpassed her quickly, as I was meant to do for her to become me. But the ink-black thing did not have a chance to find its power here in this realm. It might have, if Abyssia hadn't met it and torn it apart and sent the shards spraying across myself.

I am the forest and the tree.

The shards went everywhere—every time, every place. Then they all were mouths. But eventually, some of them cooled, calmed, became other things than they were. They became loved. They died. Lived again. Became more. And as each shard cooled, I was hopeful, and so was sister-mother-me. But there was one who continued to burn. And now it understood this realm and its own power, and it was still ink-black need, despair, and mouth and devouring. And there was nothing any of us could do for it except let it feed. It burned out whole trees this way. Do you understand? It was a rot. But for a while, we could contain it.

Before, I am told, it was a greater thing, capable of burning whole forests. Do you understand? No, not just what you call a universe. Or a multiverse. The world above the forests, that binds the forests. But also its cradle. It could eat it all. And the gods too. It would all become ink-black mouth. Here, in my forest, in myself, I pressed all that want in, concentrated it into coal, and then smoothed it into clay. And made a new thing of all that pain. Except the one place I couldn't. Do you understand?

I am sorry. Perhaps it is better to say that I am one thing even as I am many, even as I am vast, and that my maker was vast and had made other vastnesses. And that this maker had parent-sibling-sister-brother-lover-children who were also vast and made vastnesses and that all these vastnesses lived in a higher, greater vastness, which could contain vastnesses, all the way down to the smallest vastness. And that this vastness was made from my mother-maker-vastness to keep out the cold. The cold, the thing no one understands, is also the thing the ink-black-need-mouth-devourer wants to be. It is also where we come from, our cradle, though it doesn't love us, because it cannot. But the inky-black-mouth-need-devourer wanted to be loved and so tried to become it, become less than vast by becoming more.

The *nothing* that somehow becomes the *something*.

This part, no one knows. But it is also the part that makes us. We want because we don't understand how we can want. Because we came from unwant, or not-want. But we don't know how or when or why. Do you understand? I ask because I do not. It breaks me. It is what breaks you too. It is all of us, and we can't find it, so we keep searching. But it isn't made. It is maker. And it does not exist.

Without voice. We can hear it when it gets quiet, because it fills the quiet. All the empty spaces, it fills. And something in us senses it there, but it is not there at all, so we keep getting pulled to it. To calm ourselves, we become makers. To face away from it. To want what can be wanted, instead of unwanting.

The inky-black-mouth-need-devourer did not turn away.

I will tell you, but it will not help.

You are falling.

Yes, I know. It scares you, but I can speak with you down here, at the bottom. It doesn't know that I am also here. There is less static in the belly of need.

CONVERGENCE

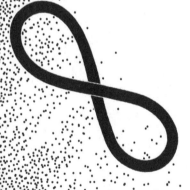

36

I wake up in a soft bed, sheets drawn over me. A fire burns mere feet from my face, crackling over logs. I feel warm, which is the fireplace and the quilt, but I'm groggy as hell. I take my time lifting my head, propping up on one elbow to get a good look at the room. Not my house or the hospital bed. Not anywhere I've ever been. A cabin—small but cozy, well kept, everything in one square room. I can see an open kitchenette, a door in one corner leading into a cramped bathroom, and next to the kitchenette a little square table, two chairs. Someone is sitting in one of the chairs, watching me, as if he just materialized as soon as my eye drifted past him.

I startle—quick electric surge up my spine.

"It's okay," he says. "I'm a friend. Promise."

The man is stocky, broad and thick-limbed. Someone whose work makes him fit but who still has a healthy appetite. Gray-black beard and bushy eyebrows, brown skin. Like someone's kindly grandfather who has worked all his life, who knows nothing but work.

Hesitant, I ask, "What's your name, *friend*?"

"Gishmul."

Something about his voice, about his face, feels familiar. "And how do I know you?"

He smiles, and it is the very picture of a gentle patriarch, cut right out of the dictionary. "You don't know me, not exactly. I am *part* of the Zsouvox."

The first image that comes to mind is the white one.

Seeing my terror, he clarifies: "No, the other one. The one on your side."

"My side," I repeat.

"The side that wants this all to end *without* your whole universe being wiped from existence."

I nod, trying and failing to process what he has said. "Where are we?"

Concern marks his face. "Now, listen, I'm going to need you not to panic. There's a way out of this, promise."

Of course, this has the opposite effect. I am off the bed and going to the only window. Before I touch the sill, I see it, where the firelight is hitting the walls. It looks like wood, standard for a small cabin. But it isn't. Or it is wood *and* something else. All the knots and blemishes on the wood slabs are . . . moving, animated—swirling around and into each other like paintings stitched together; the details shift with each new frame.

I step away from the window as if it will burn me. "Where are we?" I ask again.

He sighs. "Inside the other Zsouvox."

I find the bed again, sit down before I fall over. I am *inside* the other Zsouvox. I try to make sense of that fact but can't.

"When we grabbed you," he says, "we pulled you into us. And then we pushed ourself into the other Zsouvox. It was the only thing to do, the only way you wouldn't end up obliterated."

My first thought: Can't he obliterate us from the inside? But I answer that question for myself. Obviously not, or I wouldn't be here.

"I don't suppose you'll tell me what's going on?" Something is in my ears, I notice, like the sound of the ocean, but with words hiding inside that sound. I can't make it out, but I vaguely remember a conversation I've just had even as it drifts out of reach.

Gishmul is looking at me. "You want some tea?"

"Yes. *Please.*"

Gishmul gets up and pours water from the faucet into a kettle. He whistles as he does this—a tune I've never heard that barely sounds like a melody as I understand the term.

"Every time I've asked someone like you what's going on, I don't get an answer," I say. "Just riddles."

He nods, sage-like, places the kettle on the stove, and lights the flame. I don't see how he lights it. Of any of the gods I've met, he comes closest to my image of one. That fact only makes me more suspicious.

He lets out a breath. "Well, no point in keeping anything from you. How do you want it?"

"From the beginning."

"You sure? Okay, okay." Another breath. "Let's see. All right. Now, this was before my time, but I've heard the story. Just letting you know where my gaps are."

I nod.

"At the beginning of creation—and I mean all creation, not just yours. Your universe came much later. I am talking about the world above this one, the world of the gods—"

My head is swimming, but I don't interrupt.

"—there existed two aspects: Creation and Void. Again, not like your void of space. Absence. True nothing. I've never seen it myself, mind you. But I've heard the story of it. We all have. The gods, I mean. And we were obsessed with it, tried to wrap our heads and our hands around it. The opposite of us. Anti-creation. Apeiron. The closest we gods have to God."

He smiles, all bashful warmth. Naturally, I am unnerved.

"It is a paradox, the beginning of everything. How can something come to exist out of nothing? At first, we were separated into our own god realms, thinking we had always existed. Some of the elder ones, like me, knew there were other gods, had made other gods to try to answer the question we had of ourselves: Could we have been made? We made more of us to see if it was possible. And when we discovered that it was indeed possible, we were scared silent. We dared not reveal ourselves to these gods we'd made. We locked them away from us and closed the door. We left them to their infinities and lived in our own. Until Asha made Akasha, the world above."

The kettle starts to scream.

Gishmul stands and goes to the stove. "When we gods came out of our realms into this vaster realm, we were like children being born. Now we were all there looking at each other, making space for each other, making new infinities together, and sharing our secrets and our fears. A world for us, a meeting place for gods that numbered in the billions. Made by the daughter of that first initial spark of creation."

He laughs as he pours the hot water from the kettle into a mug. He retrieves a tea bag from a glass jar and puts it in the water. "I can see you're struggling to fathom all this. Don't try too hard. Sugar?"

I shake my head, and he passes the tea to me. The mug is brown, the surface swimming like everything else.

"The best way I can explain it is this: Like you, *we* have our world, and there we ask the same questions you do. The difference being that we have infinite time and infinite power to try to answer those questions. How do we exist? Why do we exist? We were excited by those questions. And terrified by them. How's your tea?"

I nod. "It's great. Thank you."

He laughs again. "Wonderful. See, here inside the Zsouvox, the tea is both idea and reality. It tastes like you'd expect, right? And this place: It looks near right, doesn't it? But this is a world inside a being that once spanned god-realms and universes past counting. This place here is a little thing, a pocket world the Zsouvox was allowed to make inside your universe. A tiny island reality."

"So is that what the Zsouvox is? *Nothing?*"

Gishmul shakes his head. "No, no. The Zsouvox could never be that, no matter how much it wants to be. Oblivion does not think, does not want. True oblivion is *not*."

I shake my head, trying to quiet the noise in my brain. "Then what is it?"

The question makes him look sad. "The Zsouvox was made out of our insecurity. Some of us wanted to understand Nothing.

So they tried to make it. They tried to hold it in their hands. It was a group of gods who did it, a secret society. Worshippers of the Question, the Nothing That Created Something, the Prime Paradox. They called themselves the Cult of the Zsouvox."

I sipped my tea. It was hot on my tongue, earthy.

"They didn't know their mistake until it was too late. Eventually, it stopped wanting to be held. And they lost control of it. Before we knew it, the . . . *entity* was bigger than any of us could contain, eating everything, devouring gods and universes and Akasha itself. Taking its fill, with us powerless to stop it. We got lucky. Right before we might have been wiped out, Yun, Asha's living multiverse, gained sentience. No, something more than that. It would be the equivalent of what you'd call a singularity. A created thing, ascending to godhood. Unprecedented. And just what we needed: something big enough, new enough, that the Zsouvox wouldn't know what to do. Somehow Yun knew what was necessary. She devoured the devourer, taking the Zsouvox into herself. She set to work trying to heal the Zsouvox, trying to quell its hunger.

"I am from the part of the Zsouvox that has healed. We are inside the part that has not."

Do I understand what he is saying? Yes. Mostly. Certainly more than I understood when any of the other deities talked to me. A place where the gods lived. Infinities within infinity within an infinite void. Hugh Everett, the physicist who proposed the many-worlds interpretation, had an obsession with infinite regression. That's what this is, or some version of it.

"Why now?" I ask. "Why tell me all this now, after all this time?"

The look on Gishmul's face is pitying. "Friend," he says,

"you're at the last stop on the road. Here . . ." He lets his eyes wander around the cabin, taking it all in for me to see. "What you're inside of is the true reason for all the contracts with your universe, the silence pacts—everything. What we're here to do, in this place, will either destroy everything or save everything."

I stare at him for a very long time.

Eventually, he stands up and walks to the door, pulling a coat from the rack there. "Well," he says, "this will remain abstract to you if you stay here. You have to see it."

I'm standing before I know I'm going to do so. I pull the only other coat from the rack by the door. It fits perfectly.

These coats, this cabin, an old man in regular clothes. None of these things are of the truest reality. But it *feels* real. It makes me wonder: What is the difference? The smile the man gives me as he opens the door feels like many I've seen. The opposite of uncanny. Warm enough to distract me from the bite of cold outside.

"Come on," he says. "Let's go meet the Devourer."

37

As we walk, I draw the coat tighter around me. The *idea* of a coat. It is so cold here, even the trees shiver. The smell of dirt and dead leaves, the feel of deepest winter. A whole world inside a monster's belly that looks and feels like memory, a place I've been but since forgotten. This isn't actually my body, I remind myself. I am lying in a hospital bed at least two realities above this one. The thought makes my head hurt. A real feeling, however improbable, in this place.

I follow Gishmul down a path between the trees. A path made for whom, exactly? I force myself not to think about it.

It isn't far. Through the trees I see a small village. And then we're inside the village. Gishmul's steps remain patient. I take his lead, though I am shaking like crazy, from cold and terror.

As we pass through the village at this center of the Zsouvox, the whole scene descends from eerie to insane. Every house we pass is a different color, made of different materials, designed in ways previously unimaginable. Houses that look like natural structures: anthills and bee nests and coral reefs—organic, living, dynamic, ever-shifting. Houses that have extra dimensions, that hurt to look at, that have tails reaching into the sky. Houses that swirl and amble—stacked, hitched, swollen, heaping structures that glimmer and pulse, phase in and out of existence. It is as if someone took the idea of a house but started from scratch each time. And the gods themselves, looking out at us from windows and holes and gaping mouths, are alien entirely, living beings without referents in this reality. These are not gods defined by anything thought up by human minds.

None of the gods speak. They perceive us, direct their attention to us. Even the ones without eyes I can feel watching me. I try to keep my own eyes fixed on Gishmul's back, as everything in my periphery slips into madness.

"Those . . . people," I say.

"Are ruled by the Devourer. See the castle there?"

Before us is a hill, a winding path leading up to a squat structure crowned with what I can only describe as a halo of antilight. Though I wouldn't call what's ahead a castle, I must admit that it has the aura of something powerful.

Time and distance shrink. Suddenly, we are at the entrance, the door already open. Gishmul enters first, not even pausing before the threshold. I continue behind him. Our footsteps echo in the expanse. The walls are made of some kind of stone, iced over with something viscous that is the color and texture of tar. Every surface reflects us, multiplying our bodies, stretching them thin, curving them into geometric shapes. Above us is a straight line of burning orbs of fire, small suns hung as chandeliers. The floor beneath us is made of glass, a river of black water under that glass, roiling and angry, caught in an endless scream. I keep my attention on Gishmul, tethering myself to his human shape. My heart beats in my ears.

When we reach another open doorway, I lose my courage. "I'll stay behind," I say. The words echo off the walls, shatter beneath my feet.

"You are needed," Gishmul says. "As witness."

"What does that mean?"

Gishmul doesn't answer with words. He puts out his hand for me to hold as if he were guiding a child, and steps through the doorway with me trailing behind him. We come to an inner chamber, red like the inside of a heart, and beating just the same. The walls are flesh. The floor is blood. A tall figure sits on a throne before us. The throne itself has eyes, is made up of eyes. The figure on the throne is humanoid, at least in the sense that it has bilateral symmetry and the requisite number of limbs. That's where the comparisons end. Again, my head hurts just to look.

As we get closer, the figure stands. Fifteen feet tall. I look up to its face, which isn't a face at all but a mosaic of shattered rainbowed glass, set into grout. Only the grout hasn't set. Black and viscous as the stuff on the walls of the castle, roiling like liquid, the thick sludge pulls our awareness inexorably to the eyes: three of them, like churning whirlpools, like indigo suns, bright and shining. They burn the air, and the shattered glass on that face pulses and rattles and bobs, each shard, each slab, hitting against the others atop that whirling black murk as thick as tar.

"Ox-ai," Gishmul says. "It has been a long time."

The figure says something, but not with its mouth—it has none. The voice erupts from the center of its chest and is so deep that the whole room trembles. My skull aches as it speaks. When it stops, the pressure releases.

"Please speak so the witness here can understand," Gishmul says.

The figure speaks again, and this second utterance has me holding my hands over my ears to protect myself. But nothing I can do can stop me from hearing that terrible sound.

"Please. It is in the contract," Gishmul says.

"I signed no contract," Ox-ai says. This time, I can actually understand it, though there is no indication that Ox-ai has even noticed the change. The sound of its voice hurts just the same.

Gishmul says, "We signed the contract in your stead."

Ox-ai smiles, a row of broad glass teeth unhinging from its not-mouth, parting skin that isn't skin.

I want desperately to run, but I hold myself to the spot, returning its gaze.

"What an amusing little thing," Ox-ai says.

"Lower your voice," Gishmul says. "Calvin can't take it. Speak as I speak."

"Is that its name?" Ox-ai says, with an expression I have no context to understand. I have to clench my jaw shut to keep the sound out of my insides. But its voice feels less likely to explode my brain this time. The rattling in my skull ceases, and I take my hands off my ears.

"Now that we've wasted enough time on your pet there, can we get on with it? What do you want to say before you take your place among my subjects?"

"Your subjects," Gishmul repeats. He says something else after that, but it is in another tongue, unmoored from any history of human language.

Ox-ai replies in the same language, then condescendingly says, "But let's not be rude to Calvin."

"I came to say I'm sorry," Gishmul says. "And set things right."

Ox-ai does something with its mouth. Amusement? "You have no reason to be sorry," it says. "I've won."

"Yes," Gishmul says, his face unreadable. "You 'winning' was how we established trust. Our goal: get you to integrate with us and *not* obliterate us. All the fuss, all the fighting, was to sell you on the idea. Convince you that merging was something you wanted, that it was your way out."

Ox-ai's face shifts several times, churning and churning until it crashes like water on rocks. Then it resets back to its standard viscoid mess. "I don't believe you."

Gishmul nods with something like approval. "You were the first of the gods I made, the first of my line. I created you to help me overcome my greatest fear, the gnawing suspicion that I did not know myself, that someone had kept some core part of myself hidden from me. I tried to answer that suspicion myself and couldn't. The paranoia ate away at me."

Something begins to move inside Ox-ai. I can see it, a storm seething in the belly of the god.

Gishmul continues: "I wanted to know if an alien, opposing force could live inside a god—a force that resisted being known to that god."

And suddenly, Ox-ai is shouting. I have to cover my ears again as the whole chamber threatens to shudder apart.

I've missed something. I look to both of them to determine what it was.

"What did you do to me!" Ox-ai yells.

A chandelier in the ceiling falls and crashes behind us, a sun shattering against black glass.

Gishmul continues, louder: "I made you. I made the antithesis of you. I placed your antithesis *inside* you. And then I told it to hide."

Ox-ai is cracking, shattering. Fissures form all around us; suns fall into the black current below; the walls bleed.

"I did it because I could," Gishmul says. "To know if it could have been done to me. I didn't know then that you would help make the Zsouvox. I didn't know that the Zsouvox would latch itself to the thing inside you. It is the reason you haven't been able to heal. I am here to undo that part of you so that you can finally heal."

Ox-ai screams.

And Gishmul starts *singing*, a series of notes that are also words. But not words uttered from any human mouth. Something else: a voice, a song, with no referent in this reality. It goes on for a long time, in this place where time has no meaning. The only marker is Ox-ai: Ox-ai screaming, Ox-ai sobbing, Ox-ai softly crying, Ox-ai silent. And as this happens, other changes occur. Ox-ai shrinking, becoming that other child . . . Ox-ai transforming into the pale Zsouvox, eyes the color of eggshell. Ox-ai—the pale Zsouvox—in tears.

Gishmul is in tears too. "It was a terrible thing I did. And so much suffering because of it. This has been an education. For us all."

More song, and Ox-ai transforms again. In the place of the pale child: a black egg, dripping darkness, the floor beneath opening, peeling, the inky water parting to reveal . . . void.

And somehow I know. We are staring into the edge of things.

Gishmul does not pause. He presses his hands together, steps forward, touches both palms to the egg. The song crescendos, rises to a new plateau. And beyond that plateau are both sight and sound. In the song, I can see other universes, multiverses—an omniverse of worlds breathing in and out, sharing breath, finding voice together. Light shines up from beneath the black egg, blanketing everything with warmth.

I feel myself slipping, sliding toward the center of the light. Gishmul reaches out one hand to stop me.

Step back, he instructs, his voice in my head while his song continues uninterrupted. *If you fall in, no one will find you.*

I obey. I can still feel it pulling at me, that pit radiating light. I hold myself back. I listen to the music of Gishmul's voice but try not to get too caught up in it. There is a greater flash of light and the sound of chimes, and my mind is transported. I am on the floor, staring up at snowfall, snow all around me. I am standing on the rim of a deep cavern, a pink sky above. I am under still water, rain falling on the surface above me as if onto rippling glass. Then I am in front of the pit again. Only there is no pit, just Ox-ai, blinking at us both. The child form of Ox-ai. Still pale white, but the eyes are now a strangely iridescent shade of gray.

Bewildered, I watch Ox-ai. And it watches me, the same expression reflected.

"Is it over?" it asks, I ask.

Gishmul nods. "It is," he says to Ox-ai, adding, "That feeling inside you, that other emptiness. It is what we all feel, always. Ignore it."

Ox-ai says nothing. Again tears begin to fall from its eyes. But these tears are different. Ox-ai is experiencing . . . joy.

Gishmul turns to me. "Time to go. We're done here."

"How do we get out?" I ask.

It is Ox-ai who answers. "Close your eyes."

I do as I'm told, and I feel it. Actual hands, not a metaphor, and a cliff that I didn't know was there—a sort of metaphor—and me falling off that cliff. The sensation makes me open my eyes, but by the time I do, I am stumbling on grass, back in the clearing we left. A quiet battlefield around me. Everyone is staring in our direction—looking past me, actually. Because standing next to me is the Zsouvox. Neither pale nor dark, but smooth gray, like clay on a pottery wheel. Clothes the same color: a simple short-sleeved shirt and pants. Androgynous, with eyes that same uninterrupted gray, the pupils large, like a deer's. A face so serene—docile, even—that I know its power just by looking.

"We are sorry," they say, this new and great god.

No one living responds.

And then the Zsouvox is gone.

For those who remain only seconds have passed: the Zsouvox appearing, their apology, the flash of brilliant light, the Zsouvox gone, the silence afterward full of grief.

The battlefield is littered with corpses and people huddled in mourning.

Dragon looking at the place where Georgie fell. Connor resting in a crater made of his own body, blood pooled around him. Laina, a limp thing lying between two wailing wolves. Ossi watching over everyone, predictably vigilant.

Only one place holds anything but torment. There, a naked Sondra stoops to embrace her naked father, who, because of Damsel's magic, has been able to shift out of the form he has worn for over a decade. He is crying quietly and she is crying quietly, both out of relief. They exchange whispered words, holding each other tightly.

Footsteps approach, too light for any human ears to perceive. But not for the ears of weredogs. Sondra turns her ear to the sound, then her nose. A faint smile, delicate on her tear-streaked face.

"Sister," she says, and to her father: "Your other daughter is here."

He looks up, smelling her too. Renewed sobs of gratitude.

Sonya stops a foot from them, still uncertain, still afraid that this goal she has fought so hard for will be swept away, taken from her. So many things have been taken from her.

"Are you coming or not?" Sondra asks.

Sonya, invisible, takes one step toward her father and her sister, takes another, and then is running to their side, stooping down and throwing her hands over them both. She releases a gentle sigh. So does her father—a rumbling of deep contentment from inside his chest.

"We've gone through hard times," Sondra says to her beautiful sister. "But we've also been lucky. Most people don't get to have this. A reunion, after all this time."

"Your mother," their father says.

"We'll take you to her." The words rise out of Sonya's throat at the same time that Sondra says them, the two utterances perfectly synchronized. For the first time in ages, they are completely on the same page. No prophecies or misaligned allegiances between them. No impossible tasks to complete. Just this moment, their father between them—the very last thing Sonya needed to do so that she might be free.

38

In those days after the battle outside Moon, the community center is converted to a large hospital room. The doors and windows are left open to let air in, the fans hung from the high ceiling spinning lazily. At every hour of the day, people pass in and out of the community center to grab food, to talk, to visit the dying or those trying to live. To hope.

There are now five cots in the room. There were six after that first night, but the occupant of that sixth cot is now lying in a fresh grave. On the other five are Jesmeen, Espeth, Georgie, Laina, and Alex.

It is nearing eight o'clock, and the sun is setting. The lights are all on, mixing with the last of the sunlight.

The gods and all their high servants are all long gone now. The monsters and the people remain. And the ants, which continue to monitor their charges on the cots. It is not unusual to see an ant crawl out of the mouth or ear or nostril of the sedated, or cut into or out of the skin with delicate precision, leaving no blood or scarring behind.

Watching an ant crawl out of Laina's glistening neck, Rebecca is reminded of a recurring dream she used to have, of little people carving her father's body out of bread. The strange malleability of Laina's flesh in the mandibles of machine ants disturbs her. She imagines, under Laina's skin, spongy layers of dough . . . breathing.

Against the wall, Manny sits, hair shading his eyes, a book in his lap. Rebecca has gotten so used to this . . . She doesn't know what to call it. Stance? Stature? The way he can exist at near stillness. She's gotten so used to it, sometimes she forgets he is even there. Manny turns a page, releases some soft sound from between his lips, returning him to her awareness. What is he feeling right now? He doesn't even argue with her anymore, so she has no idea what he feels in general, let alone in this specific moment.

Laina's breath is even, calm despite the thin sheen of sweat on her skin. Her mouth is soft, the muscles there at rest, but the terrain between her eyebrows is bunched up as if in quiet contemplation.

She has asked the ants if Laina will wake up. So far, they have opted not to answer.

Ridley approaches, holding out a tuna sandwich.

Rebecca shakes her head.

"You need to eat," Ridley says.

Rebecca bunches up her nose. "I don't want it." It occurs to her that she's behaving like a child, but she doesn't care.

Ridley looks to Manny: "Help me out here?"

Manny just shakes his head.

With a huff of frustration, Ridley says, "I heard your stomach growling a while ago."

"I'm not hungry."

Ridley doesn't point out the contradiction. He puts the extra tuna sandwich on the table near the cot and sits in the fold-out chair he's been occupying.

Compared to Rebecca, he seems almost calm. She hasn't confronted him about why, because the "almost" is important where Ridley is concerned. She knows him well enough to understand how much worry he carries behind those small outward signs of distress. He is controlling himself in hopes that the same control will manifest in the world around him. He always does this, and most of the time it annoys Rebecca, but not now. She's glad he is there trying to be okay so she can lean on him.

"I have good news," Ridley says. "Probably not what you want to hear right this minute, but it might give some small comfort."

Rebecca turns to look at him with an anger that she has to push out through her breathing.

Ridley notices this, of course, so he doesn't continue right away. He waits for her to calm down. Minutes later, he says, "I didn't mean it that way. You know I didn't. Nothing can make your worry better."

"What is it?"

"We're going to try to permanently defend Moon."

Rebecca asks how.

"I've been talking to Alex. She's doing better, by the way."

"I don't care."

"Yes, you do. Don't be like that," he says. "Alex knows Shaya

Joshi. She's the progressive Democratic candidate, currently ahead in the polls . . ."

Rebecca tries very hard not to turn away from Ridley. Why should she care about this person? Nothing outside Moon matters. And soon Moon won't matter. No matter what he says, they'll have to leave.

"Are you listening?"

"Yes," Rebecca lies. "Go on."

"We're going to use the ants to visit her, make a deal. And if she wins—"

"What?" Rebecca says. "She'll get the National Guard down here to camp outside Moon?"

"No," Ridley says. "Okay, I see now isn't really the right time."

Rebecca turns away, shutting down any curiosity she has. Besides, nothing they've ever tried on their own has done a lick of good. Since the beginning, they've always been reacting to the plans of other people.

The next ten minutes pass in silence.

"She looks better today," Ridley offers.

"She looks the same."

Ridley doesn't argue. He picks up the extra sandwich and starts eating it. If this is him being petty, it's useless effort.

Rebecca watches another ant come out of Laina's nose. Then three more. A startling increase in number compared to what she has witnessed over the past few days.

All these years together, and Laina has never looked more like Lincoln than in this moment, in sleep. All that armor—and, yes, Laina, too, has armor—at rest, revealing the person underneath, vulnerable yet strong.

She replays the moment the giantess squeezed Laina, that feeling of helplessness and fury, that wishing to be able to twist time back on itself, send it backward so she might save her love. She felt something like it when she watched Sarah die. She felt it when she heard that Lincoln was dead. She wished she could say she felt it when Connor finally died, but for her it felt like bargaining with the universe. Take this one, but not her. She wishes she could feel awful about that, but first Laina has to live. She can mourn, beat herself up, grieve her latest lost friend, if Laina lives. For now, she remains arrested, unable to do anything but wait.

The sound of her stomach growling brings her back to the moment. She can feel Ridley's eyes on her, his silent judgment. She continues ignoring him.

"Say the word, and I'll bring you another sandwich," he says.

This time, she considers eating. "I don't want tuna. Put some cold cuts and mayo on some bread. Untoasted."

Ridley groans. "I'm sorry. I have to say it. You eat like a white kid from the suburbs."

"You'd know," she says.

Ridley laughs, just a little, putting a hand to his chest as if wounded. "Good to know you're still sharp beneath all that sulking."

Rebecca doesn't reply. She has used up all her energy in the short exchange.

A sigh escapes her as Ridley stands and quietly slips away. With that second sense, that little bit of magic that allows her to sense others, she feels him moving away from her.

Five minutes pass.

"Haven't you read that before?" she asks Manny, nodding to the open book in his lap.

First, he simply shrugs. But then, a miracle: "I'm reading it again."

"Why?"

"Until Laina wakes up."

His response is more a clarification than an answer to Rebecca's direct question. And yet . . .

Rebecca tries to meet her brother's eyes.

As usual, he's hiding, his body language remaining closed off.

But Rebecca knows her brother, recognizes the tone of his voice. When their father died, Rebecca was all outward emotion, all rage, trying to intimidate the world into being what she wanted it to be. Like their mother, Manny made statements, poured all of himself into them, all his will. Perhaps, if he believed hard enough, the world could be what he wanted.

"It'll be okay," Rebecca says, parroting Ridley.

Briefly the hair in front of her brother's face parts like a curtain, like the Red Sea, and she can see his eyes. A moment of connection, there and gone in a blink. But enough.

More minutes, and another ant leaves Laina. Rebecca watches it move across Laina's clothes—a sterile white linen shirt and pants—until it reaches the hem of the shirt and stops. Rebecca can't say what possessed her to put her hand down next to the ant. She only registers it as strange once the ant crawls onto her hand. It crawls up her arm, her shoulder, her neck, and then along the curve of her jaw until reaching her ear.

When it speaks, she listens.

• • •

Across the room, under the tent, Dragon and Ossi and Alex are talking.

"Will you come?" Dragon asks.

Both Ossi and Dragon are standing over Alex's cot. Despite being awake, Alex remains bedridden, her chest a crater, making it hard to speak more than a sentence at a time.

"Where will we go?" Alex asks.

"Anywhere," Dragon says. "All over."

"We'll follow the stories," Ossi says. "Find the monsters that need us, and take care of the people who want to harm us. Be proactive, for once."

Something about the way Dragon isn't meeting her gaze makes Alex ask, "How's Georgie? You check on her?"

This gets a glare out of him. "Will you answer us or not?"

Alex gathers herself, which takes a great deal of energy. It feels as though she has to inflate her chest, force air into it as if into a balloon, before she can speak. She says, "This is not something I can bring to Shaya."

Dragon shakes his head. "We're not asking you to do that. Besides," he says, "no one else can know—only us. They won't understand."

Is he right? she wonders. Would they not understand? It is true that the rest of the Moonites come from a world of clear lines. Alex and Ossi—Dragon too, she must admit—come from a world where you sometimes have to be the aggressor to protect someone. But continued aggressive actions coming from within the monster settlements will keep these communities from ever finding peace. Vigilantism isn't something they can afford to implicate Moon in.

"I won't play their game anymore," Dragon says. "I'm not

sitting around waiting for things to happen or for anyone to tell me what needs doing. I want to find my own will."

Looking at the boy, Alex can finally see what he will become. The reality both fills her with hope and terrifies her. Like her, Dragon is ready and willing to stare into darkness and not flinch. But with Dragon, the darkness will cower. He will be a terrifying, burning light.

Luckily, he's on their side.

"And you, Ossi?" Alex asks. "Why do you want to do this?"

"Because someone needs to be at the door defending places like this," she says. Then she pauses, thinking for a moment, and in a very quiet voice adds, "Because this is all I've known. I'm useful this way."

Alex must admit that this is also true of her. She is meant for the shadows. She climbed all the way down into the depths, and no matter what she has done or will do, she can never climb out again. She sees her mother at the bottom of a well, only now she is down there with her, looking up, the mouth of the well high above her head, opening to a gray sky.

"You're quiet," Ossi says. "Does that mean you're with us?"

"I am with you," Alex says, having to gather herself. She puts up a hand so she can say more. "Who else?"

"Sonya," Ossi says. "And Karuna, when she chooses. I don't trust anyone else from the Order of Asha."

"Not Sondra?"

"She needs to leave Moon," Dragon says. "But we should keep her hands clean. She will advocate for us politically."

Alex nods, because of course that makes sense. "You've grown so much," she says to Dragon, and for a moment, standing between them, she can see Tez. They both look like him, each in their own way—Dragon so tall now, slender but strong, and Ossi carrying a truer physical likeness and that same force of will, perhaps even greater than Tez's.

"Well, you've thought it all out," she says, gasping. She feels suddenly overwhelmed by exhaustion. "Okay. Okay. I'm with you. Just let me rest."

When they leave, a voice comes out of the darkness of the tent. "I am sorry to say that even this is according to their plans."

Alex smiles. It takes a whole lot of effort for her to speak again, but Sonya waits.

"We're all set comfortably on our little tracks," Alex says. "And now, with no more deus ex machinas to save us, or blame when things go badly, it's all up to us now."

"Dragon will do well," Sonya says. "It is foretold."

"And the rest of us?"

Sonya takes a while to answer. "I don't know. We're not meant to know, I guess." Another silence. "I used to be so good at that: accepting. Now . . ."

Alex endures a bout of coughing before saying, "Now you've lost too much."

It is a statement of fact and of solidarity. No confirmation required.

And Sonya doesn't offer one. Alex only sees the tent flap open ever so slightly, leaving her alone again with her thoughts.

Alex thinks of Tez, the way the world rippled before he was blown apart. And her mother, face destroyed, heart ripped from her chest. And Mister, the last time she saw him, right before he sank his teeth into her neck.

Seconds and hours and days and months and years. They are only different demarcations of time. She may live centuries after this. Or pull herself out of bed right now and step into sunlight.

No. She won't do the latter. She doesn't have that kind of courage. She is a monster. And Mister was right—she has been one for a long time, even before the change.

A monster keeps on living. A monster survives out of spite.

• • •

Ridley returns with another sandwich. Seeing the expression on Rebecca's face, he absently sets it down where the last one was.

"What? What is it?" he asks.

"Georgie is brain-dead," Rebecca calmly says. "The ants are keeping her alive, but they can't restore brain activity. The head trauma was too severe. They say—"

"We have to decide when to let her die." Ridley is a mirror of calm, though she can see a slight tremble in his right hand.

Rebecca nods. "We'll do it at sunset. Give people a chance to be there if they want, say goodbye."

"I know you don't want to hear this," Ridley says, "but considering our odds going into that battle . . ."

Rebecca doesn't lash out verbally, but the look she gives him is enough. She lets her expression soften, though. "You're right. We were lucky."

He doesn't say anything, only watches her as if she were a bomb set to explode.

"Laina is improving," Rebecca says. "Espeth and Jesmeen too."

"What?" Surprise on his face, and the first signs of unaffected relief.

Manny looks up from his book.

"They are responding well to treatment," Rebecca adds. "Laina especially."

"I knew it," Ridley says. "She was looking better."

The relief on Ridley's face is a thing to behold. Manny's too. He is *smiling*. She never sees him smile anymore.

"I'm sorry for snapping at you earlier," she says to Ridley.

"I understand. I'd snap at me too. I'm not good at this. Comforting people."

"Which is strange. You're good at almost everything else."

This gets a laugh out of him—a little self-conscious, a little desperate, like a child's. "I love you both," he says. "You're everything to me."

"We love you too. It might have taken me and you longer to figure it out, but thanks to our girl here—"

Ridley's gaze has traveled down to Laina's cot, mouth open. Rebecca turns to see.

"Look at you both," Laina rasps. "Getting along without me. Finally."

39

Later, Ossi knocks on Dragon's door. As she enters, she looks around the spare living room: a single large rug under the coffee table, a television set against one wall, a large couch opposite. She nods approvingly. "Nice."

And, yes, in comparison to Ossi's own living situation, it *is* nice. Alex had little interest in decorating, and Dragon possesses little talent for it. So this is the result: a nice, spare, lifeless living room that matches the rest of the house.

Dragon doesn't smile.

"We don't have to talk," Ossi says. "I'm just here."

Georgie kept a nice house. Dragon took that place for granted, but he liked visiting because her house had a certain aliveness. It felt like a home. Before Georgie's, in the last place Dragon stayed that felt like a home, he had imagined a whole different life—one where he was a normal boy who did normal things. Those dreams had lasted one day before the family in that house was murdered.

Dragon wipes at his eyes, gestures to the couch.

Ossi gives a satisfied sigh as she sits down. "Comfy," she says. And then: "Alex was looking for you at the burial."

"I wasn't there," Dragon says, joining her.

Ossi nods slowly. "Seriously, why is this couch so soft? Mine's so stiff."

"What are you doing?"

Ossi looks surprised. "What?"

"Why are you talking about the couch?"

"I'm engaging in small talk." Ossi frowns. "And it isn't working. Forgive me, you just look . . ."

Distantly, Dragon is flattered that he could move Ossi, of all people, to small talk, to asking forgiveness, to being rendered speechless. His more immediate emotions, however, remain frustration and anger.

"You know the last thing she told me, after we scared off the Black Hand the second time? 'Don't let anyone use you.' And then she hugged me."

"She was a sweet woman. Kind."

"How many people have you lost?" Dragon asks.

Ossi's frown deepens. But she pays him another compliment. She answers. "My entire family. And before this, many of the people I swore my protection to. Life . . . is loss."

Nothing could make Dragon feel better. But this makes him feel less lonely, along with other, more complicated emotions. "I'm sorry."

"Why apologize? Besides, most of these wounds are old now. And the newer ones have already started to lose their sting." She sits for a moment, staring down into her lap, considering something. "When I found out that my brother was dead, the most surprising feeling was the lack of feeling. The numbness."

Dragon nods at this too. "I've been there."

"There are different kinds of numbness. There's shock." She looks at him, eyes searching his. "And there's the numbness of not being surprised, of meeting your tragic expectations. You're young, but . . ." She continues watching him, eyes unblinking, expression resolute. "You've already had a long life. You know what it means to expect the worst and greet it when it inevitably meets you."

"I really liked your brother."

"I did too. He was an idiot, but I liked him. I love him."

"How old are you?"

"I don't know. Those early years, we didn't keep track. Over three hundred, maybe. If I tried hard enough, I could probably guess down to the decade I was born. But that's not your real question. You want to know if it gets easier. No. It doesn't. You're still growing. I can tell that eventually your aging will slow. As the people around you die, you will live on. And with a life like ours, full of violence, maybe eventually death will find the both of us too."

Dragon doesn't need to say anything. The understanding is in his eyes. Life is loss.

"I was supposed to come here and comfort you."

"You're not good at it," Dragon says.

She laughs softly.

"But I like this better."

She laughs more. "I have at least one good thing to say."

"What is it?"

"I think you'll be easier to keep alive."

The laugh that escapes Dragon startles him, but he lets it come and go without shame. "You too."

"Now, Alex might be a problem."

"You think?"

"The girl's got a pretty persistent enemy." She smirks at Dragon's bafflement. "The sun."

And for the second time, Dragon laughs.

"It is a miracle any vampires survive at all. Living for eternity and can't even go to the beach?"

That sends him into a fit of tearful laughter. How wonderful that there are other reasons to cry.

"I've never seen the ocean," Dragon says.

"You're not serious."

"Well, I've seen some lakes. The Charles River. Oh, and the Dorchester Bay, but only from a distance."

"That's not what I meant by 'beach,' anyway. I'm talking about the tropics." She smiles, clarifies. "Down south, near the equator."

"I've never been that far south."

Ossi reaches out, pats him on the shoulder. "Well, let's make a deal. You still owe me a flight, so if you take me up," she says, pointing skyward, "then I'll take you down. I can show you some beaches, take you to where I was born. And from there, we'll see."

Dragon grins. "An easy deal to make."

SHAYA JOSHI

Shaya receives two unexpected visits. The second one is in her office at the Capitol, late at night, after her staff has left. After she would have left too, if she hadn't used the Senate gym's pool that night and then stopped by her office for a change of clothes.

As she turns on the lights, he's there standing by the door.

"Senator Joshi."

Shaya isn't an easy person to frighten, but she screams. When she realizes he is in fact someone she knows, she removes the hand from her chest, even as her heart continues to race. "What the hell are you doing here?"

"You remember me," he says. "Good."

Shaya laughs, but it comes out a little shrill—she is still catching her breath. "You look exactly the same," she says. "I mean, *exactly* the same. I'd have to have head trauma to not recognize you. *Significant* head trauma."

Good grief. She is repeating herself. Shaya takes a few quick breaths before crossing the room to her desk. She sits down.

He sits across from her, shifting his body in the chair to face her. When he's comfortable, he crosses his legs and steeples his fingers together on the top knee. "Since we're old friends—"

"That's not how I'd put it."

"—I think we should just be direct with each other. I come to you as a representative of an organization. It is very old, and we've recently experienced . . . well, I guess it could best be described as an internal restructuring. Over the past few months, I've managed to rise in influence within this organization."

Shaya is watching his mouth open and close, looking for sharp teeth.

"And I've convinced them that you are someone we should put our substantial influence behind."

Shaya clears her throat. "So, this is a sales pitch, right? You want to know what price I'd demand for my soul."

"You catch on fast," he says.

"I've had these conversations before. Not quite like this— no one has shown up in my locked office before—but you don't get this far without powerful people waving carrots in your face so you'll do what they want. Or sticks." Shaya squints at him. "What's the stick?"

She has to hand it to the man. He doesn't skip a beat. "I'm sure you're old enough to realize that your parents could not have amassed their own power and influence without allies. And certainly not without getting their hands dirty every once in a while." His smile is all polite remorse. "Their misdeeds could be made known, which will surely cause a scandal you don't want when you're so close to getting elected."

"I'm not leading in the polls currently," Shaya says, trying to appear unruffled herself.

"Yes," he says, "but you'll win nonetheless."

Shaya folds her arms and leans back in her chair, relaxes her posture. She is steadier now, and she needs to tell her body that this isn't a life-or-death situation, even though it is. She'll need to be calm for the next several minutes.

He continues: "Without our help, you won the primary. The general will be close—you're far too progressive for a lot of Americans—but it will ultimately go to you. So you might be wondering: Why would you need our help? Well, the House is blue, but the Senate is split. And we have several . . . *sticks* that can help your first term in office pass smoothly, and with major wins under you since I know you intend to come in with an ambitious agenda. An agenda that can fail if you can't get the right support. Sure, you've prepared for that outcome. But what if you didn't have to worry about that? What if support comes to you?"

"And what does your organization want in return?"

"Nothing yet. Just your ear. And a heads-up on any policy you plan to implement."

"I'm surprised," Shaya says. "I was expecting you to try to stop my progressive ambitions, nefarious organization that you are."

"That's a reductive label. I wouldn't call us nefarious. Any large system needs an invisible hand."

"Invisible hand," she says with a huff. "I can't take you seriously if you talk like this."

Again she has to give him credit. His laughter seems genuine—disarming, even—and might have worked on her if she didn't know who he is.

"I'll put it another way," he says. "I've managed to convince my organization that social and economic change is good for us. A worthy compromise. It will help stabilize our current situation."

"You mean the monster situation."

"Yes. But also all the other perils of late-stage capitalism. Stability prevents another French-style revolution, but on a global scale. We're trying to head that off, if we can."

"By 'we,' you mean the Order of the Zsouvox, right, Mr. Trapp?"

At this, Mister can't hide his astonishment, and, oh, is it satisfying!

"Or do you prefer your surname from birth?"

All the time Shaya and Alex were best friends, she had never seen Alex's adoptive father ever display any outward affect but perfect calm. It is delightful to see him panic now, even a little.

"I'll give you a moment to collect yourself," Shaya says. "In the meantime, I'll summarize my position. Unfortunately—for you, I mean—I won't be accepting help from your organization. But I won't be actively seeking your destruction either. That's the carrot, by the way."

Mister's eyes, which were darting about—trying to put some things together, if Shaya has to guess—finally settle back on her.

And, mercies above, there it is again: that perfect calm, returned. "You've talked to someone in the Order of Asha."

"No. They didn't go by that name, though I believe some of them might once have been a part of that organization."

"Right," Mister says, mouth pursed.

He's coming to some conclusion, she observes with a little disappointment. She wants to fuck with him a little more, but alas, there's more business to discuss.

"So why won't you destroy us?" he asks her. "I assume the invisible woman gave you her burn book. All the world's secrets she's been able to uncover."

"No, not all. She was explicit about that. Enough to topple your organization, force you into the light. A den of vampires with ex-presidents among its membership. Presidents and prime ministers, royalty, notable political and business figures. And several great men." She winks at Mister. "Information that's sure to raise some hell."

"And you're sure people will believe you."

"There's a lot of evidence. Honestly, I don't know how she got all that stuff."

"The tech mage," Mister says without elaborating.

"And you won't be able to steal it either. Anything happens to me, it leaks. You step out of bounds, it leaks. Look at me funny . . ." Shaya laughs. "I'm overdoing this whole intimidation thing, aren't I?"

Mister watches Shaya with serene curiosity. "Why not destroy us now?"

"Right. You asked that." Shaya lets the pause drag on for an uncomfortable few seconds.

Mister does not budge.

She sighs with exasperation. "*Because* it doesn't serve me. I want to be president. I want to change things. Better to have you in my pocket than out you to the world."

Mister unfolds his legs, gracing Shaya with a devious smile. "This is desirable for me as well."

She raises an eyebrow.

He continues. "With the Order of the Zsouvox suitably muzzled, we can build a better world."

"We?"

"Yes. You and me. I've always wanted to find the spider at the center of the web. Now we are that spider."

"You're not understanding the situation," Shaya says. "You work for me. We don't work together."

Mister nods, the same awful smile. "Yes, as you say, of course." He stands to leave. "Good night, Madam President."

Shaya waits for him to reach the door before she speaks. She has one small stick she can throw away. "Good night, Mr. Marx."

Infuriating to the end, Mister doesn't turn or pause or do anything else that Shaya can savor later. He simply walks out the door.

When he is gone, Shaya allows herself to fall apart. She collapses to the floor under her desk, curling up in the tight space, knees pressed to her chest.

She desperately needs a smoke, but she promised Brit that she would abandon that vice. The antianxiety meds aren't working right now either. The only thing to do is sit with this, roll through the panic.

In all this craziness, Shaya is completely out of her depth. But what else is new? She has always punched above her weight. Today is no different.

For three weeks, Shaya has been battling with herself, keeping her psyche intact by sheer force of will.

Mister was late by three weeks.

There were five who came, out of a rent in reality. Alex, she obviously recognized. But she also recognized the former Senator Paige, from the Virgin Islands. Wife of the murdered Senator Reed, whose body was recovered in his living room. The room was strangely empty of furniture. The cracks and bullet holes

in the floor and walls, however, could not be removed. Except
for his blood, there was no other DNA evidence anywhere in
that house. And his wife had disappeared. Shaya followed the
story and knew that Reed was championing pro-monster legislation, knew that former Senator Paige had been revealed as a
monster sympathizer if not a monster herself, and knew that she
had disappeared on the same day her husband turned up dead.

The other three people who showed up at her house were
a teenage boy, a woman who looked to be in her thirties but
carried herself with the authority of a matriarch, and an invisible woman.

And they came with their own offer.

A noise below, in her living room, had woken her. The
noise wasn't loud. It sounded like someone knocking on the
door, but from the inside—someone knocking on the walls
inside her house.

She woke with a start.

Brit rolled over. "What is it?"

"Nothing," she had replied, caressing Brit's back. "Go back
to sleep."

Brit wasn't fully awake, so she settled easily.

Shaya kept listening. The knock came again, softer, as if it
knew she was awake.

Shaya wasn't afraid as she descended the stairs. As a child,
she had heard noises in her parents' house—this house—all the
time, and it always turned out to be nothing, so she expected
the same outcome. But what she saw, after she came down the
stairs and entered the living room, she would never forget for
the rest of her life.

The living room was the same: large fireplace with

the big-screen television she had installed above it, the L-shaped couch where she slept sometimes on lazy weekend afternoons, the huge framed portrait on the wall, of her with her parents when she was a teenager. Only now there was a hole right next to it. A hole in reality, shaped like a doorway.

Shaya had walked up to that doorway, entranced. Across the threshold, she saw a small, nondescript apartment, and four people seated around a small dining-room table with five chairs, one empty.

Alex was one of them, and she smiled. "It's all right," she said. "Come in so we can talk."

Shaya had done so, stepped right through the portal. After she stepped through, she heard soft footsteps behind her, and the brush of what felt like another person slipping through the portal behind her. She looked back. Heavens above, she looked back, purely on instinct, just in time to see the hole in her living room close. What remained was a closed door, rimmed with what at first looked like a strip of metal but then, as Shaya looked more closely, proved to be . . . ants. Metal ants, the head of one ant clamped by its mandibles to the abdomen of the ant in front, all the way around the frame of the door. A uniform pattern, like a design on wallpaper, but the abdomens of the ants had been glowing and were now starting to dim.

Shaya couldn't help it; she shouted out in alarm. Finally, fear had taken over.

"Calm down," Alex said. "It's okay. You're safe."

"What the fuck just happened?"

Alex laughed nervously. "I think I'll freak you out if I try to explain that. But I can explain other things. Please. Have a seat with us."

Shaya stared at her former best friend, incredulous. She looked to the other two women again and sat, her fear momentarily replaced by curiosity.

"I know this is a bad way to show back up in your life," Alex said. "But we need a favor."

"And who is this 'we'?"

"Monsters," Alex said.

Shaya shuddered but didn't speak. She watched her friend's eyes, which were as they had always been, how she remembered them being. But there was now something different, unnamable but clear behind those eyes. She had changed somehow, and that change wasn't superficial. The change had reached down into her friend's very being.

Shaya glanced over at the boy, who hadn't taken his eyes off her the whole time. He had leaned back in his chair, the only change in his body language. He wasn't glaring menacingly anymore, Shaya observed, but he remained obviously unimpressed with her.

"Don't worry about him," Alex said. "He is not a fan of consorting with you and what you represent."

"And what do I represent?" Shaya said, deciding in that moment to meet the boy's gaze without flinching away.

"He's distrustful of authority," Alex answered. "Not in the way you think, but it's hard to explain."

The boy said nothing, but he did look at Alex and made a face very close to petulance.

Shaya took the chance to look away herself.

Former Senator Paige spoke next. "Getting to the point. We

need government support for the hidden monster settlements. Protection. Special status."

"What?" Shaya felt the flash of panic again, the urge to flee. Hidden monster settlements? What was this? Why would she want anything to do with this?

Alex smiled at her, reaching out a hand to touch her forearm. "Okay, let's slow down, everyone. I'll explain everything."

Alex recounted the series of events leading up to this meeting: the riots and the following exodus to hidden settlements, the trickle of monsters relocating to these settlements as anti-monster sentiment grew, the attack on Moon, their own settlement, the need now to protect that settlement and the others that were likely to be found.

Then Sondra explained what she meant by *special status*.

This was when Shaya had no choice but to chime back in. "Reservations are an interesting system in theory, but complicated in practice."

"Well," Sondra said, "that's something you'll need to fix."

"What are you asking for exactly?"

"Sovereignty."

Shaya had to consciously will her mouth shut. "You're all crazy."

"Listen," Alex said, "we can help you do it. We just need your promise to help us."

"And why would I do that?"

"Because you are in danger and don't know it yet."

A flash drive appeared on the table in front of Shaya. She had seen no hand put it there, but there it was.

"In that drive are enough secrets to topple our society. Or save it." Alex gazed into her eyes with that look Shaya remembered from when they were friends. The same love and compassion. When Shaya had realized that her parents were not good people, Alex had been there with that same look. I am here, it said. I am with you. Shaya had missed her friend. A million small things, this most of all.

"You won't understand what we mean until you have a look," Alex said. "But what we're giving you is the knowledge to pull almost any lever of power you want."

"And if I pull a lever and someone decides to kill me, who will help me then?"

"I will," said a voice. It came from her right, in the corner, where no one was. "I'm Sonya," said the voice. "I'll be your spy and your guard. Pleasure to finally meet you."

"Uh, pleasure to meet you too," Shaya said in a tone expressing only half the terror she actually felt.

"It's a lot, I know," Alex said.

Shaya laughed. "Sure, yeah. And what will the rest of you be doing while I risk my life?"

"What you can't," said the boy with fire in his eyes. "Protect our own on the ground."

"I can't condone violence," Shaya said.

"*Condone*," the boy repeated, putting odd emphasis on the word. "Violence is already happening. We're responding to it."

Shaya met his stony gaze. There was no version of this conversation that would convince this young man that he shouldn't kill anything that shot first.

"Okay," she said. "I don't need to know about any of that."

Another hour of conversation passed, and by the end, Shaya wasn't convinced, but she wasn't afraid anymore either. Strangely, a sort of exhilaration had come over her. She could feel it in her body—a tangible sensation of weight. The unknown had reached out and touched her. And now she had to find out why.

"I won't be your pawn," Shaya said before stepping back through the portal to her living room.

"That's not what we want," Alex said. "None of us can do what you can do. But we want to equip you with the tools to do it well. And completely."

"You'll hear from us soon," Sondra added.

Shaya slipped back into bed but couldn't sleep. Then she went to her office and started looking at the files.

Brit found her there in the morning, one hand propped under her chin, eyes fixed to the computer screen. Shaya was so transfixed, she didn't hear Brit open the door, didn't see her standing there.

"Are you okay?" Brit asked.

Shaya looked up. How must she look to Brit? Her eyes were certainly red from lack of sleep, but what was her expression? What was she communicating with her tired face, eyes fully open for the first time in her life?

This information could not be shared. It was hers to carry, at least for as long as she could alone. "Ready to have breakfast?" Shaya asked.

"Sure. Okay." Brit was no fool; she understood the need for certain boundaries. To protect them both. But Shaya would eventually have to prepare some version of the truth, with as little *actual* truth as she could get away with. She didn't want to destroy the love of her life.

After the late-night visit, the next few weeks passed with terrible speed, and Shaya had found out that the truth—or whatever she would call this cache of secrets—might destroy her as well. Just knowing was enough to collapse parts of her psyche. But what about the danger of knowing? Surely she could not be protected at all times.

Mister could have snapped her neck minutes ago if he had thought it prudent. But luckily, he is a man like her, interested in long-term benefit over short-term advantage. Luckily, he needs her for his own ends.

Well, she can't stay under this desk forever.

On the drive home from the office, she thinks, she plans, she calms. The version of herself that Brit meets at the door is a comforting whole, Shaya's shattered bits drawn back together again.

They have dinner, watch an episode of a Korean drama, complete their bedtime routine, go to bed.

Shaya closes her eyes, makes a valiant attempt at sleep, but images swim behind her eyelids and swarm inside her brain.

So she is awake when the knock comes. Dutifully, she slips out of bed and goes to her office, the place where the voice likes to meet her now. She steps in and gently pulls the door shut.

"Were you there tonight?" Shaya asks.

"Not in the room," the voice says, "but close by."

"Oh, great. That would've been helpful if he tried to kill me."

"He wouldn't have harmed you. And if he had tried, I'm very fast."

"Sure, fine. What's the point arguing now? I'm alive. You're here. What is it?"

"We have another request."

Shaya folds her arms. "And what if I refuse?" She's still standing by the door. The voice is coming from her bookcase. Shaya likes a little distance between her and her "guard."

"You can refuse anything," the voice says. "You're not our hostage."

She is mostly right, Shaya thinks, relenting. The things that trap her are her own ambition and her own folly. And no matter the hardships of her current situation, she must admit that she would have been helpless against Mister if the monsters hadn't given her what they did.

"I want to hear the request before I make any promises," Shaya says.

"It is about the American territories."

"Let me guess. Sovereignty?"

A short pause. "Sondra doesn't know yet. It might go that way. It might not. What she's asking for, what we're asking for, is your explicit support of the movement."

Shaya considers. She supposes she could ask, What movement? But she understands context. She also understands that no one person can determine which route a people will take. Statehood, independence, sovereign nations within the United States (God, that's a mouthful), or to remain exactly as they are, for their own purposes—all paths that have to be determined collectively.

"So, Senator Paige has decided to step back into the limelight."

A longer pause this time. "She's decided to honor the wishes of someone she loves, who isn't here to do it himself."

Shaya nods, unfolds her arms. "She has my support. And any resources I can bring to bear. I'm happy she isn't wasting all that talent."

"Me too," the voice says with surprising tenderness.

"I'll leave you to it, then," Shaya says. "The leaving, I mean."

She definitely doesn't want to see it happen. She opens the door again, letting it hang open as she returns to her bedroom.

She slips back into bed. It is so strange—her mundane life, this lovely woman beside her, a monster in the next room, and in her head a mare's nest of unimaginable secrets and horrors. Still, she is a body moving through the world. She has a job to do. She'll keep punching up until her will gives out. It hasn't yet, which provides a certain kind of comfort.

Reaching into the drawer beside her bed, Shaya pulls out her headphones. She'll have to fill her ears with someone else's voice if she's going to get any sleep tonight.

As the audiobook plays, Brit turns and nestles into her. On the outside, a normal scene. On the inside, a storm.

She will uphold this reassuring fiction for as long as she can.

ST. THOMAS, USVI

EARTH 0016

JUNE 26, 2074

FIFTY YEARS AFTER THE MASSACRE OF MEN

Yacht Haven Grande is quiet this late on a Thursday, something Patrice was betting on. Even after all the years and all the changes to St. Thomas, this late-night sleepiness remains. Rock City isn't bustling at this hour. There are pockets of noise, of vibrancy: a boat ride floating out from the harbor, its music carrying on the wind. There's also music from Dog House nearby, one of the fixtures of old St. Thomas that remain.

But in front of her, in the bar she is entering, there are only a handful of people. This place, which used to be called Fat Turtle a long time ago, and then the Box Bar for a time, and now Remembrance, pipes soft music from its speakers, and the chatter is so subdued, Patrice actually has to strain a little to pick up the bits of conversation happening at the different tables.

Leaving her Secret Service detail at the entrance, Patrice

sidles up to a bar stool and sits down. The bartender, a young woman with dark glistening skin, has her back to Patrice as she rinses a glass.

Patrice waits patiently. As the woman turns, Patrice says, "Good evening."

The blessed woman almost drops her glass. "Madam President," she says, eyes wide. "I'm sorry, I didn't hear you. How long were you sitting there?"

"Only a moment. But please, call me Patrice."

The woman is clearly horrified by the suggestion. "Ana," she says, gently, like a tender offering.

"I know. You've been working here for a few months now, right? It's my business to know things."

"Right," she says, flustered. "Uh, what you looking to drink?"

"Rum on the rocks. Your best stuff."

"Right away, Madam—I mean, Patrice."

It's been over a decade since she was president. She hates that people continue to call her by a title she's vacated—hates also that eventually she'll have to pretend to die, so that people can move on, forget her. And after that, the decades—centuries, possibly—of working behind the scenes to make sure that all that she has built endures.

Ana puts the glass of rum on a coaster in front of Patrice. "Nice night, no?"

Patrice smiles, drinking her rum on the rocks. "A lot of nice nights lately," she says.

"You probably hear this all the time, but I want to thank you for all that you've done for us."

Patrice bites back the urge to insult the poor girl. "We've all done it," she says. "You're too young to have witnessed the

Massacre of Men, but you should know. We all needed each other then, all had to work together to build a bright future after all that loss. Nothing makes up for it. No brightness could banish the shadow of those years. But because we didn't lie there, because we kept going, it hasn't been for nothing."

Jesus, what is she even saying? Was that from a speech?

Ana watches her, transfixed. "Yes, Mother." And that snaps Ana out of it—those words, Patrice's expression, and the flash of hatred she didn't manage to hide. "I'm sorry," she says. "You must hate being called that. I'm sorry."

Admittedly, out of some morbid curiosity, Patrice came to this bar because she knows that Ana is a fan. She even watched some of Ana's political videos online. All praise for the senator who became governor, who became president—once statehood had been secured (her doing as well)—the woman who helped bring the Virgin Islands out of tragedy into greatest light.

Patrice drinks. "It's fine. Sometimes I get angry because I wish I could have done more."

"But you've done everything," Ana counters.

Why is she playing this game with this young woman? Did she really believe that if she came and basked in all this adoration, it could help her? That it would remind her of the reason she did those things? It isn't helping her. In fact, it's making her sick.

Her drink is done. "Can I have another?"

A look of concern crosses the young woman's face, but she hides it.

The next glass of rum goes almost as quickly. And the next.

"It's the anniversary of the massacre today," Ana says. "This time of year must be hard on you."

Not particularly, she wants to say. Nothing is hard on her except herself, the only one left to be hard on her.

She could tell this woman she killed someone today. A correction. The corrections are so small these days. She's not saving lives anymore, not really, only preserving the absence of premature deaths.

Premature deaths that aren't corrections.

The reefs: *There are high levels of alcohol in your bloodstream.*

Leave it.

Not advisable.

"Leave it."

Ana startles.

"I'm sorry," Patrice says. She should probably go now that she has frightened the woman. Or at least offer an explanation to mitigate the abruptness. "I lost my best friend during the massacre. No, that's not the whole truth. He was my best friend, and I was in love with him."

"That's terrible."

It is so easy now, so natural, to manipulate people. Like second skin. "I should head out. Past my bedtime." Patrice reaches into her purse and retrieves three very large bills. No one uses cash anymore, but oh, does she love her quick exits.

Ana takes the cash. "I'll get you change."

"No, no," Patrice says, already getting up. "You keep what's left. You've been so gracious, indulging an old woman like this. Though I suppose by today's standards, I'm middle-aged." She laughs nervously. "Enjoy the rest of your night."

Ana's expression is all confused reverence.

Patrice rushes out, letting her legs carry her God knows where.

"Madam President?" When she whips around, Feder is speedwalking toward her, the other two Secret Service agents trailing stoically behind.

"I need a moment alone," she says.

"Can't do that," Feder says with feigned remorse.

"Fucking hell," Patrice whispers.

The reefs again: *Should we sober you?*

No! Just help me smile at this fool.

And the reefs oblige, seizing her facial muscles and forcing them into a smile. "Fine. Let's go."

When she was younger, Patrice used to walk the pier where all the yachts docked for the night. It's only a short walk.

And quiet even here: the lapping water, the soft lights of drowsy luxury boats. Now most of the yachts are owned by Virgin Islanders. Her influence once again. And beyond the small wonder of the dock, the space elevator—a gleaming marvel shooting up from Water Island Extension. The colonies and military bases on the moon, on Io, on Titan. The Martian Defense in development. All that grandness above her head, above the calm water and ocean breeze, and these twenty-five yachts that could belong to almost any Virgin Islander foolish enough to waste a few yearly loss allowances on such luxuries. Everywhere her eye goes, that her mind reaches, she has influenced. And yet, with each passing day, her hatred grows. The burden of influence, with little reward.

We can increase your serotonin, the reefs suggest.

No. She should go home. She should go to another bar, get even drunker. She should go visit Lee in Okinawa, take a vacation. She should shoot herself into space, to find her Derricks. She should kill herself. Throw herself right off this dock.

She should sleep.

Patrice is escorted to the parking lot and then escorted home. As the vehicle winds along silent mountain roads, she allows the reefs to sober her up.

The house is dark as she enters, quiet. Patrice's footsteps echo off the walls, the high ceiling.

Her son isn't here. A few years ago, he packed up a few items of clothing, a laptop, three cell phones, and a smartwatch and left. He was in northern Spain, South Korea, Mauritius, South Africa, and then he went up in a space elevator. He was on the moon for a year and decided he would build himself a small ship, put himself into cryonic sleep, and launch himself into deep space. Patrice learned of this decision via voice note:

I am going into deep space, details in your inbox.

She tried to respond, but he was already gone and was not receiving any messages. As expected . . .

Now she lives alone.

Patrice walks through the largish house and up a flight of stairs to her bedroom. As she enters, lights flick on, set to their dimmest setting. She undresses. Though she has the outer appearance of an elderly woman, with appropriate wrinkles where they can be seen, beneath her clothes is the same youthful body, and here in the privacy of her own home, she can smooth away the superficial signs of aging, except for her hair, which she likes to leave bone white. The body that slips under the bedsheets is as youthful-looking as Patrice in college, when she used to run track. The same strong body, maintained now by her mind and the reefs instead of by athletic effort. This too makes her feel hatred, even though she would never change it. This privilege she has become dependent on by default. If you can choose strength, can maintain it with mere thought, what's the value of that strength?

Doesn't matter. At this moment, it feels good to wear her young skin, to be clean under clean sheets.

A whisper inside her head: *Call incoming.*

Who is it?

Your sister.

This is the word the reefs use, as first instructed by Patrice's sister herself. "I am more than a friend," Lee had said then. "We are a sisterhood."

Patrice was amused by that. And it warmed her heart.

She sighs, sitting up in bed. *Answer.*

First, a voice: "Hey, what's this? Let me see you."

Another sigh. "All right." With her mind, she directs the reefs to project Lee's face onto the wall opposite her bed. Patrice's bedroom brightens: the image of Lee on the far side of the world, sitting in front of her desk, daylight shining through from a window to her left.

"You're in bed," Lee says.

"It's late."

"Not so late," she says. Worry creases her brow.

Patrice pretends not to notice. "What's up?"

Lee folds her arms in feigned offense. "It's the anniversary."

"You don't call every anniversary."

"This is special. You didn't think I would call on the fiftieth?"

Patrice laughs. "What does that mean to us?"

This time, the offense isn't feigned. "Don't be an asshole. Are you okay?"

"Why wouldn't I be okay? Everything is as it should be."

The deepest frown marks Lee's face, but before she can say

anything, a woman enters the room. Behind Lee, Mari is quick, darting to a dresser, where she shoves in a stack of freshly folded underwear. She tries to rush back out of the room, but Lee stops her, smiling. "Come say hi."

A moment's hesitation before Mari rushes over to the computer, smiling brightly. "Hello, Patrice."

"Hey, Mari."

The woman is younger than Lee. In her forties. But Lee does not look her age, doesn't try particularly hard to put on the ruse of getting old. Mari must know, Patrice guesses. Somehow, in some way, Lee must have explained it to her. Patrice doesn't know what to feel about this. Certainly, she shouldn't be worried. If Mari were to share this with anyone, who would believe it? Easy enough to take care of her if . . . She stifles the thought.

Lee's frown returns. "I'll just be a minute," she tells Mari. Her wife nods minutely at the screen and disappears from view.

"She knows," Patrice says.

Lee shrugs. "She knows that the ambassador gave us a gift." She spares a moment to look to her right, to where the door must be. "Nothing else."

Patrice nods, orders the reefs to clear any concern from her face. The slight manipulation of her facial muscles doesn't bother her anymore. When did it stop?

"Actually," Lee says, uncertainty showing on her face, "I wanted to talk to you about something."

"You want to give Mari the gift."

Lee raises her eyebrows. "What? No, no. That's never come up. And even if it had, Mari doesn't want that."

"How do you know? Who wouldn't—"

"This isn't about Mari. It's about you."

Patrice commands the lights in the room to turn on. She sits up fully. "What about me?"

"Your son talked to me before he . . . left. He said you weren't doing well."

"Not you too. I got enough of this tactful concern from him."

"If not me, who's left?"

Patrice glares at the screen.

"Listen, sis," Lee says, "if anything happens, I can take over. I promise."

"You won't do what needs to be done."

"No, I won't do it the way *you* want me to," she says, returning Patrice's glare. "I'll use a gentler hand in general, but I promise, if someone terrible needs a good shove off a ledge, I won't hesitate."

"You should've sent me this through the reefs," Patrice says.

"I needed to see your face."

"The answer is no."

"Patrice, you need to stop this. It's destroying you. It's *been* destroying you."

"I'm fine."

Lee huffs her exasperation. "Do you know why Derrick left?" She doesn't wait for Patrice to answer. "To get away from you. He got tired of watching you do this to yourself. And to get away from that look of yours. Like the whole world spins because you will it to. His whole life, under your thumb. And no, that's not what I mean, so shut it. He let you hole him up in that house. He did it for you, because he knew that's what you wanted. You don't tell him what to do, but you do tell him where to be. So you can protect him—from what, I don't know."

"You do know."

"They're gone," Lee says. "The Ynaa left fifty years ago. They want nothing from us. There's no reason for them to come back."

"What about—"

"I thought you outgrew that rationalization. No other aliens are coming to kill us. That's paranoia. And even if they did come, what else could you possibly do? Our trajectory is set. Humans have been advancing since long before you started handing us the answers."

"So I am something else now," Patrice says. She is yelling. Distantly she understands that she has lost control of herself. The reefs send her imperatives to calm down, offers to lower her heart rate, her breathing. She pushes them aside. "It's 'us humans,' huh? And I'm what? *Them?*"

Lee's face is pure remorse. "You know I didn't mean it that way. I'm just tired of watching you carry this burden on your own."

"You're not watching anything. You're not here!"

Silence. They stare at each other, Patrice's anger bright on her face, Lee's sadness on hers.

Footsteps interrupt the moment. Lee looks away to the door again. She smiles at what must be Mari standing there.

They exchange words in Japanese, Lee reassuring, Mari asking what's wrong. Lee saying she's fine before they say their I-love-yous. Mari's footsteps retreat.

Lee turns back to the screen. "I'm sorry. I'm being a pushy asshole."

This seemingly earnest admission, instead of comforting Patrice, fills her with shame. "I didn't mean to turn this into . . . whatever this is."

"I know. Me neither. Let's table it for now."

"You seem happy."

Lee beams. "I am. She is an amazing person, certainly more than I deserve. I don't know what I'll do when . . ."

Patrice doesn't need Lee to finish the thought. Lee is the last of the Reeds since her brother Derrick died. She has no interest in raising children, adopted or otherwise. Until Mari, she had little interest in even a life partner. To have to perform aging for them or, worse, confess to being ageless, while forced to watch said life partner slowly die. Or, worse, if she were to grant the gift to said life partner, only to find out they could not endure eternity together. Or, worse, when the relationship ended, to have to deal with said life partner's eternal resentment for gifting unceasing life.

Every time Patrice has told Lee she can grant someone the gift, Lee's response has always been the same: "Tempting. If only we had divination too."

She has always been wiser than Patrice. Even her comparative lack of world-saving ambition seems wise. Lee is content to stand still, to move little, to affect little, and if she does have an impact, to do it the slow way. Hours and effort. She has all the time in the world, she says. The Lee in front of her is a millionaire by her own hands, a social activist and recluse, a long-term partner to the woman she loves.

And to love that way, willfully without permanence. The sort of love that requires open hands.

"Are you doing anything for the fiftieth?" Patrice asks.

"We did something yesterday."

"Right, you're ahead."

Lee nods. "You'll be okay?"

"I'm fine, promise. I will call you tomorrow. You can try to convince me again."

Lee's laugh does little to hide her sadness. "Tomorrow, then."

Such infuriating wisdom. Patrice disconnects and plunges the room back into darkness.

When did she go too far? Was it when she blackmailed the governor to support her push for statehood? Was it when she engineered a hostile takeover of three tech giants so she could quietly manipulate advancements in quantum computing and nano-defense? Was it when she killed Orlov and made it look like a stroke? Was it when she repeated the move six more times under the cover of a pandemic? The pandemic was not her doing, but was it wrong not to stop it? Had she gone too far by considering the advantage of not stopping it? Was it too far when she repeated the blackmail maneuver with eight senators, a vice president, and five billionaires?

All those small choices—little nudges, careful removals of people who were a blight on their nations and on progress. When did she take it too far? What if it wasn't far enough? What if the threat comes and humanity still cannot meet it? What if the threat never comes?

Her father's words in her head, the disappointment on his face. What if all she has really done is blacken her soul? There are colonies on the moon, on Mars, on Io, on Titan. Her doing. Deep-space recon. Her doing. Weapons so small and so lethal, an enemy force wouldn't see them until they were all dying. Bombs so tiny they could be inhaled, but so powerful they could wipe out a city, push a small star into supernova. Her doing.

When did she cross the line?

Patrice remembers that this all started when she looked at her son and saw someone defenseless, someone in need of protection. Now her son is gone. And she has no more excuses.

Is it her? Has she become the threat? Is she still needed here? Or does the world need her to disappear?

Patrice nestles in but doesn't order sleep from the reefs. She watches the far corner of the bedroom, which has begun to sparkle. Her eyesight is very good even in darkness, but she doesn't need superior eyesight to know that she is being visited again.

"You're here," Patrice says.

At this, the Night Lady detaches from the corner's shadow and gracefully steps into a strip of light coming in from the window. The Night Lady eats that sliver of light; it falls into the negative space of her body and scatters. As always, her eyes, which are nebulae, swirl lazily.

I am asking you again, she says, and this is the way their conversations have been starting for years now. *Come with me.*

It is true that Patrice is feeling better now that she is in her own bed, where she might stay for a few days, monitoring her world, making small lethal and nonlethal corrections through the reefs as she sleeps or watches old episodes of her favorite television shows. Better now that she is, in fact, looking forward to seeing no one for a while, canceling any commitments due to bad health—which she can get away with at her advanced age. This is true, but something else is also true. Patrice is curious, has been curious from the beginning.

"Will you tell me this time," she says, "where we will go?"

I'll show you.

It is as if the Night Lady were following a script.

"Is Derrick alive? Both Derricks?"

I can show you.

Patrice tries another tack. "This isn't really a choice if you force me by withholding information."

I am not withholding. Everything you ask, you will know. But you'll know when I show you.

Now, that's new. "You're saying it's some kind of determinism thing."

For the other versions of you, the ones I tell, you don't leave. You stay here. You waste away. You are the one I never tell.

"And so I am the one who leaves."

The Night Lady offers nothing. It is not a question. The distant stars inside her sparkle; her body continues eating light.

"I'm going to sleep," Patrice says.

At that moment, Mera flickers—a fraction of a second when she is gone and appears again.

"Where did you go?" Patrice asks.

She does not answer, only continues waiting for Patrice to stop wasting time.

She has already decided that she will go the next time Mera asks. She's already prepared her will and the detailed instructions Lee will receive for maintaining the world, keeping it on its path. And the message she will leave behind for her son, who she hopes is still alive out there somewhere. Patrice is not in control, or if she is, she doesn't want to be. For once in a very long time, she wants to be without control. She wants to be surprised.

"What is the price?"

Death, Mera answers. *Transformation.*

"Like you?"

Not like me. You will become something else.

"Okay, let me get dressed. I'd rather not be found naked." Purposefully, she puts on a nice pair of pajamas. Then she slips back into bed.

Let me die, Patrice tells the reefs.

The reefs protest for only a moment. They knew this was coming. When her heart stops beating, they will leave her, construct a small body from their collective self—an insect, perhaps—and find Lee, where they will fuse with her, passing on everything that Patrice was that might still be useful in ensuring the future of Earth. Lee will take what is needed, discard the rest. A fitting end to all this.

The reefs begin a countdown. *10, 9, 8 . . .*

"Will everything be okay?" Patrice asks. As she speaks, the countdown continues.

You will see for yourself.

It is not a satisfying answer, but what can she do? She can't force an answer, which is what she wanted after all—a loss of control.

5, 4 . . .

Will we meet God? she wants to ask, but she doesn't believe in God. And yet she has decided to end her life, to see what's on the other side. She believes in . . . something, even after all this time.

2 . . .

She could stop it now, and the reefs, sensing this thought, pause the countdown.

But she has done everything. All that's left to do is surrender.

"One," she says.

CHITLANG, NEPAL

EARTH 0539

JUNE 14, 2029

ONE YEAR AFTER THE ATTACK ON MOON

If you start in Kathmandu and drive out to the eastward hills, you'll eventually reach a point where the paved road turns to gravel. Take that road up for forty-five minutes (a truck is your best bet, or a jeep) and then down the other side until you reach an overlook about halfway into the adjoining valley. From there, you can see Chitlang with its squat one- to four-story houses and other buildings peppered amid terraced farmland and bounded by wilderness. And beyond, more hills and valleys, stretching all the way to the Indian border in the south. Drive down to the first village and through it, past storefronts and small hotels and terraced fields, then up a series of winding dirt roads—not as bad as the ones through the hills, but close—and keep going until you reach a little hill. There sits a four-story house surrounded by a stone-and-mortar fence and a hillside of terraces that give way to an uninhabited wood of dense pine. It is here where Karuna settles. Not far from where her mother lived most of her life, before her mother's husband took her to Kathmandu, before that husband died and left her mother penniless and with child, before her mother gave that child up in hopes that it might have a better life.

Karuna learns all this through her ants, quietly finding the answers to mysteries she could not penetrate on her own. And in response, she goes out to her mother's home village and starts looking for a plot of land to invest in. And she does. The inhabitants of the village note quietly and to themselves just how fast the house on the hill goes up, as if sprouted from magic beans overnight.

There are a lot of questions at first about this stranger and her seemingly infinite wealth, but soon those questions go away. If a few old women recognize something in her face, they keep it among themselves. They know the story, know the sadness of that long-ago tragedy. They know where her mother is buried. But a person should find one's own way outside the shadow of calamity. If Karuna asks, they'll tell her, but they won't offer that story unsolicited.

Though Karuna is not that friendly with the locals, her white companion—no one is sure exactly who he is to her: Friend? Lover? Husband?—spends a lot of his time in town hunched over his typewriter and speaking to the villagers in halting Nepali. And the farm around Karuna's big house yields abundance—enough to sell and more, which she can offer freely. No one in the village is starving, and many of the villagers wake up to find that their own homes, their own fields, have slowly, quietly begun to look as if they were touched by the same magic hand. Nothing too noticeable. It isn't as if their houses have sprouted new rooms—nothing so blatant as that. But their homes are noticeably less dusty in the dry season, the bricks look newer, and their fields are free of pests, their goats and chickens and buffaloes healthy and clean. Animal waste seems to vanish overnight back into the fertile soil.

Some of the villagers have begun to call Karuna their "little spirit of compassion"—fitting since her name means *compassion* in Nepali. And the fear they feel at first, that there must be some price to all these blessings, passes with time. Despite the neighbors' efforts, Karuna doesn't seem that interested in getting to know them, let alone receive any explicit gratitude. But when they do come to her with a problem, they soon learn from her quiet thoughtfulness that this is what she is: a woman who finds all she needs inside herself and looks out to the world only for confirmation of what she already knows.

All this in a year—a whole new life. Like Moon, Karuna's house on the hill has a series of doors that lead to other settlements in the Distributed Monster Territories. By just passing through a few doorways, Karuna could be almost anywhere on Earth. But on the day of the meeting, all those doors are closed. Except for one. And through that door, each of the attendants will arrive.

"When should I be back?" Harry asks.

"Five hours," she says. "But before you go . . ."

She rushes off, disappearing through a standard open doorway deeper into the house.

He waits, knowing she'll be back. This isn't unusual behavior for Karuna.

She is there and shoving something at his chest before he

fully registers what it is. He holds it there with his good hand, and she releases the gift, stepping back.

At first, Harry can't read the expression on her face, and then he realizes, that's because he has never seen it before. Karuna is nervous.

The object is a hand. A hand and a forearm, the same shade as his skin but with none of the pliancy of flesh. He holds it out, mouth open, unsure what to say or ask.

"It's for you," Karuna fills in. "I should've packaged it, or something, but—"

"That's not your way." Not what she was going to say, but just as true. "No, this is better. Saved me the trouble of having to open a package."

Karuna's eyes are unblinking, searching. "I wanted to give it to you earlier, but I kept messing with it. I wanted it to be perfect."

Harry is surprised by the tears in his eyes. "It is. Thank you."

This seems to be enough for Karuna. She sounds much surer of herself when she says, "Right now it looks like a nonfunctional prosthetic, and it'll appear that way for a short while. But soon it will start responding to your mental directives."

Harry blinks away the tears. "How?"

"The same way portals are possible," she answers. "But truly, the current human tech is very close to what I'm describing."

"What about your . . ."

"I don't need it," she says. When he frowns, she reaches for him, resting her arm on his shoulder. "But it is okay if you do."

He slowly nods, focusing on the point of contact between them.

Despite its size and sturdiness, the prosthesis is very light.

Harry looks into the forearm's end and notes that it isn't hollow, though there's an irregular concave divot, as if something had taken a bite out of the prosthesis. Harry is doing it before he can think it through or lose courage. He slots his scarred stump into the divot. The stump slips in with ease, and the prosthesis tightens around him. For a moment, it feels a little like the squeeze of a blood-pressure cuff, but then the tension releases. Harry removes his other hand from supporting the prosthesis, and it holds firm, doesn't fall off. He moves this new, complete arm in careful circles.

"If you need to remove it," Karuna says, "just apply some pressure to the wrist with your thumb and it will come right off."

Tears again, his body starting to convulse with the sobs he is helpless to stop.

And Karuna comes right to him, wrapping her arms around him in a firm embrace. "I'm glad you like it," she says. "I got you. I got you." She kisses him on the cheek and then gives him a quick, gentle kiss on the lips.

She is patient, waits for the emotion to pass through him. And after it does, she steps back again. "You're still okay to leave?"

Harry laughs. Because how else could this moment end, but like this. "Yeah, sure, I'm okay to leave."

"Good."

Harry is walking down the hill into town when a finger on the prosthesis twitches for the first time. Tears begin again.

In the house, after he's gone, Karuna continues her preparations. An hour later, she activates the portal.

First through the door is a black house cat. Asha saunters in on light feet, and Karuna points her to the meeting room.

Next is Damsel. A curt nod to Karuna as she enters. Again Karuna points the way. Damsel looks at Karuna, taking her in.

"Fully awakened, I see," she says. "What name do you go by?"

"Just 'Karuna' will do."

"And is Melku in there somewhere?"

"They are, but I am still myself."

"How interesting," Damsel says dryly, and then goes to the room.

The Historians enter next. Three of them, and what a sight they are in their flowing maroon robes and long golden boots. What a sight they are even without those adornments.

Karuna points the way. "Just down the hall."

The Historians all nod and thank her for the courtesy and proceed as directed.

Karuna's other guests come one by one—some through the door, some materializing out of the very air. For each, she points the way to the meeting hall, where they sit quietly, waiting for the others to arrive. Appetizers are arranged in one corner of the room—finger cakes and cured meats, crackers, cheeses, and little Nepali dumplings with various dipping sauces.

Once all the attendees have arrived, Karuna welcomes everyone.

"We're here to conclude all our business," she says. "Before you are the terms of each of your contracts with the universe."

They glance to their paper, return their gazes to Karuna.

"Right. We'll go one by one to give each of you a moment to discuss or amend any items of your contracts. Once you've signed, we'll move on to the next person. We'll go clockwise. Now, as you can see, the Sisterhood is not in attendance. This was by choice. They wish to be 'left alone, to finally live out their lives in peace.' Given their service to all this, the universe has agreed to conclude dealings with the Sisterhood privately."

"How convenient for them," Damsel says. "And not at all ominous."

Karuna ignores her. "With that settled, we will begin deliberations. Starting with me. As stand-in for Melku."

"A useless distinction." Damsel again.

Karuna remains unruffled. She begins by reading from her contract, skipping the specifics of what she had to do to fulfill the universe's requests, and going straight to what she will be granted in return for her service. As a child of Asha and sibling to Yun, the living multiverse, Karuna is granted a choice of staying here within Yun where she may continue to reincarnate into new individuals (as she has done since arriving in Asha Verse 7). Or—and this choice may be granted now or at any point of death—she may be untangled from the universe and return to Akasha, where she may live again as a god, creating realms of her own, and exist within the realm of gods.

Karuna answers: "I choose to stay until the end of this life. And I will defer this choice to my future selves. Is this acceptable, Yun?"

There is no verbal answer, but a signature appears on Yun's line in the contract.

Karuna nods, signing her own name.

She then moves on to Damsel, and the terms are similar. Damsel may return to Akasha.

"You're neglecting to mention something important," Damsel says. In demonstration, she swings her right hand down, and instead of slapping the table, the hand passes through it—a ghost. She reverses the action and then displays the hand to everyone to show that it is still there, if only in spirit. For a moment, the hand shimmers, its subtle translucence dimming back to the appearance of solidity.

"And what would have happened if I didn't mimic the Zsouvox's obliteration right before Asha and I were truly destroyed! What then? Look . . ." She repeats running her hand through the table. "No matter what I do, I can't bring the hand back, can't make it any more than a convincing glamour. This is my dominant hand, Yun. What if I return to Akasha and I am still incomplete, some important part of myself missing. How will I be compensated for this loss? How will I be made whole again?"

Yun says nothing, but an amendment appears on the contract that Yun will personally give a part of herself to Damsel should Damsel return to Akasha incomplete.

"And what of the emotional hardship?"

Yun offers nothing for that, the unspoken response clear: Get over it.

"I should return the favor," Damsel says to the gray Zsouvox.

The Zsouvox stares back, sage-like, seeming neither offended nor remorseful. They are innocent, after all. It was the taint that caused this, and the actions of a few guilty parties within them. What exists within them now is a cooperative of gods.

Damsel's glare turns to a sneer.

It is pointless to direct anger at them now, says Asha. As always, she communicates this telepathically, broadcasting to everyone in the room. *Let it go. It is done.*

They all have lost things, they must all be thinking. And what they've gained has come at the cost of immense, unfathomable hardships. But no one is tactless enough to say that or offer a solution. Damsel will have to come to one herself in that strange and infinite above.

"Fine. I accept the terms," Damsel says, eyes rolling. She signs the contract, which renders her service complete.

Asha is also offered the option of staying or returning to Akasha. She has performed her service as a guide to the others. And there is also her greater service of returning to mankind over the centuries, in her cat form, speaking with each successive generation of the Order of Asha, keeping that lineage intact for the final days.

What could Asha be feeling at this moment? For five thousand years, she performed a duty—as a central figure in one very small community's divine pantheon. One can imagine her sober amusement at witnessing all the other deities that mankind has made for itself. Here she is, the grand cause among these surprising, destructive, wondrous people, and she has never been compelling enough to even be known as a significant god to any culture, any group of peoples. Just her order. This relative obscurity—the contract says—was preferable, both by her and by Yun, the latter being the truer god of this place. Now, unbeknownst to mankind, Yun has created realms within herself where these deities exist, for her own purposes. To know something of herself. To *understand.* Asha could take a place among them if she chooses. This the contract offers. But would such a place be acceptable to her? She was not dreamed up; *she* was the dreamer.

No. She will not go to the made god-realms of Yun. But Asha must feel a pang of sadness now that she can finally leave this place, now that she is not needed. Will she go? Will she relinquish this place back to itself without further intervention?

A span of moments passes during which Asha doesn't say anything. No telepathic message passes through the assemblage. What multitude of thoughts must pass through the mind of a god?

I will go, she says. And ominously, she adds, *There is still much more to do, much more to become.*

It is a grand reply. Fitting. She says nothing more, signs her name on the line with a thought. This time, Yun's signature follows. Proceedings pass to the next.

The Historians are sitting together as a group, and for this occasion they appear corporeal, able to enjoy the richness of true life in this room. Yun has granted them this corporeality for the purposes of this meeting. Otherwise, they would have appeared physically but would have been unable to affect anything around them. There is a realm where they enjoy corporeality, a universe that exists as one immense university, each habitable world a wing of this vast institution, whole worlds rendered into campuses so that the community of Historians may gather and discuss and write down and share the great mysteries and never-ending knowledge of the multiverse. But here in this moderately sized room, there are only three Historians. All of them are familiar. Two of them I know intimately. The third I have met twice: in the great hall of the Cult of the Zsouvox and in my car, right before I missed the curve.

Karuna continues to read the relevant part of their contract. I've missed most of the first part, staring at the other two more-familiar Historians. One stares back, smiling softly.

I remember to pay attention.

For their part in the conflict's resolution, they have been granted greater control of their organization. Yun has abdicated her authority over them. This must be a grand prize because the female Historian looks very pleased. Now, as an independent organization, they can work to address their own desires and goals. They'll still have to perform their main duty, however, which is to collect all the stories of all sentients across the multiverse and create a soul for each sentient made from those stories. Those souls will remain under the auspices of Yun, where they will be collected in afterlife realities designed for their continued life and for Yun's continued understanding of herself.

A final offering: The Historians will have an office in said afterlife realities—with minor duties, of course, but mainly for purposes of recruitment.

"How strange it is that I am already a beneficiary of this clause," says the woman Historian. "Time is indeed a tangled web." She signs her name in the spot reserved for her: Reina Calvary.

The eldest of the three Historians smiles. He says, "Indeed, as there are two of me here to witness this moment." A quick glance in my direction.

The eldest Historian has gray hair at his temples, a fully gray beard, crow's-feet at his eyes, frown lines around his mouth. Specks of milia under his eyes beset a constellation of black moles. Some of these features I already possess, but many of them still lie ahead of me. Already my facial hair has started to gray. But the major revelation here is that this version of me isn't that old. Early sixties at most. Which means . . .

He nods when he is finished signing the contract under his name: Calvin William Turner.

Next to him, as if waiting for his superiors to finish, the final Historian looks down at his contract and signs. When he is done, he spares a glance at me. It isn't with reverence or real recognition. This Cory Turner is not mine. But he recognizes me as a brother to one of his alternate selves. He looks at me and, with words that are solely for me, says, "I've met your Cory, and he sends his regards. He is well, but unfortunately, your reunion still lies ahead of you. He wants you to live. He says, 'Don't waste a single moment more mourning me. All my tragedies are to my back.'"

Of course, I have questions, but this Cory turns away from me to follow the remaining proceedings.

Next is the Zsouvox. Once again, they appear as an androgynous human with soft features, both masculine and feminine, but holding so much of either possibility that it renders both descriptors meaningless. This is, of course, by design. The Zsouvox has no interest in assuming any gender. They are what they are: a conglomerate, a multibeing. Plain clothes, again giving away no hint of a preference toward any gendered sense of fashion. Two distinguishing qualities, however: long dreadlocks that seem to obey their own sense of gravity, and skin a uniform gray, like volcanic ash. This is just what they have chosen given limited materials. Human is how they should look, so they have accepted a version that is unobtrusive to their interior sense of self. Even their eyes have taken on the color, the irises and pupils only successively dark enough to distinguish one from the other.

Karuna observes the Zsouvox impassively. The cause of so much conflict and loss of life sits before her, right there. But this is business. She reads the relevant part of the agreement.

Because of the harm the Zsouvox has committed in Akasha, they must remain within Yun for a period of time before Akasha can accept their reintegration into the world above. This isn't punishment. It is the best option given the circumstances.

Naturally, Akasha is wary of another incursion, the Zsouvox trying once more to consume all gods and their verses in an attempt to remerge with Apeiron (Yun's favored name for the nothing-that-created-something). Distance and planes of existence must isolate the Zsouvox from that goal until the gods above can replenish their number and put safeguards in place against future potential attempts to obliterate everything. Surely, the Zsouvox must understand the logic of all this.

And the Zsouvox does. They nod and quietly sign the document before saying, "We are content within ourselves as long as Yun continues to ensure a place for them within herself. We are uninterested in the specifics of such a place."

No need for Yun to answer. The contract is signed.

Karuna turns her attention to Abyssia, paying no attention to the person next to her, a young woman I have met in another universe. A woman who is now more than a woman: an immortal being who has vacated her world for a promise of something greater.

Patrice takes in the spectacle the same way I do: wide-eyed and open-mouthed. Finally, there is something above her head, beyond her grasp, and it reminds her of the fear and awe she has lost since the days of the Ynaa.

It is unclear whether Karuna can see Patrice. It is unclear whether she can see me, for that matter. But if she is anything like Melku, I suspect that she can but has chosen not to acknowledge us. We are witness to the proceedings, nothing more.

Karuna reads the relevant part of Abyssia's contract.

Abyssia will continue in her unique position, a superposition of all her divergent selves across all universes, brought into power by the spark of Yun's waking mind. It is impossible to reverse such a thing, and unnecessary. Abyssia can leave the body of Yun if she chooses, or she can continue to grow and become greater within Yun, as part of Yun. Her reward is an unfragmented self—all the pieces of her that exploded and fractured at the moment of her inception, now made whole. She can be sane again.

By all appearances, this has already happened, though it is always unclear whence Abyssia comes. This version of her could be an Abyssia from a distant past or a far future. The lack of unbridled chaos around her suggests something closer to the latter.

Abyssia signs under her true name, Ssasmeran, though she has many names from different chapters of her many parallel lives. Ssasmeran is who she was before she diverged down different paths—her common self. Of all the Ynaa, she has come the closest to escaping this black prison. She is the only Ynaa who knows the prison's name.

Abyssia says, *I choose to stay within Yun but reserve the right to change my mind at a later time. I have things I still need to do before I can go beyond this place.*

This, apparently, is agreeable to Yun, for out of the ether above the congregation of higher beings, she speaks for the first time: *There is a part of me that you've been cleaved from, sister. And you are dearly missed.*

Abyssia's nebulae swirl in acknowledgment of her sibling and her future.

With that, Karuna says, "This is the end of matters. You are free to enjoy more refreshments until you choose to depart."

Karuna, obligations met, leaves the room first.

Pockets of conversation linger as the remaining gods and cosmic beings engage in chitchat.

I waste no time interrupting the Historians, who are in the midst of fevered discussion.

"Cory," I say. I carefully avoid looking at my future self. I am sure he is that now. He is talking to the female Historian, and she smiles at me before returning to her conversation.

This Cory turns to me. "Cornelius," he corrects.

"You're joking."

"Mom's idea, at the last minute. Divine inspiration, she said."

"But if you shorten that—"

"Yes, I know. Every student in K through twelve came to the same clever conclusion. Never heard the end of it."

I am closer to him now and getting a good look. There's a scar through one of his eyebrows, cutting through the hair there, forcing that brow to a premature conclusion. Same eyes, same nose, same mouth. Three piercings through one ear, so definitely not my Cory.

"You're young," I say.

"Car accident," he says. "Not like your Cory. I never went to war. Never developed . . . PTSD." He watches my expression change, readjusts. "Lots of us lived to old age, and many of my parasiblings have had good lives. There's no curse or anything, if you're thinking that."

I've seen many of these other Corys, so I nod. "I wasn't thinking that. Parasiblings?"

"Same DNA, but not me exactly. You know."

I do know. It is a good name for all the *mes* I've seen who weren't quite me or weren't even close, though I shared the same parents with them, same birthday. And a good name for all those other not-quite selves, further removed.

I feel that we've hit against the end of the conversation.

There is nothing in his eyes that will give me any peace. There has never been a Cory in existence who recognized me as his brother. All the Corys I've seen, and no closure.

This Cory—sorry, *Cornelius*—smiles sadly at me. "He knew you'd take it hard. He said to pat you on the shoulder." Cornelius does this now, awkwardly. "And tell you that a time for a reunion is coming. But you have some time to get through first. He said, 'Get your shit together.' Said you'd know what he meant."

I laughed. It was a cruel joke for him to use my own words against me that way, but I welcome the chastisement all the same.

"Let me talk to him," says the other me.

I finally look at him again, but I don't say anything. Midfifties, for sure. Not so many years ahead.

"I'm supposed to tell you that you're wasting your life," he says. "That's what I remember, anyway." He laughs. "The future me said it just like that. I found it annoying at the time. Are you finding this annoying?"

I nod.

He laughs again, no doubt remembering all this and being charmed by it.

I am not charmed.

"You don't need me to tell you to stop wasting your life," my other self says. "You've already gotten the message. But you probably do need me to tell you that it'll work out with Tanya. It'll work out for as long as breath is in your lungs. And after you die, there will be more to look forward to, much more. But none of that afterlife will ever be like the years of true life you have ahead of you. The time you have left in life will be your sweetest." He grins. "Don't fuck up."

Reina leans over and kisses me on the cheek. Her smirk is all mischief. "You'd never let me get away with it," she tells future me.

He looks away, a complicated emotion hidden behind his smile.

Up close, I can see the resemblance to Laina Calvary. Definitely a parasibling.

"Be good, now," she tells me. She claps her two fellow Historians on the back. "Off we go. More things to discuss, you know." With a wink from Reina, they all pull themselves back out into the fractal sea. I can actually feel the force of it, the quiet pull beckoning me too, though I do not follow yet.

I return to Abyssia and Patrice, wedging myself into the middle of their conversation:

There is a multiverse out there—countless people in need of ensouling so that they may live on in other realities beyond their deaths. If they choose it. Your father could be one such person. You could do the work of ensouling him.

Tears come to Patrice's eyes so swiftly, they are falling before she can wipe them away. She does not understand everything Abyssia is saying, but she understands enough. "He will not have me."

The face of this goddess shimmers—some sort of expression that Patrice cannot read. *You may be surprised. Forever is a long time. Even a hundred years is a long time. Yours may be exactly the face he wants to see at the end.* When Patrice remains quiet, Abyssia says, *And the you that greets him there at the end doesn't have to be the same one you are now. Take your time and consider. Time is a flat canvas for such as us. He'll be there whenever you're ready to retrieve him.*

"So, I will be a Historian?" Patrice asks.

If you desire it.

"And after?"

Abyssia does not respond. There are things that even the gods don't know.

Patrice seems to understand. She does not appear to see me standing there as she accepts her new role. And suddenly, without another word from Abyssia, she is pulled out into the fractal sea.

Abyssia finally turns the force of her attention on me: *This is the last time you'll see me for a while,* she says. *I can take the power back. Do you want me to take it back?*

I consider the question for a long time, thinking of what future me said. Once I do this, it can't be undone. But somehow that prospect doesn't scare me, maybe because I know that not long from now, I'll have the power again, and a whole community to join with.

But I don't need it at the moment. Time to get my shit together. "Take it back," I say.

And again there is no grace period. One moment, I am there in that room, catching one last glimpse of Abyssia; the next, I am floating up from sleep, my legs swinging off the bed and onto the floor.

Tanya is there by the hospital bed, a puzzled expression on her face. "What just happened?" she asks. "Why did you sit up like that?"

Gina is there too, looking up from her phone and watching me with knowing eyes.

I reach for the power and find . . . nothing. Not even the ghost of it that I feel when I am awake. The gift, the curse, is behind me. And ahead.

I smile, and then I start laughing, and then I start crying. I look at Tanya, and Gina, tears falling freely. The power is gone. I am myself, only myself. I cannot enter other people's minds in other universes. I cannot live as other people.

For now. For the rest of this life.

"Seriously," Tanya says. "You're freaking me out."

"You good?" Gina asks.

"Yeah," I say. "It's nothing. Just a weird dream."

ACKNOWLEDGMENTS

We've arrived. The end of the Convergence Saga. Or at least this part of it.

This is going to be a long one. Like end-credits-to-a-movie long.

I want to start with thanking you, the readers. For making it this far. For sticking this out with me.

Not enough is said about how much changes while writing a book series. I wrote this over six years. If I include *The Lesson* (which I should), then it has been more like twelve. If I include the underlying cosmology, it has been even longer.

Over these years, I've changed a lot. I've gone through quite a few ups and downs. Had my first panic attack while working on this trilogy. These growing pains have made it into the work. But I am proud of every bit of the Convergence Saga, for what it has taught me about writing, about being an author, about myself. And I'm grateful to you for taking this journey along with me.

I want to thank my usual conspirators, but I first want to give a special (long-overdue) thank-you to Dion Graham. He lent his many considerable talents to this series, and as its narrator brought countless readers to this story. I am also grateful for our many conversations, some lasting hours, where he grappled deeply with the details and ideas in this series: some on the page, some implied, some just in my head. Over the course of all that talking, he became a friend. He told me, frankly and kindly, to put *more* on the page. I tried. And this series is better for his honesty.

My editor, Michael Carr. These last two books were especially difficult for me. For my first two books, I submitted manuscripts that were complete to the best of my ability. For *We Are the Crisis* and *A Ruin, Great and Free*, I submitted messier manuscripts with my own very long critique letters attached. Michael helped me sort all of it, and quite a bit of things I couldn't see. Once again, I was encouraged to make things clearer. But Michael also gently pointed out where my other idiosyncrasies were getting in the way of the story, guidance that certainly improved these novels. I could say so much more. Working with Michael has been a dream. He'd laugh at this, but I truly feel like he saved my writing career.

My copyeditor, Ananda Finwall. The last line of defense against my bad memory. These books required getting a lot of details right. I failed to do this often. Ananda was there to catch me, on top of her other duties as a copyeditor. It would be too embarrassing to list all the times she's caught something I'd missed even after dozens of readings. Trust me when I say she is very good at her job (and mine).

My former agents, Nell Pierce and Martha Millard. My

current agent, Kim-Mei Kirtland. I have been lucky every time when it comes to representation. Some of my greatest champions have been my agents. Even when I told them I wanted to add more POVs in the next book, they somehow continued to trust me. Kim-Mei has tolerated many phone calls from me, mid-panic over some narrative choice I was making. She held firm and kept me steady. And took a risk on me from the very beginning.

For my first two books Lauren Opper was my publicist and fiercest advocate. Every year I continue this work, I realize just how much I should be thanking her. She believed in what I was doing, and when I doubted myself, she told me to cut it out.

For *Crisis* and *Ruin*, Sarah Bonamino became my publicist and advocate. She's wonderful and it has been amazing getting to work with her. And I am hopeful that we'll continue to work together on future books.

I want to thank everyone that worked with me on a regular basis at Blackstone Publishing. In no particular order: Addi, Haila, Jeff, Vikki, Anthony, Greg, Sean, Jesse, Rachel, Kyle, Candice, Nikki, Isabella, Francie, Brendan, Benjamin, Mike, and Bryan. And so many more I'm positive I am missing. Please feel free to yell at me for my bad memory the next time we talk. And please know that this is the very least I could say in thanks. Each of you deserve pages of my gratitude.

Special thanks to Josie Woodbridge for being one of the kindest, most genuine, most incredibly thoughtful and helpful people I've ever had the pleasure of meeting.

Special thanks to Josh Stanton for never laughing me out of the room when I came to him with another wacky proposal. Particularly *Many Worlds*. And for trusting me and my work.

Kathryn G. English, for designing every single one of my covers and for making each one better than the last. I have yet to see the limits of her talents. And her work has even inspired a tattoo on my arm. She is that good. And also just an absolutely wonderful human being.

Elena and Brianna from Wunderkind PR. For all you've done to help readers find this series.

The darklies at *Many Worlds*: Darusha, Ben, Josh, and Craig. For being incredible and supportive. For writing books with me.

The Many Worlds Collective in its entirety. For joining this crazy thing. I'm looking forward to what we cook up together in the coming years.

My Cambridge Friends writing group: Ian, Jess, Andrea, Isabel, Jae, Alyssa, and Cherae. For offering guidance every time I needed. For telling me it was okay to take a week off, more than once. I really tried to listen.

My fellow Cryptids from the Clocktower: Mary, Aylin, Shirin, Heather, Nel, and Abby. For being the inspiration for several plotlines in this series. And for being great supporters and friends.

My La Roche Writers' Center crew: Jess, Michael, Ashley, Vanessa, Therese, Anju. And honorary member Larry Ganni, the greatest drummer I know. For being huge supporters and great people.

The Gannis and Barszczowskis. For being a home away from home.

My La Roche University professors: Chris, Josh, Sister Rita, Janine, Michelle, Ed, and others. So hard to use first names when talking about yinz.

My friends at North Island Workshop: Travis, Rebekah,

Marie, Nora, John, and Riley. For letting me take a breather when I failed to turn in work for months. For letting me come back. For being incredibly talented writers and brilliant critiquers.

Grassroots Economic Organizing Collective: Josh, Jessica, Michael, Ajowa, Matt, Abe, Sarah, Malikia, Megan, and Jim, to name a few. For being a source of education and challenge when it comes to solidarity economics. For being, each of them individually, some of the best activists I've had the privilege of meeting. My love for this group is endless.

My friends, students, and colleagues at North Carolina State University. My fiction mentors: John, Wilton, Jill, and Belle. For teaching me everything they know and forgiving me whenever I fell short. For supporting my work in so many ways. My linguistics mentors: Walt, Agnes, and Robin. For teaching me to think critically about the politics of language. For supporting me.

All my people at Clarion West. All my people in Team Arsenic. All my people in Team Tuesday. My Clarion West students. Seattle, generally.

My teachers and mentors from Gomez and Ulla and Cancryn and Charlotte Amalie High.

Caroline and Aaron. Scott and Kelly. For getting me through some hard times just by being there.

Helena and John. For barbecues and long talks about books. For letting me play with their dogs.

Morgan and Dylan. For conversations over bubble tea.

Jessica and Staige. Cat and Amy. For always having the best advice.

People I talked to while writing this series (some repeats): Wayne, Jake, Cat, Mary, Nel, Heather, Sarah, Josh, Miriam, Kyra, Paul, and Jeremy.

The many books I read while writing this series.

The authors who have inspired me. Le Guin and Butler and Jemisin and Mandel.

Author friends who've supported me (some repeats): Maria, Ted, Sylvain, John, Wilton, Andrew, Rebecca, Isabel, Tiphanie, Tobias, Sam, Phenderson, Tananarive, Kris, M. K., Annalee, Marty, Elizabeth, Paul. Many, many others. For showing love even when no one knew who the hell I was. More should be said about the effort it takes to blurb and review books. It is hard to do. And yet authors do this work often, despite the paltry recognition.

Brandon and Shaun from *The Skiffy and Fanty Show*. For many great conversations.

Pam Stack and Florenza Lee. For the same. And just being the coolest people.

Kiki from @ifthisisparadise. L. P. Kindred. For returning to my work and bringing others with them. For showing love to this series and defending its strange choices.

Cindy from @BookofCinz. For doing the same with *The Lesson*.

So many other book lovers who've built platforms out of their love of books. They are the unsung heroes that keep this industry vibrant.

All the awards institutions that have shown love to my work and this series.

Kelly Justice from Fountain Bookstore. For being an ally from the very start.

My best friend, Elliot. For the many conversations about music, movies, TV, and books. For the enduring friendship.

My boy Dian, whom I miss deeply.

My in-laws. My brother-in-law, Anup. My wife's entire extended family. For welcoming me and caring for me and making me feel like family. For taking me to the best places in Kathmandu to eat and see and write.

Sumitra-Aunty, for letting me stay at her beautiful home. For letting me write there and take inspiration from being there. For her many admirable qualities.

My mom, sis, big bro, aunties, uncles, cousins, nieces and nephews, grandparents. My dad. Everyone still here and those who've passed on. For supporting me and putting up with me in equal measure. For raising me and raising me up. For being patient with me and never giving up on me. I love you, Mommy.

All my friends, colleagues, and supporters I haven't named. The certainly droves of people I've missed. Acknowledgments are hard as hell! Especially when one decides to start naming names, like I have. I might have overdone it and, by doing so, not done enough. Please forgive me. Thank you so much.

To my wife, Anju. For always, always, always being there. For building a life with me. For listening to me explain things for hours. For reading my work and being the realest one. For keeping my head on straight and keeping me grounded. For forgiveness and support and care and warmth. For believing I could do this long before I published a single word. For believing I could still do this. For everything. For your love.